TAKING A CHANCE

"Charlotte . . ." Max stepped between her and the door, his expression soft and easy, his eyes deep midnight blue. He shouldn't have been a nice guy. Not with his looks and his reputation, but she was starting to think he was one, and that could prove a very dangerous thing.

"It's late, Max. You need to get back to Zuzu." She tried to get him moving, but he didn't seem eager to step out of the way.

"What are you running from, Charlotte?" he asked.

"I'm not running."

"Could have fooled me." He tucked a strand of hair behind her ear, traced a line from there to her temple and the scar she'd had for so many years she'd almost forgotten how she'd gotten it.

Almost.

But it was hard to forget something that haunted her dreams.

"You took a pretty hard hit," Max murmured, following the scar with his finger. She could have stepped back, but she didn't. It felt so good to be touched, and it had been so long since anyone had bothered, that she let herself stay right where she was. . . .

Books by Shirlee McCoy

THE HOUSE ON MAIN STREET

THE COTTAGE ON THE CORNER

Published by Kensington Publishing Corporation

THE COTTAGE ON THE CORNER

SHIRLEE McCOY

ZEBRA BOOKS
KENSINGTON PUBLISHING CORP.
http://www.kensingtonbooks.com

Chapter One

November 27.

The worst day of the year.

The worst day of *her* year, anyway.

Usually Charlotte Garrison spent it with a box of tissues and a bagful of mini Reese's. If she were feeling particularly sappy, she rented a romantic movie and watched it on her two-decades-old TV.

No need for that today.

She had a real live romance to watch.

Cade Cunningham and Tessa McKenzie's wedding was the most talked about event in Apple Valley, Washington, since Miriam and Daniel Riley had married over a hundred years before. The happy couple had asked Charlotte to make the wedding cake. If she hadn't loved them both so much, she'd have said no. But she did love them, and she hadn't been able to open her mouth and say what she should.

That was Charlotte's problem. One of her *many* problems. She loved the people in her life, and she'd do anything for them. As long as it wasn't illegal or immoral. Which . . . when it had come to her husband . . . had proven to be a problem.

"Do not even go there," she murmured.

The nineteen-year-old kid working salad prep at the counter a few feet away smiled quizzically.

"What?" he asked.

"Nothing." She placed the last sugar flower on the five-tier cake. White on white to go along with the Victorian Christmas theme that Tessa had chosen for the wedding. The cake was beautiful, every flower sparkling with shimmery powder. Anemone for unfading love. Bluebells for constancy. Lavender for devotion. Violet for faithfulness.

Such fanciful Victorian ideas.

She'd have snorted, but Town Hall's oversized kitchen was nearly bursting at the seams with people preparing Tessa and Cade's catered buffet. The last thing she wanted to do was give any of them reason to talk about her.

Not that people weren't *already* talking.

Charlotte and Cade had dated shortly after she'd moved to Apple Valley. It had been a moment of weakness on her part. She'd been new to the area and wavering in her conviction that being single was the best thing a woman could ever do for herself. Cade had asked her to dinner. She'd said yes.

Two very nice dates later, they decided that they'd be better suited as friends than they would be as lovers. That had worked out well since Tessa had returned to Apple Valley to care for her nephew Alex a couple of months later. It had taken Cade all of two minutes to fall for his childhood friend. It had taken Tessa a little longer, but she'd eventually realized how inevitable their love was.

At least that's what the blue-haired ladies said when they met at the diner every Thursday morning. Charlotte heard their whispered gossip when she delivered muffins and Danishes. They loved to try to pull her into it, but she wasn't big on gossip.

Besides, while they were all talking about how perfect the couple was for each other, she was secretly worrying that things wouldn't work out and that her friends would be disappointed, hurt, betrayed.

She wanted a lot more than that for them. Tessa and Cade deserved their happiness. Personally, she'd had her shot at happily ever after. It had been more like a nightmare than a dream come true.

But that was another story for another time.

Tonight she was going to roll the cake out into the reception hall and hightail it back to her little house. She'd park herself on the love seat she'd bought from Tessa's antique store, read a book, eat Reese's, and wait for the twenty-seventh to turn into the twenty-eighth.

"That cake about done, doll?" Gertrude McKenzie walked into the kitchen, her bright orange hair curled to within an inch of its life. Forty minutes ago she'd walked Tessa down the aisle, her sturdy white shoes peeking out from beneath a floor-length pink skirt, her face softer than Charlotte had ever seen it. Now she looked ready to party, the Victorian-style gown she'd worn to the ceremony exchanged for a short fuchsia dress that hit just above her knobby knees. "'Cause the crowd has eaten every one of those fancy appetizers Rylie made, and we're about ready to move into the reception hall."

"I just finished," Charlotte replied, stepping aside so Gertrude could see the cake.

"Wow!" she said. "Just . . . wow! You've outdone yourself, Charlie."

"Think they'll like it?"

"Like it?" Gertrude exclaimed. "They're going to love it! Come on, let's get it out there. Tessa is insisting on tossing the bouquet before we eat. You don't want to miss that."

Actually she did.

The last thing she wanted to do was stand in a crowd of clawing, jostling women, all of them bent on being the next Mrs. Somebody. Been there. Done that. Had the heartache to prove it.

She rolled the cake into the reception hall. Tables had been set up, a fire stoked in the oversized fireplace. Still a month out from Christmas, but the place had been decorated with white Christmas lights and pine boughs. Each of the twenty tables had been set with ivory linens, white candles, and a single pink rose.

"Right over here, Charlie!" Event planner Martha Wright-Randolph called. Thirty, with a fake smile and perfectly highlighted hair, she'd married Henderson Randolph the year she'd turned twenty-five. He'd been ninety and, according to people who'd been in Apple Valley back then, had died trying to keep up with his young bride.

Martha had inherited a million dollars, a house, and forty acres just outside of town. Charlotte could have done a lot with an inheritance like that. Purchased a storefront, bought new baking equipment, put new windows in her house.

Martha had apparently spent her money on clothes, cars, and brand-new double Ds. Now she was on the hunt again. The sapphire-blue dress she'd squeezed her curves into was designed to let every man in the vicinity know it.

Charlotte pushed the cake to the spot Martha indicated.

"Perfect," Martha cooed. "Just perfect."

"Thank yo—"

"This event will be the talk of the town for generations to come." Martha cut her off. Apparently it wasn't Charlotte's cake she thought was perfect. "I can't believe that I've pulled it off."

"You're a one-woman marvel, Martha," Charlotte replied without even a hint of sarcasm in her voice.

Martha's eyes narrowed, her Botox-filled forehead nearly rupturing with the need to wrinkle into dozens of frown lines. "What's that supposed to mean?"

"Just that the reception hall looks lovely. The historical society did a great job decorating it last night." Led by Cade's grandmother, Ida Cunningham, the committee had cleaned and polished the tables the local boys' club had brought in, set up the chairs, put out the decorations. They'd been there for hours while Charlotte worked in the kitchen.

As far as Charlotte knew, all Martha had done was stand in the corner barking orders.

She decided against pointing that out.

"Under *my* direction," Martha huffed, her sleek

chignon vibrating with the force of her indignation. "My design ideas. My sense of style."

"It's lovely," Charlotte conceded. Mostly because she didn't want to rile the woman up during Tessa and Cade's wedding.

"I'm glad we see things the same way." Martha glanced at her gold watch. "I'd better get people moving in this direction. We're on a pretty tight schedule."

Charlotte wasn't sure what schedule that was. Cade and Tessa were going on their official honeymoon during Tessa's nephew Alex's spring break. They *were* going away for a couple of nights, but they were driving. There was no limo waiting to take them to the airport, no flight to catch. The wedding reception would probably go on into the wee hours of the morning.

Charlotte would be sound asleep by then.

Hopefully.

She hadn't been sleeping well the last few weeks. This time of year she never did. Too many memories. Some of them wonderful. Some of them not. All of them tainted by what Brett had done.

She grabbed her coat from the closet near the front door and slipped outside before any of the wedding guests made it into the reception hall. It was quiet there. Everyone who was anyone in the community was inside with the bride and groom. She'd parked at the far edge of the lot, her old station wagon squeezed in between a snazzy sports car and a Toyota sedan. She hurried to it, trying to swallow down the hard lump of sadness in her throat. It didn't matter how much she told herself he didn't deserve it, she always spent the anniversary of Brett's death on the verge of tears.

"Charlotte! Hold up!" someone shouted.

She kept right on going, because she knew the voice and had no intention of stopping to chat with Max Stanford. Not when she was so close to tears.

"I know you heard me," he called. "And since you're not nearly as rude as I am, you may as well stop. If you don't, you'll spend the rest of the night feeling guilty for not doing it."

She hesitated with her hand on the station wagon door.

Darn the man for being right.

She *wasn't* rude, and she didn't make a habit of ignoring people.

There was a first time for everything, though, and this was going to be it.

She unlocked the station wagon and slid behind the wheel.

Max grabbed the door before she could close it, bending down so they were eye to eye. He had midnight-blue irises, thick golden lashes, and the kind of movie-star-handsome face that made women swoon.

"Maybe I was wrong about your capacity for rudeness, Charlotte," he said dryly.

"What do you want, Max?" she asked. Not a date. He'd asked her out once. She'd said no. As irreverent as the man could be, he knew how to take no for an answer.

His dark blue gaze dropped from her face to the front of the dove gray sheath dress she'd bought for the occasion. "You."

"Forget it." She tried to yank the door from his grasp, but the man had more muscle than any human being had a right to.

"For the flower toss," he continued, a smile tugging at the corners of his mouth. He had a nice mouth. Firm full lips with a tiny scar at the left corner.

She looked away. "You mean the bouquet toss?"

"Whatever it is the bride does. Tessa asked me to get you."

"Tell her I went home."

"But you didn't," he said reasonably, snagging her hand and tugging her out of the car. "You went to your car, and now you're going back inside to participate in the festivities."

From the way he said the last word, Charlotte got the distinct impression that Max was as excited about the reception as she was.

"Sorry," she said. "But I'm not. It's been a long day, and I'm ready to go home."

"And disappoint Tessa on her big day? Would you really do that to a friend?" His thumb ran across her wrist as he spoke. An unconscious gesture, Charlotte knew, but it reminded her of things she'd rather forget. Things that could get a woman into a world of trouble if she let them.

She pulled away, wiped her palm on her skirt. "She won't even know I'm missing."

"Then why'd she send me to find you?"

Good question.

She couldn't think of an answer.

No matter how hard she tried.

And God knew she was trying.

"Fine," she finally said. "If it means that much to

Tessa, I'll go stand in the group of desperate single women and wait for the stupid flowers to be tossed."

"You sound bitter."

She ignored the comment as she walked back across the parking lot. She wasn't bitter, but at some point in her life, she was going to have to learn how to say no. Loudly and with feeling.

Unfortunately, sometime was not *this* time. For Tessa's sake, she was going to squeeze herself into the pack and pretend that she actually wanted to catch the bouquet.

She'd rather catch a basket of vipers.

But that was just her.

She jogged up the porch stairs, the sound of piano music drifting from inside. Alex Riley, she'd bet. Tessa's nephew had a gift for music. After his parents' deaths, he'd struggled to communicate, autism preventing him from connecting in typical ways. Music was his language, and he used it well. From the sound of the music, she'd say the wedding had made him happy.

She was glad, but she still didn't want to go back inside.

"You going to stand there all night?" Max asked, his breath ruffling the hair at her nape as he leaned past and opened the door. He nudged her forward, and half a dozen people swooped in. Martha in the lead.

"There you are! Tessa is absolutely refusing to toss the bouquet without you. If we don't hurry, the food will get cold. Come on." She snagged her arm and dragged her toward the banquet room.

Tessa was there, resplendent in a vintage lace gown, her red hair pulled back, her face flushed with happiness. She saw Charlotte and smiled. "I see Max completed his mission."

"I never had any doubt that he would," Martha cooed, shooting the man in question what was probably supposed to be a beguiling smile.

"Thanks for your vote of confidence, Marti," Max drawled, giving her a once-over that would have made Charlotte blush.

Martha preened. "How about you thank me with a dance?" she asked. "First, though, the bouquet toss."

A cheer went up, dozens of happy women jockeying for position. Widows. Divorcees. Singles. Teens. Couples crowded around as Tessa positioned herself at the far end of the room, Cade a few feet away. He looked happy and content. Charlotte wanted so much for this to work for him and for Tessa. If she could have willed it to be so, she would have, but all she could do was hope and pray that they'd make a lifetime of beautiful memories together.

Cade must have felt Charlotte's gaze. He glanced her way and winked. She returned the gesture.

"No flirting with the groom," Max murmured near her ear.

"I'm not—"

"Better get into place." He nudged her into the crowd of women.

Tessa glanced over her shoulder and looked straight into Charlotte's eyes. Typical of the happily married, she wanted all her friends to be happily in relationships, too.

Wasn't going to happen.

Ever.

Martha handed Tess a simple bouquet of white

roses wrapped with a hot pink ribbon. One white feather peeked out from the flowers. Silky and soft looking, it added a touch of whimsy to the traditional and suited the bride's taste perfectly. Charlotte had seen the feather in a vase on the fireplace mantle at Tessa's house. When she'd asked about it, her friend had laughed and said that Gertrude thought it was from an angel's wing and would bring love and good fortune to whoever had it.

"One," Tessa said, lifting the bouquet dramatically. "Two."

Charlotte braced herself.

"Three!"

Girls screamed with excitement. Women jumped and clawed. Charlotte dodged, barely avoiding the bouquet. It landed in the hands of town librarian Daisy Forester. She held it up, squealing gleefully while everyone around her cheered.

Something fluttered near Charlotte's face. No, not fluttered. *Floated.* The feather, just drifting lazily in the air. She grabbed it before it could drop to the ground, tucking it into her pocket as Daisy whirled around in circles, clutching the roses like they were a winning lottery ticket.

"There we have it!" Martha announced loudly. "The next Apple Valley bride."

People cheered and laughed, closing in around Daisy and patting her on the back like she'd done something more impressive than snatching a bunch of dying roses from the air.

Careful, Charlotte's better self said. *Your bitter is showing.*

Yep. It sure was.

Time to go.

She sidled to the left, scooted around Lesley Wagner, and nearly collided with Rod Lancaster. Tall and lean with a runner's build and a too-confident smile, he taught math at Apple Valley High. "Charlotte!" he said warmly. "I was wondering when I'd see you."

Why? was what she wanted to say, but her mother had raised her with manners. "Hello, Rod. Enjoying the wedding?"

"Yes, and getting ideas for my own. Wink, wink."

"Daisy Forester just caught the bouquet. Maybe you should check in with her and see if she's available."

Rod laughed. "You've got a good sense of humor, Char. I like that in a woman."

"It's Charlotte." She hated being called Char for reasons that she preferred not to think about while she was at her good friends' wedding. "If you'll excuse me, I really need to get going."

"Before you go, I had a question for you."

"What's that?" *Please, don't let him ask me out. Please, please,* please *don't!*

"I thought it might be beneficial for some of my lower-level students to see how math can help them in the real world. Cooking seems like a good way to demonstrate that. I was thinking that we could borrow the home economics room—"

"We?" She shoved her hands in her coat pockets, felt the silky feather brush against her knuckles.

"Sure. I don't know anything about cooking, but I know plenty about math."

Next thing Charlotte knew, Rod was explaining exactly what he knew in excruciating detail.

Maxwell Stanford wasn't sure what all the excitement was about. Sure Daisy had caught the bouquet, but he was pretty damn sure that didn't mean her longtime boyfriend was going to propose. From what Max had heard, Jerry Webber had been stringing Daisy along for five years, promising that he'd marry her as soon as he was making enough money to support them. In the meantime, he lived in Daisy's apartment, ate her food, and pretended to be writing the next bestselling murder mystery.

If a few white roses changed that, Max was going to have to reevaluate everything he knew about men.

And roses.

He waded through the throng of people and clapped Cade on the back. "You did good on this one, Cunningham. You and Tessa are going to have a lot of good years together."

"That's an awfully nice thing to say, Stanford. Are you going soft on me?" Cade asked with a cocky grin.

"Just throwing you a bone, since I'm still a better shot than you."

"I think I outmarked you the last three times we went to the gun range," Cade pointed out.

"Only because I didn't want to embarrass you. You're the sheriff, after all. It wouldn't look good for you to keep getting bested by one of your deputies."

"Bullsh—"

"Folks!" Martha Wright-Randolph's voice rose above the rumble of the crowd. "The buffet is open.

We'll have dancing in the meeting hall in an hour. For now, let's all enjoy the wonderful meal provided by Apple Valley Fritters."

Max didn't have to be told twice. He was a good cop and a decent handyman, but he sucked at cooking. A free meal anywhere was always a good thing.

He hadn't even taken a step toward the buffet tables when Martha approached and dug her too-red and too-shiny nails into his bicep.

"Max," she purred. "How about we get our plates and find a quiet place to talk?"

Not in this lifetime.

Or the next.

He liked women. No. He *loved* them, but Martha had trouble written all over her. "I think I'll have to pass on that, Marti," he said.

She frowned. "You didn't bring a date, did you?"

"No." But right about then, he was really wishing he had. *Hell hath no fury like a woman scorned.* His grandfather's favorite saying. One that Grandpa James had good reason to know was true. Max had learned a few lessons in that area himself. He had no intention of taking a refresher course.

"Then what's the problem? You don't think I'm attractive?" She smoothed both hands down her shapely hips and smiled the kind of smile that said she knew that couldn't be the case.

"Your attractiveness has nothing to do with it. I'm just not interested." Short and to the point. That was the only way to deal with women like Martha.

"I bet I could make you change your mind," she purred, running her hand down his bicep.

He took a step away, nearly falling over Charlotte.

He grabbed her elbow, realizing a second too late that Rod Lancaster was holding on to her other arm and staring at her with the starry-eyed gaze of a man in love.

Were the two dating?

If so, he hadn't heard anything about it.

In a town the size of Apple Valley he should have. Unless they'd kept it secret. An interesting thought. Charlotte did tend to stay to herself, baking in the kitchen of the little cottage at the corner of Main and Wesley and selling whatever baked good she could to whomever she could.

Not the kind of life Max would have chosen, but he had to respect her for doing things her own way.

"Sorry," he said, holding on to her arm until she regained her balance. "I didn't mean to knock you over."

"You didn't. Much." She laughed lightly, extracting herself from Lancaster's hand in a practiced move that barely seemed to register with the high school teacher. "If you'll all excuse me, I have—"

"To get something to eat?" Max suggested, because she didn't seem any more eager to stick close to Lancaster than he was to be around Martha. "How about we go together?"

"I was planning to—"

"Don't make me beg, sweetheart. Not in front of strangers." He slid his arm around her waist and hurried her toward the buffet table.

"What are you doing?" she whispered, shoving his arm away.

"Just trying to keep you from announcing to my stalker that I'm going to be eating alone."

"Your stalker?"

"Martha. She's got a thing for me."

"She has a thing for any man with two legs, a car, and money."

"You forgot hair. She likes men with hair."

"Her ninety-year-old husband had hair?"

"A full head of glossy white curls," he said, even though he'd never met the man in question.

"Really?" She eyed him from beneath thick lashes. She'd pulled her glossy brown hair into a high pony-tail, and he could see the scar at her temple. He'd wondered a couple of times how she'd gotten it, but since she'd turned down his dinner offer, he hadn't thought it was any of his business.

"You never even met him, did you?" she accused, her dark eyes flashing with indignation and just a hint of humor.

"No, but telling you that I did distracted you long enough to get us into the buffet line."

"That doesn't mean I'm going to stay here."

He glanced at Martha. She was hanging on to Rod's arm and looking at him like he'd hung the moon and the stars just for her. "No need to. We've lost our shadows."

"Hopefully they'll make each other very happy."

"I'm not sure anyone can do that for Martha." He nudged Charlotte forward, eyeing the food that stretched the length of three tables. Apple Valley Fritters Catering had done itself proud. "Looks good enough to eat," he said, but Charlotte had stepped out of line and was making her escape.

He couldn't say he blamed her.

If he weren't so hungry, he'd have done the same.

Chapter Two

He stayed until the last guest left the reception. Not because he had a sudden overwhelming desire to socialize, but because Cade had asked him to keep an eye on Gertrude and Alex. You didn't tell your buddy no when he was on his way to a mountain cabin to spend a couple of nights alone with his new bride. Cade and Tessa had left a half hour ago, and Max had been counting the seconds as the remainder of the guests trickled out.

"Well, that's that. The most beautiful wedding in Apple Valley history is over," Gertrude said, tugging a cigarette from behind her ear and tapping it on her thigh as she surveyed the empty reception hall.

"Don't light up in here, Ms. Gertrude. I'd hate to have to cite you." Max glanced at his watch. Just past one. The reception had ended a little earlier than he'd thought it might. He couldn't say he minded. He was on the schedule at work for the next two days, pulling double shifts so that Cade could have a little time off.

He liked work, so it didn't bother him, but he figured that when Cade got back, he'd take a drive to Seattle. Enjoy a nightlife that didn't shut down at ten. Bright lights, loud music, maybe a visit to Erin's. They'd met in college, hit it off right away. Neither believed in the hokey kind of love their friends had fallen into.

Which probably explained why neither had ever married.

"Come on, Alex," Gertrude called to her nephew. "We need to leave."

Alex didn't respond. Not surprising. Most people talked to Alex without anticipating an answer. Every once in a while, the kid shocked someone with a few words. Mostly, though, he was silent, moving through the world like a wraith.

"Alex Riley, I said we need to leave!" Gertrude barked.

Alex looked at his aunt, his expression quizzical as if he had no idea why Gertrude would be irritated.

"Okay," he finally said, folding his hand around something.

"What do you have there?" Max asked as the boy approached.

"Angel kisses," Alex responded, opening his fist to reveal several white rose petals.

"Angel kisses?" Max asked as they walked outside.

"The boy has a good imagination." Gertrude opened the door of her old Cadillac and motioned for Alex to get in. "Nothing wrong with that, is there?" She scowled in Max's direction, and he shrugged.

He didn't have an opinion on it one way or another.

He knew nothing about kids, and he really wasn't interested in learning.

"Well?" she demanded. "Is there?"

"Doesn't seem that way," he said.

"Humph!" Gertrude responded, climbing into the car. She yanked the door closed.

That sealed it. Max was on the old lady's shit list.

Hopefully not for long. He ate dinner at the Riley place once a week thanks to Tessa. She thought it was good for Alex to have more than just family around. Max thought it was good to eat something besides take-out or frozen meals.

The back window of the Cadillac rolled down, and Alex stuck his head out.

"Here," he said, holding something out to Max.

"What is—"

"Just take the da—arn thing, so I can get out of here," Gertrude grumbled in normal Gertrude fashion.

Max held out his hand, and Alex dropped a rose petal into it.

The window went back up, the car pulled away, and Max was left standing in the parking lot alone. He almost dropped the petal on the ground, but that felt . . . wrong, so he tucked it into his coat pocket and walked to the 1967 Corvette he'd bought the year he'd turned thirty. A birthday gift to himself, and the beginning of the end of the longest relationship he'd ever been in.

He frowned. He generally didn't waste time thinking about the past. What was done was done. There was no way to change or undo it, so why dwell on it?

Besides, he didn't regret his relationship with Morgan, and he didn't regret their break-up. Morgan had been fun for a while. She'd stopped being fun right around the time she started wanting more than a little house in a small town.

Her need for more had seemed ironic to Max, since Morgan had been the reason he'd ended up in Apple Valley. She'd been the one who'd insisted on leaving Los Angeles and returning to the town she'd grown up in. She'd inherited a house on three acres and twenty-thousand dollars. Not enough to live on, but a good little nest egg. That's what she'd said when she'd told Max she planned to move back. Since they'd only been dating a few months, Max hadn't had much to say about it. He wasn't sure if he'd have said much even if they'd been living together.

When she'd invited Max to visit for a weekend, he'd been sure he'd hate Apple Valley. He certainly hadn't anticipated living there. Small towns weren't his thing. Had never been his thing.

This wasn't just any small town, though. It was Apple Valley, and of all the places he'd been, it felt the most like home.

He pulled out of the parking lot and wound his way through town. He passed Riley Park, the courthouse, the sheriff's department, drove along Main Street and onto the long driveway that led to Ida Cunningham's house. Everything felt familiar and right—the quiet neighborhood, the empty streets, the distant mountains backlit by the setting moon.

Home.

How many years had he looked for it?

How many years had he spent wanting it?

If someone had told him ten years ago that he'd

have found it in a little town in eastern Washington, he'd have laughed himself sick.

Ida's oversized white house jutted up from the center of a beautifully landscaped yard. Christmas lights shone from every window and wrapped around every tree. He'd helped her put them up, and she'd made him enough clam chowder for a week's worth of meals.

He parked in front of the garage, frowning as he caught sight of a sporty little Mazda. Not Ida's car. Probably not one of her friends' cars either. They tended toward sedans, trucks, or SUVs.

He got out of the Corvette, tucking his keys into his pocket as he walked up the stairs to his apartment door. He never locked it. There wasn't any reason. Even if someone had broken in, there was nothing of value to take. His firearms were locked safely away. His money was in the bank. He had a laptop and a television, none of them the top-notch stuff he'd had when he and Morgan had lived together. She'd kept everything when he'd moved out. He'd been happy to let her do it.

He opened the door, loosening his tie as he walked into the dark living room. Usually, Pete sauntered over, but the one-eyed cat didn't make an appearance.

Max flipped on the light and frowned. The place looked the same. Same plaid sofa and leather armchair that had been there since he'd moved in. Same green throw rug. Same curtains hanging listlessly at the windows.

Something was different, though. He felt it tugging

at his gut, clawing up his spine. He didn't question the feeling. He'd had it enough times to know to pay attention.

He walked into the kitchen, turned on the light in there. A small glass sat on the counter, a piece of toast abandoned on a plate beside it. He hadn't left either there.

He turned, stalking down the hall, pulling open the bathroom door. Nothing. Spare bedroom. Empty. His bedroom . . .

Bingo!

A lump lay in the center of the bed. He could see it even without the light on. He flipped the switch on the wall, and bright yellow light illuminated the room. The lump on the bed moved. He didn't know who he expected to emerge from under the covers. Maybe one of the women he'd dated in the past year.

He wasn't expecting the blond-haired beauty who sat up and smiled at him. "Hello, Max. It's been a long time."

"What the hell do you want, Morgan?" Because there was no way in the world she'd showed up without wanting something.

"How about we talk about it over some coffee?" she asked, dropping her legs over the side of the bed and standing. "So we don't wake Zuzu."

"Zuzu?"

"Our daughter."

"Our *what?!*" He crossed the room in two long strides, peeled back the blankets. Sure enough, there was a kid in the bed. A little girl. Maybe three years old. Splayed out like she didn't have a care in the world.

He turned on his heel and left.

Walked out into the hall, into the kitchen, grabbed a beer from the fridge. Changed his mind and grabbed a soda instead.

Morgan padded into the room behind him. "I know this is a surprise."

"A surprise?" he growled, swinging around and slamming the soda down on the counter. "A surprise is when an old friend comes for a visit. Not when your ex brings a kid to your house and says it's yours."

"I can explain." To her credit, she looked uncomfortable, her tan skin a shade paler than it probably should have been. She had dark circles under her eyes, and her hand shook a little as she twirled the edges of her bleached hair. When they'd met, he'd loved her processed look. Perfect body, perfect hair, perfect manicure, perfect tan. Now she just looked . . . brittle. Used up. Maybe even a little sad.

He glanced away, not all that happy with the twinge of sympathy he felt. *She'd* been the one to call it quits, and it hadn't been because she wanted to live in a bigger town than Apple Valley. By the time they'd split up, Max hadn't cared enough to make accusations or sling mud, but he'd known she'd met someone else. Probably on one of her many trips back to L.A. or to visit friends in Miami.

"Go ahead," he prodded when she didn't continue. "Explain."

She bit her plumped lip in the sexy little move that used to make his blood run hot. Now it just irritated him.

"Come on, Morgan. It's late. I'm tired. Get on with the story."

"It's not a story," she insisted. "I realized I was pregnant after I left town."

"Uh-huh."

"It's true."

"How long after? Four or five months? Six?"

"A couple of weeks. I was already with Kenny. I figured that you'd rather not be burdened with the responsibility of raising a child. I mean, we *did* talk about kids, and you *did* say you didn't want them."

True. But if he had one, he sure as hell wanted to know about it. He *didn't* have one, though. He'd always been careful for exactly the reason Morgan had said. He didn't want kids.

"That was really thoughtful of you, Morgan," he responded, every word oozing with sarcasm. "But I'm not buying your story. The kid is Kenny's or someone else's. He dumped you. You need someone to support you, so you came here."

"You're an ass. You know that, Max," she said mildly. "You always have been."

"So you told me about a thousand times before we split."

She pressed her lips together. Probably to keep all the venom from spewing out. Then sighed. "Look, I didn't come here to dredge up the past."

"Then why did you come?"

"To tell you about your daughter. And because I have a job opportunity in Las Vegas. The interview is next week. I can't have Zuzu with me during it."

"Why not?"

She studied her fingernails for several seconds. "The application asked if I was married or had kids."

"And you lied."

She looked up, her eyes blazing. "What was I supposed to do? This is an opportunity to work at a high-class restaurant on the Las Vegas strip. Decent pay. Great tips. I even have a friend that Zuzu and I can stay with while I get established."

"A guy friend?"

"What's it matter to you?" she snapped.

"I'm just trying to get the story straight, Morgan."

"Yes, a guy friend. And no, we're not romantically involved. Not that it's any of your business."

"Sure you're not."

"We're not. We met while he was on business in Miami. His partner owns the restaurant. Derrick put a good word in for me, and he's the one who told me not to mention Zuzu during the application process. This is all on the up and up, Max. I swear. All I need is someone to watch Zuzu for a week or two. Once I get the job and get established . . ."

"No."

"She's your kid!"

"Bullshit."

"I haven't asked you for one thing since I left, Max. Not one. I didn't want you in my life, and I didn't want you in hers, but Tom is dead—"

"Tom?"

"My husband. I married him a year after I got to Miami," she spat. "He died of a heart attack three months ago."

"I'm sorry." Losing someone was never fun. Even if you were just using that person to make your life easier. Knowing Morgan, that had been the case with poor old Tom.

"Me, too. He was a good guy, but he didn't leave much behind. I'm strapped for cash. I want to provide more for Zuzu than an ugly little apartment. This is the opportunity I've been waiting for. I can't pass it up."

"You probably can't, but you're going to have to bring the kid with you."

"Come on, Max. Don't be such a bastard. She's yours. I have the paperwork to prove it." She dug a piece of paper out of her pocket and thrust it at him. "See?"

He took it. A birth certificate. Zuzu Holly Stanford. Five pounds, six ounces. Born December 25. Nearly four years ago. And there was Max's name in black and white, clear as could be, listed as her father.

"I want a paternity test," he said, shoving the birth certificate back toward her.

"It's going to have to wait until I get back." She grabbed a classy-looking green coat from his closet.

"You're not leaving her here until you can prove she's my daughter, Morgan. If she really *is* mine, we'll work out child support and visitation. Until then, she's your responsibility."

"Fine. I'll take her with me. She can stay with a *stranger* while I interview for the job. If I get the job, she can stay with a *stranger* all night while I train," she snarled.

She yanked another coat from the closet. This one tiny and pink and so well-worn, most of the color had faded.

If he'd really thought the kid was his, no way would he let her go to Las Vegas to stay with strangers. As it was, he couldn't send her into the bitter cold with a coat that didn't look like it could keep a polar bear warm.

"There's no sense in waking Zuzu up and dragging her out in the cold," he said. "You can stay for the night."

"Forget it." Morgan nearly spat the words, her tight pinched expression and flashing eyes reminding him of all the reasons why he'd been happy to leave when she'd kicked him to the curb. "I wouldn't want her to spend another minute in the house of a man who refuses to acknowledge her as his own."

She stomped to the bedroom, lifted the little girl into her arms.

Despite being woken from a sound sleep, the kid didn't make a sound, just shoved her arms into her coat sleeves at Morgan's bidding, and watched Max with wide blue eyes.

Morgan lifted a small black suitcase, grabbed the little girl's hand. "Let's go, Zuzu. Your *father* is too busy to be bothered."

"I am not—"

"Can it!" she snapped, stalking from the room, the little girl running along beside her. Still not a peep out of her. She wasn't Max's kid. He was 99 percent sure of it. But that 1 percent?

Yeah. That was bothering him.

Not to mention the fact that he felt sorry for Zuzu.

She looked way too stoic for a child her age, her gaze solemn as she stood at the door and waited for

Morgan to shove her feet into three-inch heels. No shoes for the girl. She wore those footy pajama things. Blue with green and yellow cars all over the fabric.

Shouldn't she be wearing pink or yellow or some other girly color?

She stared at Max while Morgan shrugged into her coat. He stared at her. He didn't know much about kids, but this one seemed to be upset. With him.

I'm not your dad. That's what he wanted to say, but he kept his mouth shut because the faster she and her mother got out of his house, the happier he'd be.

Morgan opened the door. Frigid winter air blew in, and Zuzu shivered, reaching her arms up to Morgan.

"Mommy's hands are full. You're going to have to walk," she said, hooking a designer purse over her shoulder and grabbing the suitcase. "Come on. Let's get out of here." She grabbed Zuzu's hand a little too roughly for Max's liking. It reminded him of the years before he'd gone to live with his grandparents. Of being dragged from his bed in the middle of the night, shoved into whatever car his mother happened to be borrowing. It made him think of all the times he'd been driven to the next seedy little apartment, the next uncle or dad or whatever his mother asked him to call her newest boyfriend.

Not his problem, but the kid looked so tiny, her black hair pulled into a ponytail that listed sideways on her head. She shoved her thumb into her mouth, eyeing him suspiciously. Smart kid, but no matter how smart she was, there was no way she could defend herself from the trouble Morgan might drag her into.

Let them go, his inner voice yelled, but his gut was saying something else, and he always listened to his gut.

"Why don't you warm up the car, Morgan?" he suggested, knowing exactly what his ex would do. She'd always been pretty damn good at jumping at opportunities. "That way the kid won't freeze."

"What do you ca—" Morgan's gaze dropped to Zuzu, her eyes going from angry to calculating.

"All right," she said, just like he'd known she would.

She crouched down so she was face-to-face with her daughter. "You stay right here, okay? Mommy will be back soon."

She hurried down the stairs, the suitcase banging against her thigh. Max listened to high heel shoes tapping on pavement. Maybe he was wrong about Morgan. Maybe she'd changed. Maybe, just maybe, having a child had made her into something more than the selfish self-serving wretch she'd been when they were living together.

The sound of a car engine split the early morning silence, and he tensed.

One. Two. Three.

Headlights splashed across the pavement below, sweeping along the winter dry grass beside the driveway.

Four, five, six.

Tires whooshed over pavement and the Mazda sped away.

Morgan might have looked back, but Max doubted it.

Apparently she hadn't changed. At least not in any way that mattered. He looked at the little girl.

She looked at him. He was pretty certain she knew that she'd been screwed.

"Well, kid," he said. "I'm sorry about this."

The little girl took her thumb out of her mouth, and did exactly what he didn't want her to do.

She started to cry.

Not just silent tears. Loud wails that drilled into Max's skull and made him want to put her in his car and go after Morgan.

He'd made his choice, though. He liked to think he was the kind of guy who never made rash decisions. He'd keep the kid until he knew for sure she wasn't his, because sending her off with a mother who planned to hand her over to the first person she met in Las Vegas wouldn't work.

"Sorry, Zuzu. You're stuck with me for a while," he muttered as he scooped her into his arms and walked down the stairs. Zuzu's suitcase sat in the middle of the driveway, a car seat beside it. At least Morgan had thought to leave that.

He picked up the case, but left the car seat where it was. He'd deal with it in the morning. The kid was still wailing and shoving at his arms like he was some kind of monster set on devouring her.

He carried her into the apartment and dropped the suitcase on the floor.

"Calm down, kid. I'm not going to hurt you," he muttered.

She didn't seem convinced. He set her down in the kitchen, opened up the cupboards, looking for something Zuzu might want to eat. Maybe if she had food in her mouth, she'd stop screaming.

Protein bars didn't seem like a good choice.

Dry pasta? Nope.

He didn't have any cereal. No cookies. Nothing but a box of saltines. He pulled them out of the cupboard.

"Want a cracker, Zuzu?" He ripped open the package, and that seemed to be just enough to get the kid's attention. She stopped crying, walked to the dinette set, and scrambled up into one of the chairs.

Quiet. Finally.

He put a cracker in front of her.

Pete chose that moment to make an appearance. He slithered into the kitchen and wound his way around Max's legs.

Zuzu took one look at the old cat and started screaming again.

Sleepless nights weren't all that bad.

Sure, Charlotte was going to be tired by the end of the day, but she'd finished all her morning baking before the sun rose. Now with it just peeking out from behind distant mountains, she had enough time for a quick cup of coffee before she headed out on deliveries.

It was always good to be ahead of the game.

As an added bonus, it wasn't the twenty-seventh anymore.

"Thank God for that!" she muttered, grabbing a black marker from a drawer and scribbling out the date on the calendar that hung from the kitchen wall. It was childish, she knew, but it always made her feel better to do it.

She plugged in the coffeemaker, humming a little

to convince herself that she really was happy that she'd been up all night.

After all, things could be a lot worse. She could still be living in Billings, making boxed potatoes and precooked meatloaf for the residents of Maple Ridge Convalescent Center. She hadn't minded the work. As a matter of fact, she'd loved the elderly men and women and the stories they'd told. Lives lived long and well. Lives lived with regrets and struggles. She'd make breakfast or lunch or dinner, and walk out into the dining room to chat.

She'd loved the job. What she'd hated was going home.

She poured fresh coffee into a chipped mug that had been left behind by the house's last tenants. There'd been plates, too. Old cups and jelly jars. A Crock-Pot that she used on occasion. Not that she had anyone to cook for but herself.

A woman alone was a powerful thing. That's what Mary had always told her. Charlotte figured her friend had the experience to know. A widow since her husband's death during the Korean War, she'd never remarried, never had children, never done any of the things that women of her generation had been expected to do.

She'd been content and happy about that. Even at the end of her life, when she'd had no one but Charlotte to visit her in the convalescent center in Billings, Mary hadn't regretted her choices. At least she'd never let on that she did.

The doorbell rang, the sound so startling, Charlotte nearly dropped her coffee.

She glanced at the clock. Six in the morning. Only Tessa ever visited that early, and she was spending the next couple of nights at a mountain cabin with her new husband.

It didn't seem likely that any of Charlotte's neighbors would be up that early. Most of them were older and retired. They slept until nine or ten and then came looking for their morning fix. Quick breads or muffins or Danishes. Whatever she had left over from her baking. She always made sure to have something left.

The doorbell rang again. She set the mug down on the counter. She didn't really want to see who was standing on the doorstep, because the only one she'd ever known to be there in the wee hours of the morning or at the break of day was Brett. *He'd* been dead for three years and one day, so there was no way it was him. There were days, though, when she still thought she could feel him hanging over her shoulder, judging the things she was doing, the way she was dressed, the things she said.

There were nights when she thought she heard his heavy plodding footsteps on the wooden floor. Not real, of course. She only heard and felt and thought of those things when she was overtired or overwhelmed.

Right at that moment she was both.

The doorbell rang a third time, and someone knocked on the door. Not a gentle knock, either. A loud, get-the-darn-door kind of knock that made her pulse jump about seven notches.

"Hold your horses!" she shouted as she grabbed

the phone and hurried to the front door. If whoever it was looked like trouble, she'd call the police.

"Who's there?" She pressed her eye to the peep-hole and peered out into the violet morning light, half expecting to see Brett standing there, his hair slicked back and a contrite smile on his face.

There *was* a man standing on the porch, but he wasn't a ghost from the past. Max Stanford leaned close to the peephole, his uniform police hat low on his forehead.

"It's me. Max. For God's sake, open the door!"

Surprised, she did what he asked, stepping back as he barreled into the house with what looked like a pile of clothes in his arms.

"I need your help," he said without preamble.

"With?" she asked.

"This." He set the bundle down, a thick blanket falling away to reveal a little girl. She had dark hair and big blue eyes and the kind of chubby pink cheeks that little kids on magazine covers usually sported.

Charlotte's heart jumped in response.

"She's adorable."

"Yeah. Adorable." He glared at the child and then at Charlotte. "Except when she's screaming her fool head off."

"She's not screaming now," Charlotte pointed out, crouching down so she was eye to eye with the little girl. "Are you, sweetie?"

The girl shoved her thumb in her mouth.

"What's her name?" Charlotte asked as she straightened and met Max's eye. He looked tired, his jaw dark with the beginning of a beard, blue-black circles beneath his eyes. Even tired, he looked good. Better than good. Darn the man and his ability to make her insides melt. Thank God she'd had the presence of mind to refuse his one and only dinner invitation. Who knows what kind of trouble she could have found herself in if she hadn't?

"Zuzu."

"Cute. Whose is she?"

"My ex's," he growled. Apparently he wasn't in the mood for long conversations.

"And, you have her because?"

"It's complicated."

"So, she's yours." Otherwise she couldn't see a guy like Max babysitting a child.

"That's up for debate." He glanced at Zuzu and frowned. "Can you help me or not?"

"That depends on what you need help with."

"I need a babysitter."

"A babysitter?" she repeated. She'd been asked for a lot of things since she'd moved to Apple Valley. That wasn't one of them.

"For Zuzu," he explained as if she might have thought he needed a babysitter for himself. "I asked Ida, but she has the historical society meeting today and then she's visiting a friend in Spokane. She thought I should ask you."

"Why?" She sounded as horrified as she felt.

"Because you were the first person she thought of? Because you seem like the motherly type? How the he . . . ck should I know?"

Motherly type didn't sound like a compliment coming from Max. Not that she cared what he thought of her. "I work, Max. Maybe she forgot that."

"I doubt she forgot. You're bringing muffins to the meeting she's attending."

"I can't work and take care of a little girl." Even if she could, she didn't want to.

"Neither can I," he muttered.

He lifted the little girl, wrapped the blanket around her shoulders, and opened the door.

She knew she should let him go. She'd regret it if she didn't, but that soft spot in her heart, the spot that had made excuses for Brett's behavior because she'd wanted to give him everything he hadn't had when he was a kid, reared its stupid head. Max was a police officer. Zuzu was a tiny little girl. She couldn't go off to work with him and spend the day at the sheriff's department.

"Wait!" she said before he could walk outside.

He paused, glanced over his shoulder.

"What?"

"Let's have some coffee and discuss your options."

He scowled, but closed the door. "Charlotte, I seriously do *not* have time for coffee and discussions. Are you going to be able to help me or not?"

"Maybe," she responded, and she knew that single word was going to get her into more trouble than any single word had the right to.

Chapter Three

Thank God Charlotte hadn't let him walk out with the kid!

That was all Max could think.

"The thing is," she said as she eyed Zuzu. "I don't know a lot about children."

"Join the club."

"And, I really do have to work."

"Right," he bit out. "We've established that we both have to work. If you don't want to babysit, I understand. No hard feelings."

"If I don't take her, what are you going to do with her?"

"Bring her to work with me."

"You can't bring a baby to the sheriff's department."

"I can't leave her at home alone, either," he said impatiently. He wasn't winning any prizes for diplomacy this morning, that was for sure.

Charlotte didn't seem to notice. Her gaze was on Zuzu, her eyes soft with the kind of longing he'd seen in other women's eyes when they'd looked at engagement rings. "I guess she can stay with me for a while."

"I have a long shift today. With Cade out of town—"

"We'll work it out. As long as you don't mind me taking her on deliveries." She reached for Zuzu. To his surprise, Zuzu reached right back. Her little hands clutched at Charlotte's shoulders like she was her only hope of salvation.

"That'll be fine. I have a car seat for her. Let me grab it." He didn't run outside, but he came close. He'd dealt with a lot during his time on the LAPD, but he'd never had to deal with a screaming toddler. If he had, he'd probably have resigned long before his injury had forced him to take a leave of absence. He'd let Morgan convince him to move to Apple Valley while he recovered from a gunshot wound to the shoulder. He'd never regretted it. Although, right at that moment, he'd rather be facing well-armed L.A. gang members than spend one more minute listening to Zuzu's screams.

Charlotte followed him outside. She looked relaxed, in control. Thank God one of them was. "How about a diaper bag?" she asked.

"What the hell is that?" He dragged the car seat from his Corvette.

"A bag with diapers and clothes and stuff in it? The thing mothers and fathers everywhere pack before they take their kids anywhere?"

"I'm not a father, so I wouldn't know anything about that, but the kid is toilet trained, so you don't need to worry about diapers." He'd figured that out about three hours after Morgan left, and he'd been eternally grateful for it.

"Good to know, but she *is* wearing pajamas."

True. Zuzu had fallen asleep for an hour, and he'd fallen asleep with her. He must have slept through his alarm, because he hadn't woken until she'd started screaming for her mother again. Fortunately, Ida had been willing to watch the toddler while he took a shower and got ready for work, but he hadn't had time to deal with finding clothes that worked or thinking beyond getting her to someone who could watch her while he was on duty.

"I think she'll live," he muttered as he stalked back to Charlotte's little house. It looked cheerful, the flower boxes she'd put in the windows winter-bare, but still bright white and pretty. If he'd been in a better frame of mind, he'd have appreciated her effort more. As it was, he just wanted to toss the car seat into her living room and leave.

"You're full of good cheer this morning, Max. No wonder Zuzu's been screaming."

"She was screaming because her mother dropped her off with a stranger and left town. She's scared, and I don't blame her, but right now I've got to get to work. I don't have time to deal with it." He ground the words out as he dropped the seat onto the floor.

He didn't wait for her to respond. He didn't say good-bye to Zuzu. He didn't even glance in their direction again. He was afraid if he did, Zuzu would start crying and Charlotte would change her mind.

She was his last hope, his only hope, and if he screwed this up it would be his own damn fault.

He hurried back outside, the violet-blue sky streaked with pink and gold, a cold breeze whipping dead leaves across the sidewalk in front of Charlotte's house. Across the street, This-N-That Antiques was dark, a lone light shining from the apartment above it. Max thought he heard piano music spilling out into the morning. He wasn't sure. His ears were still ringing from Zuzu's screams.

Zimmerman Beck peeked out the window of the house next door to This-N-That, his white hair standing up around his wrinkled face. Probably collecting details for the gossipmongers. Most of the time, Max didn't mind being talked about. It came with small-town living. Right then, the last thing he wanted to do was be the center of a juicy piece of news.

He needed some time to decide what he wanted to say before he started answering the questions that he knew were going to come. Last night, giving Morgan a chance to run had seemed like a good idea. The longer he had Zuzu, the more he was questioning his choice and his sanity.

She wasn't his kid, couldn't be his kid.

Could she?

That was the question he needed answers to.

Until he knew 100 percent for sure, he couldn't just let the kid go off to Vegas to stay with strangers. The problem was that now she was in Apple Valley staying with *him*. She needed her mother. Not some jaded cop who'd seen just about everything and didn't have room for sweet or tender or loving.

If he'd wanted those things, he would have married and had a kid years ago.

He climbed into the Corvette, telling himself that

he wasn't going to look at Charlotte's little house as he drove away. Of course he did. She and Zuzu were standing in the window. Charlotte held Zuzu's hand and made her wave as Max pulled out of the driveway. As if he really were Zuzu's father, and she was saying good-bye while he headed off to work.

More than likely she was saying good riddance and hoping he'd never return. One thing he'd learned about little Zuzu, she was young, but she was smart as a whip. During the hours he'd had her, she'd managed to drag her suitcase from the bedroom where he'd put it, unlock the door, and almost escape down the stairs while he was in the bathroom. She'd dialed 911 and told the operator that a strange man had her. She'd locked herself into the guest room and screamed until she threw up. The kid was a bona fide genius. At least she seemed that way to Max. He was overtired, though, and coffeeless, so he could be giving her more credit than she was due.

He returned the wave halfheartedly and sped down Main Street. Not the best move for an officer of the law, but he wanted to get to the office, get in his cruiser, and head out on patrol. Hopefully none of the good citizens of Apple Valley would have the guts to ask him about Zuzu while he was in uniform.

He almost laughed at the thought. *Would* have laughed if he weren't so wrung out from the kid's antics. The way things worked in his adopted hometown, he'd be answering questions all day. He'd deal with it. *After* he had a cup of coffee.

He pulled into the alley beside the sheriff's department and parked. Two other cars were already there.

Emma Bailey's and Deputy Cain Lincoln's. Emma worked dispatch and was probably waiting impatiently to razz Max about Zuzu's late-night 911 call.

She was going to be waiting a long time.

Working in a small town was simpler than working in the city. There was still protocol to be followed, but the environment was friendlier and more relaxed. If he wanted to jump into his cruiser and take off without punching in, no one would care.

And he did want to do that.

He jogged to the back lot, climbed behind the wheel of a marked SUV, and pulled away from the station.

Dear God in Heaven, the kid knew how to scream.

Charlotte rubbed her forehead and eyed the little hellion. Things had been fine for the first few minutes after Max left. Then Charlotte had tried to put Zuzu down so she could pack the boxes for her delivery.

Big mistake.

Huge mistake.

Now Zuzu was screaming loud enough to wake the dead.

"Don't cry, Zuzu," she said, reaching for the little girl.

Zuzu must have thought she meant the opposite, because she backed away and ratcheted up the volume, the sound drilling through Charlotte's head and making her want to grind her teeth and block her ears.

The doorbell rang, the sound mixing with the

cacophony of noise Zuzu was creating. Hopefully Max had returned. Maybe he'd realized how inept she was and come back to get Zuzu.

She scooped the toddler into her arms and hurried to the door. She didn't even bother asking who it was. She didn't really care. As long as it was someone who knew how to deal with screaming kids, she'd be happy. She swung the door open, looked into Zimmerman Beck's wrinkled face.

"What's going on here?" he asked, shuffling into the house, his rheumy gaze on Zuzu.

"Zuzu is screaming her head off, and I'm trying to pack up for my first delivery. That's what's going on."

"Well, I'm not deaf, young lady. I can hear the child screaming. She yours?"

"No!"

"Then she's Stanford's." He spat Max's name like it tasted bitter on his lips. He didn't particularly like Max. Then again, he didn't particularly like anyone. Crotchety and a little mean, he had a reputation for complaining about everyone and everything in Apple Valley.

"I don't know whose she is," Charlotte responded honestly. The last thing she wanted to do was fuel the fire of Zim's ire. He'd go on a rant about single parents or deadbeat dads or mothers not taking responsibility for their kids. Charlotte already had a headache. She really didn't need Zim adding to it.

"Well, why's she crying?" Zim demanded.

"I don't know."

"She hungry?" Zim cocked his head to the side and looked at Zuzu.

"I don't know."

"What *do* you know, then?"

"I know that if she doesn't stop screaming, I'm never going to get the muffins packed up for the historical society. If I don't do that, I'm going to be out money and product."

"Give her to me." He took Zuzu and looked into her red face. "Pretty little thing, aren't you, doll?"

Zuzu stopped midscream, her mouth hanging open as she studied Zim's face. Finally she stuck her thumb in her mouth.

"There you are. Good girl. Now how about you and me find something to eat while Charlotte does her work?" He carried Zuzu into the kitchen, and Charlotte followed.

The silence was . . . heavenly. She'd have stood with her eyes closed listening to it if she'd had the time. She grabbed boxes from the pantry while Zim took eggs from the fridge. "Mind if I scramble a couple of these?"

"Go ahead."

"You sit here, doll," Zim said, setting Zuzu on one of the mismatched kitchen chairs. They'd been there when Charlotte moved in, and she hadn't seen any need to get new ones. Zuzu's chin barely cleared the tabletop.

"I think she needs a high chair. She can't reach the table."

"I can. I'm a big girl," Zuzu said as clear as a bell. She got on her knees, her little hands clutching the table edge. "See?"

"So you talk, do you?" Zim smiled and ruffled Zuzu's hair. "But you're not big enough to sit there yet. We'll have a picnic on the floor instead. There's a blanket on the couch in the living room. You go look for it. Bring it here when you find it." He set Zuzu on the ground, and she raced away, her black hair bouncing, her pajama-covered feet padding on the floor.

"You're really good with her, Zim." Surprising, because Zim wasn't known to be good with anyone.

"Why shouldn't I be? Had myself two daughters once upon a time."

"You did?"

"Would I be saying it if it weren't true?" He scowled and cracked four eggs into a bowl. "Both the girls died from the same cancer that took their mother. Michelle in o-five and Rachel in o-seven."

"I'm so sorry, Zim. I had no idea." She'd known him for nearly two years, and he'd never mentioned his family. Neither had anyone else in Apple Valley.

"Not something I like to talk about. A man should never live long enough to bury his wife and children. That's the way I see things, but I'm thinking God doesn't see it the same way since I'm here and they're not." He shrugged and poured the eggs into a hot pan. Obviously, he knew how to cook. That was another surprise. Based on the fact that he showed up on her doorstep every morning looking for leftover baked goods, she'd assumed that he had no skills in the kitchen.

"I really am sorry, Zim."

"Sorry doesn't bring people back. Zuzu!" he called. "Did you find the blanket?"

"Yes," she squealed, rushing back into the room, Charlotte's afghan dragging along behind her. The ivory throw had been a wedding gift from

Charlotte's mother. Brett had sneered at the simple homemade gift, but Charlotte had loved it.

She still did, so she tried not to wince as Zuzu dropped it onto the floor and sat on top of it.

"We eating?" she asked, cheeks pink from her screams, her big blue eyes still wet from tears. It was hard to believe such a tiny little package had created such an abundance of noise.

"In just a minute," Zim responded. "I'm going to make you some toast. Then you'll get a nice big plate of food to fill your tummy. Does that sound good?"

"Yes!" Zuzu said emphatically, her curls shaking with the force of the word.

She was probably starving. Poor kid.

Zim disappeared into the pantry that Charlotte had created out of an old mud room. It had taken months, but she'd managed to remove the useless old sink, repaint all the walls, put up shelves. She'd pulled from her savings and bought a new fridge and new freezer. They'd been a good investment. Business had been growing steadily since she'd moved to Apple Valley. Another six months of hard work, and she should have enough money saved to open a storefront on Main Street.

"You have bread in here, Charlotte?" Zim called.

"It's out here." She opened the old bread box that Tessa had given her. She must have realized how much Charlotte had loved the box. She'd wrapped it up and given it to her for her birthday. Now it sat in a place of honor on the counter. She took out a loaf of bread and handed it to Zim.

"Perfect!" He took two pieces and put them into the toaster. "How about fruit?"

"Fruit?"

"She's a little girl. She needs good nutrition. She needs fruit. Bananas, maybe. You have bananas, right?" He shot her a hard look, and she was pleased to admit that she did, indeed, have bananas.

"Go ahead and grab one. Cut it up into slices, then cut every slice in half. You don't want Zuzu to choke."

"I'm not choking," Zuzu said.

"And we're going to make sure you don't. Ms. Charlotte is going to cut your bananas up. You like bananas, don't you?"

"Yes!" Zuzu clapped her hands, and Zim smiled.

Charlotte would have smiled too, but she was beginning to feel like a stranger in her own home. Zim and Zuzu had known each other for less than ten minutes, and they already seemed to be best buddies.

Not that Charlotte needed a best buddy. She didn't really need a good buddy or a mediocre one, either. She was content and happy to be on her own. She enjoyed quiet nights and peaceful mornings. There was always the remnant of her dreams, though. The ones she'd thrown aside when she'd discovered Brett's betrayal—love that lasted forever, children. No matter how much she tried to drive the dreams out for good, they always reared their ugly heads when she was the most tired and the most stressed.

Right at that moment, she was both.

She grabbed a banana from a basket hanging

near the pantry door, cut it up just the way Zim had said. Her body ached from hours of being on her feet. Making the cake for Tessa and Cade's wedding had taken a lot out of her. Physically *and* emotionally.

Which seemed silly.

It had been three years, after all. Brett was dead and gone, his ashes interred in a cemetery near his other family in St. Louis.

"Hurry it up, Charlotte. This little girl can't wait forever," Zim barked as he buttered toast and put it on a plate with scrambled eggs.

"Done."

"It's about time," he muttered, scooping bananas onto the plate with Zuzu's eggs and toast. "Here you are, doll. You're all set."

He set the plate on the afghan and handed Zuzu a fork. Zuzu held it with one hand and grabbed egg with the other. Little bits of yellow dropped onto the afghan and the floor.

Nice.

Charlotte marched into the pantry, absolutely refusing to say a word about the mess. After years of being married to a man who'd wanted every piece of furniture dusted every day, every floor swept or vacuumed or cleaned, every surface wiped down, she had a penchant for a neat house that even she'd admit was a little crazy. A place for everything and everything in its place. That's what Brett had always said. It had been cute the first two or three times. After a dozen or so repeats of the same, it hadn't been cute anymore.

He hadn't been cute, either, when he'd lifted furniture to make sure no dust bunnies were hiding underneath, checked behind doors to see if she'd remembered to sweep there.

She frowned, dragging down boxes from the shelving unit that she'd installed in the pantry.

She assembled two boxes and filled them with muffins. Pumpkin, lemon poppy seed, carrot cake. She filled another box with fresh bagels. Plain and whole wheat. She'd wanted to make sesame, but Ida had said too many of the historical society members had partials and sesames would get stuck under their teeth.

"Those look mighty good," Zim said as she tucked the last bagel into the box. "They smell even better."

"I just finished making them. They're still a little warm. Want one?"

"Actually, I had a hankering for one of those pumpkin muffins of yours. If you have any to spare." He eyed the cooling racks spread out across the huge kitchen island. Another expense that had been well worth it, the molded cement surface easy to clean and difficult to damage.

"You know I do." She grabbed a muffin and placed it on a plate. "How about some coffee?"

"Don't mind if I do." He didn't wait for her to pour it. Zim had spent so many mornings in her kitchen, he rarely asked or waited for anything anymore. He knew where the mugs were, the cream, the sugar that he loved to scoop into his cup.

"You're going to kill yourself with that stuff, Zim."

"Sugar?" He eyed her over the rim of the coffee cup. "It's better than that fake stuff that's in your diet pops."

"I don't drink soda anymore. I gave it up for the

new year." She glanced at Zuzu. She'd made quick work of the toast and banana and was tossing bits of egg across the room. "I don't think Zuzu likes eggs," she murmured.

"What clued you in?"

"The egg that's spread from one end of my kitchen to the other," she responded dryly.

"She's a kid. Kids make messes." Zim shrugged, settling into a chair and stretching out his legs with a quiet groan. "There we go. This is better. You sit down, too. We'll take a little break before we make your delivery."

"We?" She topped off her coffee but didn't sit down. She had a long list of deliveries to make, and her customers weren't going to be happy if she kept them waiting so that she could have coffee and an early-morning chat with her neighbor.

"You can't do it alone. Not with little Zuzu along."

"I—"She was going to tell him that she could manage just fine, but he had a point. Deliveries usually meant more than one trip from her station wagon. She couldn't drag Zuzu along for every trip, and she couldn't leave her in the car. "Maybe you could stay here with her or take her over to your place. That would probably be the easiest thing for everyone. I could pay you in baked goods. I'm making a lemon chiffon cake for a baby shower in Spokane tomorrow. I could do an extra for you."

"Hmmmm. That's a temptation, Charlotte. I'll admit it. I do love your lemon chiffon cake."

She knew he did, but then, Zim loved everything she baked. He couldn't resist his early-morning visits, couldn't say no to her offers of gingerbread or cobbler or cookies. According to the blue-haired ladies at the diner, there were plenty of other people who couldn't resist. It seemed that men were particularly tempted by the stuff she made. Her double chocolate delight cupcakes were reported to make reluctant boyfriends and fiancés into husbands. One bite and they'd ask for the hand of the woman who'd delivered them.

Or so the story went.

The first time Charlotte heard it, she'd laughed. The second time wasn't quite as funny. When Ellie Mae Anderson bought some for her boyfriend of seven years, Charlotte had told the poor misguided woman that there was no way the cupcakes could make her Jim propose. Fifty-year-old Ellie had smiled sagely and paid for a half dozen. Two weeks later, she and Jim eloped to Las Vegas.

Next thing Charlotte knew, women were showing up on her doorstep at all hours of the day and night, begging for the cupcakes or the recipe. As if true love could be found in a chocolate confection.

She snorted and poured more coffee into Zim's mug. "I'll throw in a half dozen cookies, too," she offered, sweetening the pot just a little. "Fresh baked. I'm making them for the PTA meeting at the elementary school this afternoon."

"How about you just throw in a ride to the sheriff's department? You're making a delivery there, this morning, right?"

"Just my weekly delivery." She'd already filled a platter with leftovers from the previous day's baking.

She'd drop it off after she delivered to the historical society.

"Perfect. I'll come along. You just stay in the car with Zuzu," he crowed, looking just a little too smug for Charlotte's comfort.

"Why do you need to go to the sheriff's department?" she prodded.

"A need to do my civic duty."

"What civic duty?"

"Gertrude's growing weed in the greenhouse behind This-N-That," he said matter-of-factly.

Charlotte nearly spewed coffee across the room. "What!?"

"Pot. Cannabis. Marijuana."

"I know what weed is," she cut in, glancing at Zuzu. She'd cleared off her plate and was walking around the kitchen, tracking bits of eggs across the tile floor. "I'm just not sure why you think Gertrude is growing it in the greenhouse."

"What else would she be growing?"

"Vegetables? Herbs?"

"Then why does she keep the door locked?"

"I didn't know she did, and I'm surprised that you do. I thought the two of you had a truce." They'd been feuding bitterly when Charlotte moved in, but they'd been getting along better in recent months, going bowling and to the movies like a couple of old friends.

"We do, but that doesn't mean I'm not keeping an eye on her. The Rileys—"

"Zim, don't. Okay?" She rubbed the back of her neck, hoping he'd let the matter drop. The last thing Tessa needed was to come home to the news that her greenhouse had been raided. "Tessa grows strawberries and blueberries in the greenhouse. She has tomato plants and green beans and an entire row of rose bushes that she uses to decorate the shop."

"I'm not saying Tessa has anything to do with Gertrude's crimes. She's probably completely unaware what with how busy her life was before the wedding, but you mark my words, Gertrude is up to no good. I saw that Kenny Simpson hanging out there one day."

"I don't think I've met him." But she was sure she was about to hear every detail of his life.

"Used to live outside of town in that little trailer park off of ninety."

"That doesn't make him a bad person."

"He plays guitar in one of those seedy little bands. Goes to bars every weekend and exchanges music for drinks. He's a loser. Pure and simple."

"You seem to know an awful lot about him."

"I know his folks. They're good people. It's not their fault they birthed a bad apple."

"Zim . . ." She shook her head and didn't bother continuing. Zim had already decided Gertrude and Kenny were in the pot-growing and selling business. No way would she be able to change his mind. "Fine. Come on the deliveries with me, but you can't spend more than ten minutes at the sheriff's department. I have to make a few dozen cookies for a PTA meeting, and I've got to bake those cakes this afternoon, too."

"Lemon chiffon. My wife used to make it," he said as he put his plate and coffee cup into the sink.

"Come on, Zuzu. Let's clean you up a little before we go out. We wouldn't want the town to think Charlotte doesn't know how to take care of a child. You have extra clothes for her?" he asked as he lifted Zuzu.

"Max didn't bring any."

"The man is an idiot," Zim muttered. "We'll have to make do. Hopefully nobody will notice that she's wearing pajamas. You know how people in town are. They catch a glimpse of a child wearing pajamas out in public, and they assume the parents are inept."

"We're not her parents," Charlotte pointed out.

"Doesn't matter. She's been entrusted to our care. You have a comb in your bathroom? I can at least do the child's hair. Maybe if she looks cute enough, no one will notice what she's wearing."

Charlotte didn't know how they would *not* notice. The footy pajamas had smiling cars and trucks all over them. They were faded and old. Zuzu hadn't been wearing a coat when Max dropped her off. Just the blanket. If she and Zim got her out of the vehicle there wasn't one person in Apple Valley who wouldn't notice that.

"A brush. There's probably a couple of ponytail holders on the counter," she responded, but Zim was already walking out of the kitchen and she didn't know if he heard.

It didn't matter. He could brush Zuzu's hair. He could make cute little pigtails or curl the ends around her chubby cheeks. He could do a whole variety of things, but someone in town was going to see the poor kid. When that happened, there'd be all kinds of gossip and talk. More than likely there'd be a collection, too. Clothes and toys and all kinds of things that a little girl needed that Max might or might not have at his place. He wouldn't be happy. She didn't know him well, but she knew he wouldn't want charity.

Not Charlotte's business.

She'd agreed to babysit because Max had been desperate and because she was a pushover. Too nice for her own good. Brett had told her that dozens of times. He'd been more right than she'd known until after he'd died.

She'd been trying to change. Toughen up, close herself off to other people's demands, create a nice safe environment to grow and heal in. *No* was supposed to be her new favorite word. According to the author of *Building Brick Boundaries That Can't Be Busted,* Charlotte needed to practice saying it every day until saying *no* became more comfortable than saying *yes.* At that point, she would finally be free of her need to make others happy at the expense of her own needs and desires.

"No," she muttered, glancing at the egg-stained afghan and floor.

"No," she said again as she washed Zim's plate and mug. "No, no, no, no. NO!"

Yeah. She was getting pretty good at saying it.

When no one was around asking for anything.

Throw in a good-looking cop with heavenly eyes and sinfully sensual lips, and she forgot the word even existed.

"Loser," she muttered as she grabbed the boxes of baked goods.

"What's that?" Zim asked as he carried Zuzu back

into the kitchen. He'd scooped the child's hair into a ponytail that listed heavily to the left. Obviously, his hair-brushing skills weren't what they'd once been.

"We have to get moving. I need to be at Ida's in five minutes."

"Then let's go. Where's your coat, Zuzu?" Zim asked.

"There," Zuzu pointed to the egg-stained afghan.

Zim met Charlotte's eyes, and she shrugged. "Max must have forgotten she needed one."

"Humph!" Zim responded, yanking the blanket off the ground and tossing it around Zuzu's shoulders. "Saw a car seat in the living room. I'll grab it on the way out."

"Humph!" the little girl replied, smiling at Charlotte over Zim's shoulder.

Obviously, Zim wasn't the best influence on an impressionable little girl. Oh, well. Max should have thought of that before he'd pawned her off on Charlotte.

"No," she muttered one more time for good measure as she grabbed the baked goods and followed them out to the station wagon.

Chapter Four

Max avoided the office for as long as he could.

First he patrolled the rural routes just outside of town. Then he made a trip to the local elementary and middle school to check for vandals and loiterers. He didn't find any. He stopped for a cup of coffee and a doughnut at the local coffee shop and carried them into Riley Park. The sun had crested the mountains and the town was waking up. A few people waved as he walked the path around Riley Pond and looked for trouble that he knew he wouldn't find.

Apple Valley was a quiet town filled with quiet people.

Most of them got along. Those who didn't pretended to.

Sure there was crime. By and large, though, it was petty stuff. Missing livestock from the farms at the edge of town. Vandalism by kids with too much time on their hands and too little brain in their heads. There were a few thefts every year. One or two assault and battery charges. Nothing to write home about and nothing to keep him out on patrol for eight hours straight.

Sixteen.

He was working a double.

Too bad he couldn't find a few cases to pursue and didn't have a few criminals to track down. He'd have been happy to spend the remainder of his shift on patrol and out of the office. In a town the size of Apple Valley, there was no reason for it, though. Besides, it was cold in eastern Washington, the late-November air sharp edged and bitter. He'd grabbed his coat on the way out the door, but he'd forgotten gloves.

Had he put Zuzu's coat on?

Damn if he could remember doing it. She'd been fighting him tooth and nail by the time he'd carried her from the apartment. He'd grabbed her and a blanket, and . . .

No coat.

"Damn it," he muttered, and an old lady walking her chubby mutt frowned.

"Language," she said as she and her dog waddled past.

Yeah. Right. Language. He was on duty, wearing his uniform and badge, carrying a firearm, and representing the sheriff's office.

Otherwise, he might have let loose with a few other choice words.

Charlotte probably thought he was an idiot, bringing a little girl outside in pajamas and a blanket. *He* thought he was an idiot. Nothing he could do about it now. He'd pick the coat up on the way back to Charlotte's.

He walked out of the park and crossed Main Street. As much as he wanted to, he couldn't avoid it any longer. There was paperwork to do, a few phone calls to make. He had to go into the office.

The one-story brick building that housed the sheriff's department loomed ahead. He braced himself for what he knew would come.

Emma Bailey sat at the reception desk, her light brown hair pulled into a neat ponytail, her police uniform hugging slender curves. She had a sweet pretty face and a cutting tongue. People who'd known her while she was growing up said that the first was from her deceased mother and the second from her father, a mean drunk who'd spent more time in the bottle than he had in his home.

Max had never had reason to question the gossip.

As far as he could tell, Emma was tough as nails. She worked as dispatcher and planned to attend law school when she finished caring for her father. Rick had been diagnosed with dementia two years ago.

Most days Emma looked worn-out.

Today she looked amused.

"Good morning, Stanford," she said. "Finally decided to make your appearance, I see."

"I've been checking in all morning, Emma," he grumbled, snagging one of the cookies that she kept on a plate at the corner of her desk. Charlotte's doing. She delivered baked goods to the police department and convalescent center once or twice a week.

"Long night?" Emma asked, not even trying to hide her smirk.

"Not any longer than any other night," he lied.

"That's not the way I hear it." She smiled full out, her gray eyes sparkling with glee. "The way I hear it, you were up all night listening to your *daughter* scream."

"She's not my daughter," he argued, even though he knew it was useless.

"That's not what Ida said."

"When did you talk to Ida?"

"When she and the historical society showed up with donations. One of the ladies saw poor little Zuzu sitting in Charlotte's station wagon dressed in nothing more than faded footy pajamas, and it was obvious she was in desperate need. She decided then and there that they needed to take up a collection."

"Please tell me you're kidding." He pinched the bridge of his nose and tried to hold on to his temper. This wasn't Emma's fault. It wasn't Zuzu's fault. It wasn't the historical society's fault or Ida's or whichever one of her cronies had made the decision to take up a collection. It was Morgan's. The lying, scheming—

"I'm not. There's a two-foot pile of clothes sitting on your desk. I would have told Charlotte about it when she dropped off the cookies, but she didn't come in."

"She left cookies," he pointed out as he snagged another one. Some fancy little thing with fruit jelly in the middle and white frosting on the top.

"Zimmerman Beck left the cookies. He also left a message."

"I guess you're going to tell me what it was?"

"He says Gertrude McKenzie is growing pot in her greenhouse. He knows that the state just legalized the use of it, but he's sure that she needs a license to grow and distribute it. Plus he doesn't want the kind of riffraff in the neighborhood that he's sure her little operation is going to attract. He wants you to cut off the greenhouse lock and check the situation out."

"I'm sure he does." Zim had a habit of seeing trouble where there wasn't any. He'd caused his own trouble the previous year, and that had kept him quiet for a while. Apparently he was back to his old habits.

"Are you going to check it out? Because if you don't, he'll be back. Again and again and again."

"Trust me, I know. And I'm not in the mood to deal with him. Give him a call and tell him I'll be out there this evening, will you?"

"No problem."

"And if any historical society ladies stop by with donations while I'm here, don't send them back to my office. I have work to do, and I don't want to be interrupted."

"Uh-huh," she responded.

"What's that supposed to mean?" he demanded. He wasn't in the mood for games, and he wasn't in the mood for gossip.

"Why does it have to mean anything?"

"Because you're looking at me like you know a juicy secret that you're just dying to share."

"You're the one with the mysterious kid that no one in town has ever seen or heard of. Not me. So I'd say you're the one with the secrets. Can I help it if I want to know what they are?"

"Zuzu is not mysterious. She's my ex's kid. Morgan dropped her off at my place last night. She needs someone to watch her for a few days."

"And she left her with you?" She raised a light brown brow and tapped her fingers on the desk.

"Why not?"

"Because, as far as everyone around here is aware of, you haven't spoken to the woman in years. Not to mention the fact that you wouldn't be most women's first choice as a babysitter. You wouldn't be mine, anyway. I don't even think I'd leave you with Pops."

"Thanks," he said dryly.

"Just a statement of fact, Max. You're not a kid kind of person. You like adult companionship. Preferably the female kind, and you don't have a lot of patience for fools. Pops is nothing else if not a fool." She frowned, her gaze jumping to some point behind him.

He glanced back. A small group of ladies was decorating the lobby Christmas tree. Very *slowly* decorating it. When they realized he was looking at them, they bent over the tree's heavy boughs, pretending that they weren't straining their hearing aids trying to listen in on the conversation.

"This probably isn't the best time to discuss any of this," he murmured, and Emma nodded.

"Probably not."

"I'm going to do some paperwork," he said loudly enough for the women to hear.

"You're going to have to clear off your desk first. And your chair, and maybe some room on the floor. The historical society wasn't the only group that brought donations for your daughter."

"She is not my . . . !" He glanced at the elderly women. Their eyes were big as saucers as they waited for him to shout the denial. He wasn't going to do it. He'd take a paternity test before he made another public statement. That way he'd have undeniable proof that Zuzu wasn't his.

Or that she *was*.

The thought gave him a momentary pause, that one-percent chance that she *could* be his eating away at him. He wasn't father material. Would never *be* father material. God help the kid if he turned out to be her dad.

"You were saying?" Emma prodded.

"Never mind," he muttered. "I'll be in my office if you need me."

"Might want to take some coffee with you. You look like you need it."

He wanted to ignore her, but she was right.

He needed coffee. Badly.

He poured a cup from the carafe near her desk and retreated to his office. He planned to sit at the desk, drink his coffee, try to get his head together. One look at the room, and he knew that wasn't going to happen.

The desk was overflowing with stuff, his computer draped with a pink blanket that had little white flowers all over it. The chair was covered with more stuff. Pink stuff. Purple stuff. Little girl stuff. Even the floor had piles of clothes and toys and dolls.

"Shit!" he muttered, lifting the pile from his chair and tossing it onto the desk. He'd need a wheelbarrow to get it all out of there and another apartment to store it all.

He only had himself to blame for his troubles. He could have just let Morgan leave with the kid. He could rectify the situation. It would be easy enough to track Morgan down. He knew her name, her destination. He could put out an APB on her Mazda, find her, and ship Zuzu back where she belonged.

He couldn't make himself do it, and he wasn't sure why not. Old memories, maybe. Thoughts about what it had been like to be a fatherless kid pawned off on whatever adult was willing to take him. Maybe a generic sense of responsibility. Zuzu was a little kid. Someone needed to protect her from her mother's selfishness.

Damn his civic-mindedness. He blamed his grandparents for it. If they'd left him with his drug-addict mom for a few more years, he probably wouldn't have cared all that much about one little kid.

He did care, so he and Zuzu were stuck with each other until Morgan returned. Or until he got fed up and sent out a posse to find her.

At the rate the kid had been screaming, that might happen sooner rather than later.

Thank God for Charlotte.

There was something inherently maternal about her. Maybe it was her need to feed everyone around her. She was constantly dropping cookies or cupcakes or breads off at the front desk. Max wasn't much for sweet treats, but when it came to Charlotte's baked goods, he could pack down some serious calories.

Hopefully Zuzu had done the same.

A kid her age couldn't go very long without nourishment.

Or water.

He frowned. She'd barely even taken a sip of the juice that he'd tried to get her to drink that morning. For all he knew, she was dehydrated, her little kidneys shriveling up and shutting down.

He needed to check in with Charlotte, make sure that Zuzu had had something to drink.

He grabbed the phone and realized he didn't know her phone number. He should have gotten it before he left, given her his cell phone number in case she needed to reach him. Dang if he wasn't completely inept at this babysitting thing.

"Deputy Stanford," Emma called through his radio. "We have a 398 in progress."

"A what?" He knew all the codes, but this was one he'd never heard before.

"Cows on the interstate. Larry Beasley's son left the pasture gate open, and all Larry's prize Herefords escaped. They're trying to cross I-90 at McTravis Road. I've gotten five calls about it."

"I'm on my way."

He'd call Charlotte later. Better yet, he'd stop in. See how little Zuzu was doing. He grabbed a couple of pink pieces of clothing from the pile on his desk, dropped a pair of shoes on top of them, tucked a doll under his arm, and walked out of the office.

He was pretty damn sure he heard Emma laughing as he passed her desk and left the building.

Three deliveries down. One to go.

Charlotte glanced at the clock as she dragged a lemon yellow mixing bowl from the cupboard and set it on the counter. It would be fantastic if she actually managed to bake the cookies before they were scheduled to be delivered to Apple Valley Elementary School's PTA holiday party.

At the rate she was going, she'd be carrying in bowls of batter. Having a toddler around was really slowing her stride. Having Zim around . . .

Yeah. That was even worse.

"How's the baking going, Charlotte?" he asked as he lumbered into the kitchen, Zuzu toddling along beside him.

It would be going a lot better if you didn't keep interrupting me, she wanted to say.

"I have one more batch of cookies to make."

"What kind?"

"Oatmeal with walnuts and dark chocolate."

"Had 'em before. They're good. We're running a little behind, aren't we?" Zim asked, squinting at the dry erase board tacked to the wall. Her schedule was written out clear as day there. Anyone who could read could see that she was running behind.

"About an hour." She grabbed butter and eggs from the fridge, pulled dark chocolate from the pantry. If she worked fast, she'd still get the cookies delivered on time.

"Hmmm. Think we'll finish before those things have to be at the school?"

"I hope so."

"Well, if we're running too far behind, I can bring Zuzu to the store and we can buy a few packs of oatmeal cookies. Just put them on one of those fancy trays of yours and no one will be the wiser."

"I'd rather die," she muttered.

"No need to be dramatic."

"I'm not being dramatic. I'm being honest. The PTA paid for home-baked cookies. That's what they're going to get." She slapped two sticks of butter into the bowl, measured in sugar and vanilla. Thank God she was past the point of needing recipes.

"Take it from someone who knows. They're not going to care. Add a little fresh fruit into the mix, and they'll think they've died and gone to heaven." He stuck his head into the refrigerator. "You have any fresh fruit in here? Strawberries? Grapes?"

"Probably." But there was no way she was going to toss store-bought cookies onto the tray with the lemon bars, Russian tea cakes, and praline crunch cookies she'd spent hours baking. She certainly wasn't going to slap fruit in the center of the tray and call it good.

"Where's the tray? I'll start setting it up for you."

"I appreciate that, Zim, but it might be better if you and Zuzu just waited in the other room." She turned on the mixer and started creaming the butter, hoping that the noise would be enough to put a stop to the conversation.

She should have known better.

Zim moved closer, staring down into the bowl

while she whipped the butter and sugar into a fluffy mound.

"You want me to get some other ingredients for you?"

"No."

"You sure? Many hands make light work."

"And too many cooks spoil the broth."

"Are you saying that I'm bothering you?" He scowled, the lines in his face deepening.

"Not at all." She added vanilla to the mix, cracked in two eggs. "It's just that I have a routine, a certain way of doing things. When I'm in a hurry—"

"I'm bothering you. That's exactly what you're saying."

"No, I—"

"No need to pretend otherwise. Zuzu and I know when we're not wanted. Don't we, doll?" He lifted Zuzu. "We'll just go outside and play for a while."

"Outside!" Zuzu squealed, clapping her hands excitedly.

"That would be great, Zim, but she doesn't have a coat. You can't keep her wrapped in a blanket while she's playing," Charlotte pointed out, measuring a cup of flour into a small bowl.

"We'll find her something. You must have a spare coat around here."

"She's too little to wear my coat."

"We'll make it work. Won't we, Zuzu?"

"Yes!" Zuzu agreed.

"Even if you could find a coat that would work, she doesn't have shoes. Just those feety pajamas." Charlotte measured out baking soda and baking powder and hoped it was the right amount. Usually she baked in peace, a little music playing in the background. She wasn't used to conversing and measuring ingredients. She'd probably end up with cementlike flavorless cookies. Maybe she *should* consider throwing fresh fruit on the tray.

"Do you need shoes, doll?" Zim asked Zuzu.

"No shoes," she said.

"See?" Zim preened, his white hair standing up around his wrinkled face.

"She's barely past babyhood. How does she know what she needs?"

"She doesn't, but I'm as close to an expert as you've got, and I say she's going to be fine. Besides, I'm not bringing her far. Just out back. She'll love the baby swing you've got."

"You mean the one hanging from that rusty old swing set?" The thing looked like it was about to collapse under the weight of time. She'd been meaning to take it down, but every time she thought about it, she imagined the children who had played there and she didn't have the heart to do it.

"It's not that rusty."

"It's not that sturdy, either."

"Sturdy enough for a twenty pounder." Zim set his coffee cup into the sink. "Your coat closet is in the living room, right?"

"Yes, but—"

"Now don't fuss, Charlotte. You want the girl to be a wilting flower when she grows up?"

She didn't suppose that she did, but since Zuzu wasn't going to be her responsibility for more than a few hours, she didn't think it mattered.

She pressed her lips together and kept her thoughts to herself.

Facts were facts, after all.

And the fact was, she had about three hours of baking to do in two hours.

"Stay here for a minute, Zuzu." Zim hurried from the room.

Charlotte eyed Zuzu, wondering if she planned to start screaming again.

Zuzu eyed her right back.

She'd been doing fine since Zim's arrival, but they'd spent the majority of the morning making deliveries. When they hadn't been doing that, Zim had been entertaining the little girl.

Charlotte had always wanted children. Now that she had a child standing in front of her, she realized that she had no idea what to do with one.

Fortunately Zim reappeared, Charlotte's old sweater in one hand and one of her old coats in the other. Somehow he managed to get Zuzu into both garments. "Here we go, doll! We're all set."

He rolled up the sweater sleeves and zipped up the coat. Fabric puddled at her feet and the shoulders of the coat slipped down her arms.

"Well," Zim said with a frown, "it's not the best result, but we'll make it work."

"Zim, I really don't think—"

"You just get those cookies done and let me worry about Zuzu." He took Zuzu's hand, but the little girl tugged away when he tried to lead her to the back door.

"Where's my coat?" she asked, her little hands planted firmly on her hips.

"I think your . . ." Father? Max? "You forgot to put it on this morning."

"Where's Mommy?" Zuzu responded.

Another question Charlotte didn't know how to answer.

She glanced at Zim. He didn't seem to have any bright ideas either.

"She'll be back soon, Zuzu," Charlotte finally said, and hoped to God she was right. For the kid's sake. She deserved better than to be pawned off on two strangers.

"I want Mommy," Zuzu insisted, her chin wobbling, her eyes filling with tears.

"Don't cry, doll," Zim murmured, patting her on the head. "We're going to go have fun. Before you know it, your mommy will be back."

He met Charlotte's eyes. Maybe looking for assurance that he was right.

Charlotte had no idea when Zuzu's mother would be back. She didn't know where the woman had gone or why she'd decided to leave her child with a man she hadn't seen in years. Even if Max *was* Zuzu's father, he was as much a stranger to Zuzu as Zim and Charlotte were.

"I'm sure she will be back soon, Zuzu," she murmured even though she wasn't sure of anything except that the fact that she was behind on her schedule. Very, very behind and getting more behind every minute.

"Good. Great." Zim nodded and scooped Zuzu into his arms. "Let's go get on the swing for a while. You like swings, right?"

"Yes," Zuzu said, but she still looked like she might

start crying again. She shot Charlotte a reproachful look as Zim opened the back door, then stuck her thumb in her mouth and turned away, her nose as high in the air as it could get.

She'd learned attitude early. It would probably serve her a lot better than Charlotte's easygoing nature had served *her*. Too bad *her* mom hadn't taught her to stick her nose in the air and leave in a huff. She might not have wasted so many years on Brett.

She looked down into the bowl of butter and sugar. Had she added vanilla? Was there baking powder in the dry ingredients?

She couldn't remember for sure, and she couldn't deliver flat cookies to the PTA. Great. Perfect. She dumped the bowl of dry ingredients and started over, carefully measuring everything, chopping dark chocolate, mixing it all together. Outside, Zuzu was giggling, the high-pitched sound drifting through the single-pane glass windows.

She was having fun, but she was freezing in the process.

Charlotte glanced out the window.

The swing set stood at the back edge of the fenced yard. Old and neglected, left for decades untouched by children or adults, it had two rusty metal swings and a plastic baby swing that must have been a later addition. Mary had willed the house to Charlotte. It had been a surprise. A nice one. Charlotte had heard stories about Mary's childhood home. She'd heard all about the summers that Mary had spent playing in the backyard and planting flower gardens in the shade of the old apple tree. Mary had moved to Billings with her husband, but had kept the family home as a rental property. Other children had used the swings in the years since Mary had lived there. The red paint had faded to dingy brown, but Zuzu didn't seem to mind. Zim had her wrapped in the coat, her little shoeless feet hanging out of the holes in the swing. Her cheeks were pink, her hair bouncing as Zim gently pushed the swing.

She was a cute kid. That was for sure.

She was also a loud kid.

Charlotte's head ached from a sleepless night and hours of toddler chatter. Throw Zim chatter in and she'd had just about all she could take for the day. What she wanted to do was nap, but she had to bake the cookies and make the delivery on time. Her reputation depended on it. In a town like Apple Valley, that was everything to small businesses.

Right now she was doing well, making money, shoving it all in savings. She almost had enough for a full year's rent on the storefront she'd been eyeing. Right on Main Street, close to Riley Park, it had been a soda shop in the fifties, a five-and-dime in the seventies, and a coffee shop in recent years. The current owner planned to retire to Florida as soon as he found someone to rent the property.

Charlotte wanted to be that person in a bad way. She wanted it so much that she'd almost signed the contract a month ago. If she'd had enough money for the first year's rent, she would have, but she'd learned the value of being prepared after Brett's death. Everything she'd thought was hers hadn't been, and if she hadn't had a good job, she'd have been forced to live in her car until she'd found one.

Brett had been a bastard, but his kids had deserved better than a long drawn-out court battle over the property he'd left to them and their mother.

His other wife.

Thinking about it still made her blood run cold.

Charlotte had relinquished the house, the property, the money that Brett had been hiding away in a secret account. She'd also given up the pots and pans and linens and everything else that they'd received as wedding gifts.

She'd left all of it behind.

She wished she could have left the memories behind too. Most days, she didn't think about all the years she'd wasted with Brett, but seeing Zuzu . . .

Yeah. That was hard.

She'd wanted children more than she'd wanted anything.

Maybe after she got a little more settled, got her life a little more together, she'd adopt.

At the rate she was going, she'd be ninety by then.

She sighed and took the cookies from the oven. Golden brown and studded with dark chocolate, they were perfect.

She might not have had the marriage she'd thought, she might not be living the life she'd dreamed of, but she could make a perfect cookie.

That had to count for something.

Chapter Five

They walked out of the house with five minutes to spare. A miracle, considering how far behind Charlotte had been.

"You put Zuzu in her car seat, and I'll put these in the back. If we hurry, we'll be there in plenty of time to set up the table before the PTA meeting." She slid two trays of cookies into the station wagon.

"We have to set up a table?" Zim grumbled as he put Zuzu in her car seat. "I thought we were just bringing the cookies."

"It will only take a minute. If you can just watch Zuzu—"

"Haven't I been watching her all day?"

"Yes, and I appreciate it. Once we're done with this delivery, you can go home and . . ."

What did Zim do in the evening?

Watch TV?

Read?

"You're not going to feed me dinner?" Zim set gnarled hands on his narrow hips and glared.

"You're acting like Zuzu," she pointed out as she headed back to the house. "But I'll feed you dinner anyway."

"What are we going to have?" he called.

She didn't know so she ignored the question and walked inside. The living room was trashed, a fort made of blankets and dining room chairs taking up all the floor space. There wasn't a cushion left on the couch or love seat. They were probably in the fort, but she didn't have time to look.

She grabbed the box she'd packed with paper plates, napkins, and a tablecloth and took the old teapot she'd filled with flowers she'd purchased the previous day. White and yellow daisies. A little baby's breath. Nothing fancy, but the PTA would appreciate the presentation as much as they appreciated the cookies. That mattered when it came to building her business.

She stepped back outside, her arms full, a clock ticking in her head. Or maybe it was the headache pounding behind her eyes that she was hearing. She should have grabbed some aspirin while baking, but she'd been too busy trying to finish the order.

A car pulled up to the curb as she hurried down the porch steps. Dark blue and boxy looking, it wasn't old enough to be cool and wasn't new enough to be nice. Charlotte was sure she'd seen it around town. Probably someone wanting to place an order. She didn't have time, but she could at least get a phone number. She put the box in the back of the station wagon and handed Zim the teapot. "Can you hold these? I don't want the water to spill."

"Sure." He glanced at the car. "What's Daisy doing here?"

"Daisy?"

"Forester. That's her car." He gestured as he got into the seat beside Zuzu. "You'd better tell her you're too busy to talk. That woman knows how to gab."

"I hadn't noticed." She didn't have time to visit the library. She barely had time to read. When she did, she usually spent her time perusing old cookbooks. She also had a stash of romance novels hidden in a box under her bed, but there was no way she was going to admit it.

"I noticed. I also noticed that time is ticking away, and we're still sitting in your driveway. I'm getting kind of hungry waiting, so I hope you're planning something I like for dinner. Meatloaf maybe. Mashed potatoes. Carrots." He slammed his door.

Seconds later, Daisy got out of her car, her long black skirt brushing winter-dry grass, her black tennis shoes peeking out as she walked.

"Hi, Charlotte!" she called. "It looks like you're on the way out."

"I'm making a delivery."

"I won't keep you then." She stepped behind the station wagon, positioning herself about two feet from the fender.

"Thanks." Charlotte opened her door in some vain hope that Daisy really *didn't* plan to keep her.

"Is that Zim in your car?" Daisy asked, obviously not as anxious to leave as Charlotte was to have her go.

"Yes. He's helping with this delivery. Which I have to make in just a couple of minutes."

"Then I'll get out of your way."

Please do. The words were on the tip of her tongue, but Daisy continued before she could say them. "First, though, I was wondering if I could place an order."

"If you call me this afternoon—"

"Not a big one." Daisy offered a brittle smile and tucked a strand of mousy brown hair behind her ear. "Just a couple of the double chocolate delights."

Great. Not again.

"I don't make them any longer, Daisy."

"Why not?"

"I don't have time to go into it." Even if she did, she wouldn't bother. No matter how many times she explained that the cupcakes really didn't contain a magical potion designed to make every man who tasted them propose, she couldn't convince the women of Apple Valley. "But I'd be happy to bake a few chocolate cupcakes. Or a couple of my Boston cream. Have you had those?"

"I'm not interested in anything else." Daisy frowned. "If you don't have time to bake them, I can do it myself. Just give me the recipe."

"I don't give out recipes." Especially not for those particular cupcakes. The last thing she needed was a line of unhappy female customers outside her house.

"That's just mean, Charlotte! Everyone knows those cupcakes . . ." She glanced at the car, probably looking to see if Zim was listening. "I really need a double chocolate delight. Just one."

"I'm sorry, Daisy." She really kind of was, because poor Daisy looked like she was about to cry. "How about you give me a call tomorrow, and we'll discuss other options. Right now I have to leave."

She got into the station wagon and closed the door, hoping beyond all hope that Daisy moved out of the way so she could leave.

She stood right where she'd been, her feet firmly planted, her oversized wool coat bagging around her narrow frame.

"What's that crazy lady doing?" Zim huffed.

Making Charlotte's life miserable. That's what.

"Crazy lady!" Zuzu repeated as Zim rolled down his window and stuck his head out.

"Daisy! What are you doing back there? We've got places to go!"

"Fine!" Daisy stalked away.

Charlotte was fairly certain she was mumbling under her breath as she went. Seconds later, the boxy little car peeled away from the curb, leaving a cloud of gray exhaust in its wake.

"Let's boogie, Charlotte!" Zim demanded.

She put the car in reverse, started to back out of the driveway.

"I have to go potty!" Zuzu shouted.

"Can't it wait?"

"You're talking to a three-year-old," Zim retorted. "If you think she has the kind of bladder control it takes to wait, you just go on ahead and drive to the school."

Charlotte didn't want to be late.

She didn't want to have a pee-soaked car, either.

"Fine." She slammed on the brake, turned off the ignition, then got back out of the car.

She unhooked Zuzu's car seat and lifted her.

"Better hurry, Charlotte. Girls her age can't wait long," Zim called as she ran back to the house.

Hurry?

That's all she'd done all day, but no matter how much she hurried, she couldn't seem to catch up.

Or catch a break.

Not that she'd ever caught one in her life.

It seemed like she'd spent twenty-eight years trying to get somewhere. The problem was, she hadn't quite figured out where that was or what she was supposed to do once she got there. For a while, she'd thought Brett was the where and the what.

He hadn't been.

Maybe Apple Valley was. Maybe the little bakery on Main Street was. Or maybe in another year or two she'd move on, find another place and another thing.

Right now all she wanted to do was get Zuzu into the bathroom, get her out, and get going.

Because she *was* going to get the blasted cookies to the PTA meeting on time, come hell, high water, or potty-trained toddlers!

Giving traffic tickets to crying women wasn't exactly how Max liked to spend his days. Especially when those crying women were red-faced, red-eyed, and sobbing.

"Calm down, Daisy," he said as he took the librarian's license and registration. "Being pulled over isn't the end of the world."

"I've"—hiccup—"never"—sob—"been . . . pulled

over"—hiccup—"before." She dug through the glove compartment and took out a small package of tissues.

"There's a first time for everything, and apparently this is it." He didn't bother running her license plate. He knew her as well as he knew anyone in town. She wasn't wanted, didn't have a record, had never been in any kind of trouble with the law.

"I know, but I just don't"—sob—"speed."

"You were going forty-five in a twenty-five-mile-an-hour zone. That's dangerous, Daisy. Especially with all the houses around. What if a little kid ran out into the street? You wouldn't have time to stop." He took out his ticket pad. He didn't plan to write her more than a warning, but at the sight of the pad and his pen, she wailed so loudly, a few starlings flew from a nearby tree.

"I'm a failure. That's why Jerry won't propose!" she cried, her face blotchy and red from tears.

"He won't propose because you deserve someone better," Max said truthfully.

That was all it took. The waterworks stopped, and Daisy straightened, her eyes flashing. "I'll have you know that Jerry is the best thing that's ever happened to me. Just last week he bought me a dozen roses for no reason at all."

Max was sure there'd been a reason, but he'd said enough. "Sorry. I didn't mean to offend."

"You just don't understand, Max. You like to play the field. You want a new woman every weekend, and the women you choose want a new man every day of the week."

Ouch.

That hurt.

But it was only a slight exaggeration. Even if it hadn't been, he wouldn't have argued. He didn't much care what Daisy or anyone else thought of him.

"What's your point, Daisy?"

"Jerry and I are *exclusive.* We have been for years."

Exclusive? *She* might have been, but Max didn't think Jerry was. That was another thing Max decided to keep to himself.

"Glad to hear it," he murmured, trying his best to keep every bit of sarcasm out of his voice.

"We *are,*" she insisted even though he hadn't argued. "And Jerry is going to be *very* upset if I get a ticket. We planned on buying a brand-new high-definition TV. I'm not going to have the money if I have to pay for a ticket."

"Maybe you should let him come up with the money," he suggested.

"He would, but he had to quit his part-time job. He's finishing up his novel."

"I'm sure he is."

"What's that supposed to mean?" she asked with a scowl.

"Nothing important." He ripped a ticket from his pad and handed it to her. "I'm not going to cite you, Daisy. This time. I'm issuing you a warning. If I catch you speeding through town again, you will be cited, though. Keep that in mind the next time you want to fly through town."

"Just a warning?! Max, you're a lifesaver!" She smiled, and he was surprised at how pretty and young she looked. He'd pegged her for forty, but the smile made her look a decade younger.

"I'm giving you a break because I've never pulled

you over before. I won't be as easy on you next time." He handed back her ID and registration.

"I understand. Thanks!" She rolled up her window and pulled away, crawling down the street so slowly, he could have pulled her over for creating a hazard. There was no traffic, so he didn't. Besides, he had to stop by Charlotte's, check on Zuzu, and drop off the stuff he'd grabbed before he'd gone on the cattle round-up.

That had taken too much of his time.

Not to mention the fact that he now smelled like cow and was covered in dirt and grass stains. He kept another uniform at the office. He'd change when he got back. With any luck, the rest of the evening would be uneventful. Most days that wasn't what he wanted. He liked a little action. A couple of cases to keep him occupied. Right then, though, all he wanted was a quiet room and a little peace.

He pulled away from the curb, frowning as a station wagon passed going in the opposite direction. Not just any station wagon, either. Charlotte's beat-up 1969 Chevy was easy to recognize, the dull green paint and rusting body a dead giveaway. It chugged toward the town center, and he pulled in behind it.

She must be making a delivery. Wherever she was headed, he'd follow, give her the clothes, explain his schedule, and, of course, check on the kid. Zuzu would probably take one look at him and start screaming her head off. He seemed to have that effect on her. Apparently whatever charm he had when it came to women didn't work when it came to little girls.

Not a big surprise. Emma had been right. He wasn't a kid kind of person. As far as he could see, there wasn't a whole lot of use in having children. Sure, some people wanted to be parents. They claimed to have some innate need to procreate and produce a little mini-me or two.

Max wasn't one of those people. His parents had done a piss-poor job of raising him, and he damn sure didn't want to do the same to his own kid. Besides, he preferred freedom to responsibility. The way his life was, if he wanted to take a weekend trip to Seattle or book a flight to Los Angeles, he could do it without worrying about leaving anyone behind.

At least up until the previous night he'd been able to do that. He'd planned to take a couple of days off when Cade returned. Unless Morgan came back or he shipped the kid to Las Vegas to be with her, that wasn't going to happen.

Then again, he could take Zuzu to her mother, drop her off, spend a night or two enjoying the Las Vegas strip.

He liked that idea.

The station wagon turned into the parking lot of Apple Valley Elementary School. He followed it around to the delivery door at the back of the building. A few cars were scattered in the back lot, the playground and field beyond it empty. School was out for the weekend, the kids playing sports or participating in other wholesome activities. During his elementary school years, Max had been more into pilfering soap and shampoo from the corner 7-Eleven or snagging loose change from his mother's wallet so he could buy lunch at school than he was into reading textbooks or engaging in team sports. He hadn't had time to be a child. He'd been too busy trying to survive.

Charlotte hurried around to the back of the station wagon, shooting a quick smile in his direction. A bright pink apron hugged her slim waist and a black long-sleeved T-shirt pulled taut over full firm breasts. She had the kind of body men drooled over, and he'd seen more than one local guy make a fool of himself over Charlotte. She never seemed to notice. She opened the back of the station wagon and leaned in to grab something. She had a nice ass. Pert and round and just about perfect. He'd noticed it before. What man in Apple Valley hadn't? But he wasn't into ogling women unless they wanted to be ogled. Charlotte was definitely not the type that enjoyed long lingering looks.

He got out of the cruiser as she lifted a tray of cookies.

"Need help?" he offered, taking the tray before she could respond.

"Not unless you're here to get Zuzu. In which case I'll take all the help you want to give," she responded. No smile.

"Has the kid been screaming all day?" he guessed.

"No, but between her and Zim, I'm having trouble staying on schedule." She glanced at her watch and frowned. "I have about seven minutes to get the table set up for teacher appreciation day."

"Then I guess you do need my help. Since I'm working a double and can't pick up the kid, I'll give you a hand setting up."

"Great," she muttered, lifting a second tray. "What time will you be done tonight?"

"Eleven."

"I usually do all my prep work in the evening. How am I supposed to get that done with Zuzu and Zim under my feet?" She sounded appalled and looked exhausted, dark circles under her eyes, her skin pallid. She'd forgotten her coat. Not good when the sun was going down, the temperature dropping. He would have taken his off and dropped it around her shoulders, but she was already hurrying to the building.

He glanced in the station wagon, saw Zimmerman Beck sitting in the backseat holding a teapot filled with flowers. Great. Perfect. The guy had a mouth, and he loved to use it. He'd be talking nonstop about little Zuzu from now until the cows came home.

Max tapped on the back window, and Zim rolled it down and put a finger to his lips.

"Shhhhh! The little one is asleep," he whispered. "Best to let her stay that way."

Max peered past the elderly man. Sure enough. Zuzu was out like a light, her eyes closed, her lips pursed, her thumb hanging just to the right of her mouth. She must have been sucking it when she fell asleep. She still had no shoes and no coat, but she didn't look like she was about to die from kidney failure. That was good.

"I have some clothes and things for her in the cruiser. I'll get them after I help Charlotte."

"I hope the stuff you brought includes a coat and shoes. It's a poor excuse for a father who forgets important things like that," Zim huffed, his rheumy blue eyes filled with judgment.

"I'm not a father," Max pointed out. He didn't owe Zim an explanation, so he didn't add that he'd never laid eyes on the kid until the previous night or that her loser of a mother had dropped her off so she could interview for a job.

"That's for sure," Zim replied, thrusting the teapot into Max's free hand and rolling up the window with a speed that defied the guy's advancing age.

He'd been dismissed, so Max set the teapot in a box filled with napkins and plates, set the tray on top and carried it to the building. Bitter wind whipped through his coat and sliced through his uniform slacks. Zim was right. No father worth his salt would forget a child's coat on such a cold day. Not that Max had forgotten. He just hadn't had time to wrestle Zuzu into it. A blanket had seemed like a better solution. He probably should have grabbed shoes to go with it, but he hadn't. Which was exactly why he wasn't and never would be a father.

The delivery door swung open as he approached and Charlotte appeared, her glossy brown ponytail sliding in a silky rope across her shoulders. She looked pretty and just a little frazzled as she gestured for him to hurry.

"They're almost ready, Max. We've got to run."

"It's what? A PTA meeting? I'm sure they can wait for a couple of minutes."

"No, they can't," she snapped. "I promised the table would be set up at four-thirty. It is now"—she glanced at her watch—"four twenty-six. That gives me exactly four minutes to get things ready."

"What happens if you take five? Is the school going to implode?" he joked, and then wished he hadn't.

Charlotte didn't look amused.

She looked pissed off, her full lips pressed together, her eyes shooting daggers. "It's not funny, Max."

"I don't think I said it was," he responded as he followed her into the school cafeteria. Four round tables had been set up and covered with blue tablecloths. Yellow vases filled with blue carnations stood in the middle of each one. Blue and yellow were the Apple Valley Panthers school colors, and someone had apparently wanted everyone to know it.

A long table stood at the back of the room, empty but for the large tray of cookies Charlotte had already carried in. She lifted it, gestured with her chin. "Can you take the tablecloth out of the box and spread it out on the table? If not, just set the box on one of the tables, and I'll handle it."

"I just corralled twenty head of escaped cattle, Charlotte. I think I can handle a tablecloth," he responded.

He set the stuff down on one of the round tables and hunted through the box until he found the tablecloth. It was yellow. Apparently Charlotte had gotten the memo about the theme. Unfortunately, she didn't seem to have gotten the memo about the table size. No matter how much he stretched and maneuvered the fabric, it wouldn't cover the entire table.

"Shit," Charlotte said so softly he wasn't sure if

she'd actually cussed or if he was just hearing an echo of his thoughts.

"The table is too big." She sighed, smoothing her hand over the yellow cloth.

"Or the tablecloth is too small," he said, and was rewarded with a hot glare.

"The PTA president gave me the measurements. I made sure the tablecloth would fit. That"—she pointed at the tablecloth—"does not fit. Not only am I running late, but I don't have what I need. I'm going to look like an idiot." Her voice wobbled, and he thought there might be tears in her eyes.

He hated to see women crying. As much of a loser as his mother had been, it had always torn him up to listen to her sob after her latest conquest left for greener pastures.

"Don't cry, Charlotte," he said, because if she cried, he was going to have to find a way to solve the problem. He really wasn't in the mood to search the cafeteria for the correct size table or a bigger tablecloth.

"I'm not." Charlotte rubbed the back of her neck and blinked rapidly, doing everything in her power to not let the tears fall.

No way was she going to break down in front of Max.

"Okay," he agreed easily, but he looked irritated, his brows pulled low over sky-blue eyes. His hair was ruffled from the cow wrangling he said he'd been doing, his uniform wrinkled and stained. His hands were clean though, his tie hanging loose around his neck. Even messy and unkempt, he looked better than any man had a right to.

Not the time to be noticing.

She had a table to set up and about a minute and a half to do it.

"Here," Max said, grabbing the cloth and folding it into thirds. He spread it down the center of the table, making it into a runner.

"We'll just stick this here"—he plopped the teapot and flowers into the center of the cloth—"and these here." He put a tray of cookies on either side, set a pile of napkins on the left end of the table and the dark blue plates she'd chosen on the right.

It actually looked . . . nice. Planned even. As if she'd intended all along to set the table that way.

"Good to go," he announced as the cafeteria door opened and Wanda Mallory stuck her head in, her bleached blond hair teased to within an inch of its life.

"How is it going, Charlotte? The teachers are lining up outside. We did say four-thirty." Wanda smiled, but she had snake eyes—cold and unwavering.

Brett eyes.

Charlotte shivered and stepped away from the table. "We just finished."

"Wonderful! It looks great." Her gaze shifted and landed on Max. A single mother with three kids, she had a reputation. Not a very good one, either. According to people who said they knew her, Wanda collected men like other women collected shoes.

It wasn't Charlotte's business, but Wanda was looking at Max as if she were starving and he was a food-laden buffet.

"Hi, Max!" She gushed, rushing forward and taking both his hands in hers. "What a nice surprise!

Were you here to see me? I called you a couple of times after our date—"

"I'm here with Charlotte," he said.

"Oh. I see."

"I don't think you do," Charlotte began. Max had used her at the wedding. She wasn't going to let him do it again. If she did, she'd end up with half the town thinking she was actually dating the man. "We're not—"

"Did you need to collect a payment or anything, Charlotte?" Max cut her off, his hand settling on her lower back. She felt his palm, the pad of every finger, felt the warmth of his hand seep straight through her shirt and zip right up her spine. It lodged in her head and made thinking nearly impossible.

Which was too bad, because Max and Wanda were both staring at her like they expected an answer.

"Because I'm still on duty, and I'm sure you have plenty of work to do at home. So if we're done here, I think we should go," Max prodded.

"Of course." Wanda agreed a little too enthusiastically. She handed Charlotte an envelope. "Here's the other half of the payment and a tip from the PTA. We really appreciate you doing this for us on such short notice."

"It was no problem." Charlotte finally managed to put together a coherent sentence. "If you pack the teapot and tablecloth in the box and leave it in the office, I'll pick them up tomorrow."

"No need for that. I'll be happy to drop it off on my way home."

"I wouldn't want to put you out, Wanda." And she really didn't want her stopping by, because dropping off the teapot and tablecloth weren't going to be the only thing on Wanda's agenda. She probably planned to pick Charlotte's brains, find out what was going on between her and Max.

Which would be exactly nothing and would continue to be that way. Forever.

"You won't be. I live right around the corner. Well, not quite that close, but what's a short drive between friends? I have to go get the teachers. They're going to love these cookies! See you later!" She waved and hurried back out into the hall.

"Wow!" Max murmured as he urged her outside.

"Wow what?"

"Just . . . wow. That woman is a piece of work." He led her to his police cruiser.

"A piece of work that you dated," she responded, and regretted it immediately.

"We went on one date a year ago."

"No need to explain."

"I'm not explaining. Just stating a fact." He opened the passenger side door and pulled out a pile of what looked to be little-girl clothes. "I brought these for Zuzu. I figured she probably needed something besides pajamas to wear."

It was a little late in the day to be worried about that, but it was kind of sweet that he'd gone to the trouble. "We had her all over town in those pajamas. Don't be surprised if you get a few phone calls about it."

"Phone calls? I have about ten tons of girl stuff in my office at work." He grinned and snagged a rag doll from the passenger seat. "The good women of Apple Valley think I'm pretty inept as a babysitter."

"They're just trying to help."

"Help a man who they think doesn't know what he's doing."

"Do you?"

"Probably not. I've been thinking about tracking down Zuzu's mother. It's not right that the kid is staying with a stranger."

"So why don't you do it?" She put the pile of clothes in the back of the station wagon and took the doll. It had a sweet face with stitched blue eyes and a cute little pink dress.

"I guess I worry about who she'll go to next." He glanced at the car. "I'm not the best choice, but I'm not the worst either. At least I'll make sure she eats, bathes, and stays safe."

"How long is she going to be with you?"

"Until Morgan comes back or until I decide to bring Zuzu to her. Whichever comes first." He looked a little confused and a lot annoyed. She almost felt sorry for him.

Maybe she *did* feel sorry for him.

He could have said no, sent his ex away with Zuzu, and let whatever happened happen. He hadn't, and she couldn't fault him for that or for caring about a child. "Have you heard from Morgan since she left town?"

"No. I'm hoping she'll call tonight."

If she didn't, Charlotte would question her parenting skills. After all, what mother dropped her daughter off with a man she hadn't seen in years and didn't check in? Charlotte would have been calling every hour, making sure things were going okay.

Then again, Charlotte wouldn't have left Zuzu with Max or anyone else.

"What if she doesn't?" she asked, cold wind spearing through her T-shirt. She'd been in such a hurry, she hadn't grabbed her coat. A mistake that she was regretting more with every passing moment. She rubbed her arms and clenched her jaw to keep her teeth from chattering. The station wagon was still running. With any luck, Zim had the heat turned up high.

"You're freezing." Max shrugged out of his leather jacket and draped it over her shoulders. It smelled like musky cologne and felt as warm as his hand had.

She wanted to snuggle into it, but that seemed like a really bad idea.

"Now *you're* going to be cold." She tried to shrug out of the jacket, but he tugged it closed, holding the edges of the collar together.

"I've been in the frigid Northwest for long enough to get acclimated to the weather." His knuckles brushed her jaw as he released his hold. "Before I go, I need something from you."

"You do?" Her heart fluttered, her stomach flipped. They were close. So close that she could smell coffee on his breath, feel the heat of his body through her jeans. He had the bluest eyes she'd ever seen. Bluer than the Montana sky in the summer. A woman could lose herself in those eyes if she let herself.

He nodded slowly, his gaze dipping to her lips. "A business card," he said.

It took about thirty seconds too long for the words to register. When they did, she stepped back, took a deep breath of cold air. "You want baked goods for something?"

"I want to be able to check in while you have Zuzu. I wanted to call earlier and realized that I didn't have your number."

"Oh. Right." She dug into her purse and pulled out a business card. "Here you go."

"Thanks. I should be off the clock by eleven." He slipped the card into his pocket. "If that's not going to work for you, I can ask Ida to take care of Zuzu until I get home."

"That's okay. I'll keep her until your shift ends." The words slipped out before she realized that she was going to say them.

What she should have said, what she needed to say was *Yes, please ask Ida.*

Max smiled, flashing straight white teeth.

Of course.

He couldn't have crooked teeth. Or be missing a tooth. Or better yet, missing several. He had to have perfect teeth, perfect body, perfect reputation. Aside from his womanizing ways. Those were legendary in Apple Valley.

"You're a lifesaver, Charlotte," he said, and she had the odd feeling that he actually meant it. That he wasn't just saying words to make her happy so that she'd keep helping.

She knew all about guys like that. She'd been married to one for years.

"I don't have a crib," she said, because she was beginning to think that Max could be more trouble than Zim and Zuzu combined.

"She slept in a bed last night without a problem."

"Oh." So much for using that as an excuse to take back her offer. "You'll have to wake her up in the middle of the night, though. That will be hard."

"I hadn't thought of that." He frowned. "Want to bring her to my place tonight? You can put her in bed there."

"I . . . don't know."

"Her suitcase is there. Her clothes. I didn't check through it, but she might have some toys."

"I—"

"Charlotte!" Zim poked his head out the car window, his white hair standing up straight around his head. "Zuzu is awake, and she says she has to use the bathroom."

"Again? She went right before we left the house."

"She's three. How big is her bladder supposed to be?" Zim griped.

"I have no idea," Charlotte muttered. "And I don't want to find out. I'd better get going. I'll see you later, Max."

"You want me to take her into the school? I can bring her to the bathroom before I go back on shift," he offered as she yanked the car door open.

"That's okay. I can manage." She unhooked Zuzu's straps and lifted her from the seat.

"What's that?" Zuzu poked at the doll Charlotte was still holding.

"A doll."

"For me?"

"Yes." She handed Zuzu the doll. "Max brought it for you."

"I brought a coat, too," Max cut in, holding out a little pink coat that looked like it was from the 1950s.

"No coat!" Zuzu shook her head, her black curls flying wildly.

"Yes coat," Max insisted.

"She's going to have an accident while you sit around discussing the thing," Zim broke in.

"I'll put the coat on her later." Charlotte took the coat. "Thanks, Max."

She ran for the delivery door, terrified that Zuzu would prove Zim right.

Chapter Six

No seemed to be Zuzu's word of the night.

No coat.

No shoes.

No dinner.

No bed.

She looked pretty determined about that one, the pink dress and blue leggings that she'd insisted on changing into when they'd arrived at Max's house rustling as she ran from the living room into the kitchen.

"No, no, no," she chanted, ducking under a stainless-steel and Formica table and plopping herself on the floor.

Charlotte was tempted to do the same. Only she wouldn't plop herself down on the floor. She'd sit on the old love seat, munch on the cookies she'd packed, and open the romance novel she'd snagged from the box under her bed. Who cared if the little she-devil was still awake when Max returned? He could deal with putting her to bed and getting her to sleep.

Charlotte would just sit and read and eat cookies and pretend that Zuzu wasn't her responsibility.

Only she was, and Charlotte couldn't stomach the idea of not doing the best she could for the little girl. She'd let her stay up until nine-thirty, but it was time for bed. And, doggone it, the kid was going.

She crawled under the table, snagging the back of Zuzu's dress before she could escape. "Hold on, girlfriend. You're not going anywhere."

"I'm finding Mommy," Zuzu said, her big blue eyes wet with tears.

All Charlotte's frustration seeped away as she looked into the little girl's face. "Max is going to find her, but right now you have to go to bed."

"I need to say good night to my mommy," Zuzu insisted, sticking her thumb in her mouth, tears rolling down her cheeks. Charlotte figured that she'd be crying too if she'd been dropped off in a strange town, left with strange people, and not told when she would see her mother again. For all Zuzu knew, her mother was gone for good.

"I'm sorry, sweetie," she said gently, pulling Zuzu into her lap and pressing the little girl's head to her shoulder. Little arms wrapped around her neck, and Zuzu's silky hair brushed her jaw. Charlotte's heart thumped loudly in acknowledgment. God, she'd wanted this. She'd wanted to mother a child so badly, had begged for years to be allowed just one kid. There'd been a few times when she'd contemplated going off the pill and lying to Brett about it. A few times when she'd thought that he was away so much, he wouldn't have noticed a pregnancy or a child.

She'd hadn't given in to temptation, because she hadn't wanted to bring an unwanted child into the world. She knew how that felt. Knew exactly what it was like to be the one who wasn't wanted. She'd lived the first ten years of her life with a father who hated her and a mother who refused to acknowledge it.

Her throat felt thick with tears, her eyes hot and gritty. She'd made it through the twenty-seventh without crying, but she wasn't sure she was going to make it through the twenty-eighth.

Yes, you are! Because you are not three, and you are perfectly capable of controlling yourself.

Her brain had a lot more faith in her ability to hold the tears back than her heart did. It ached and throbbed as she scooted out from under the table, Zuzu still in her arms.

"I really am sorry, Zuzu," she murmured. "I don't know how to get in touch with your mommy. If I had her phone number, we could call her, but—"

"I know!" Zuzu's head popped up, her face so close to Charlotte's that their noses almost touched.

"Know what?"

"Look!" Zuzu grabbed her hand and led her down a narrow hallway, the old wooden floor creaking under their feet. The apartment wasn't fancy or posh. The walls were bare, the furniture old but functional. Charlotte didn't know what she'd expected from Max's place, but it hadn't been the plain and simple and obviously outdated decor.

Seriously? The guy never had a hair out of place,

and up until he'd arrived at the school fresh from
cow wrangling, she'd never seen a wrinkle in his
clothes. He drove a beautifully restored vintage
Corvette for God's sake, washed and polished every
weekend if rumors were to be believed. Shouldn't
his apartment reflect that? Maybe be decorated with
fancy furniture and stainless-steel appliances.

Zuzu opened one of three closed doors and
dragged Charlotte into a bedroom. Dark furniture
with heavy lines took up most of the space. A small
throw rug lay on the floor at the end of a huge bed.
There was a closet on one wall, a window on another,
a dresser on the third. No photographs. No pictures.
Nothing personal. Still, Charlotte was certain the
room was Max's.

Zuzu let go of her hand and dragged a little black
suitcase out from under the bed. Faded and worn, it
looked like it had been a lot of places before it had
arrived in Max's apartment. Zuzu unzipped the
front pocket and stuck her hand inside, her tongue
sticking out just a little as she concentrated on re-
trieving whatever it was she thought was there.

"Need some help, Zuzu?" Charlotte knelt on the
floor beside her, but Zuzu shook her head.

"I've got it," Zuzu responded, pulling out a tat-
tered business card. She slapped it in Charlotte's
hand with a happy grin. "My mommy's number."

"Really?" Charlotte read the card skeptically.
Morgan Fairmont, Psychic Consultant. Cell phone
number. No address. If Max hadn't mentioned
Morgan's name earlier, Charlotte wouldn't have
believed Morgan Fairmont, Psychic Consultant was
Zuzu's mother.

"Let's call her." Zuzu rushed from the room. Charlotte ran after her. The girl knew how to find trouble if given the opportunity. She'd pulled every tissue out of the box in Charlotte's bathroom, squirted toothpaste all over the sink, smeared it all over the mirror when she tried to clean it up, and somehow managed to do it all while Charlotte was cleaning the meatloaf pan and packing up a plate of food for Max.

She skidded into the living room right on Zuzu's heels, just managing to wrestle the telephone from the little girl's grasp.

"I think I'd better make the call," she panted, dialing the number that she found on the card. The phone rang a half a dozen times before voicemail picked up. A woman introduced herself as a psychic advisor. Charlotte didn't recognize the voice, of course, but Zuzu bounced up and down with excitement.

"Mommy!" she shouted. "Hi, Mommy!"

Poor little kid. All excited because she heard her mother's voice. Meanwhile, her mother didn't seem all that keen on hearing Zuzu's voice.

There was nothing Charlotte could do about it, so she let Zuzu leave a rambling message on the machine. It wasn't the same as actually having a conversation with her mom, but it seemed to make Zuzu happy. Fifteen minutes later, the little girl was tucked into bed sound asleep.

Thank God.

She glanced at the clock. Max's shift ended soon, and she'd be free to go home. She'd probably appreciate the silent empty space a lot more than she had the previous night.

Or maybe it would just feel more empty and more silent.

She walked into the living room, dragged her purse from the floor, and pulled out the cookies she'd packed. One dark chocolate oatmeal. One raspberry filled. One snickerdoodle. Three cookies almost seemed excessive, but after the day she'd had, she figured she deserved it. She'd tucked the book into the side pocket of her bag, and she took it out, too. Usually she'd be prepping for the next day's orders. Since she wasn't home, all she could do was sit and wait.

It was a strange feeling. One she didn't really like. The last few years had been hectic, one season of life changing to another and another so quickly that she'd barely had time to catch her breath. She'd thought the pace would slow down in her new home, but she'd been busier than ever. Starting a small business had been easy. Keeping it going had been the hard part.

She kicked off her shoes and stretched out on the love seat, propping a pillow behind her back, and opening the book. Something about a highland prince. She'd gotten the book from the library's ninety-nine-cent bin. A hot guy in a kilt. Why not?

She bit into the first cookie, her heart nearly stopping as something moved in her peripheral vision. She jumped to her feet, saw an ugly old tomcat slithering out from under the couch. The thing had one eye, patchy fur, and a tail that looked like it had been chewed up and spit out.

She'd never been much for cats. This one was particularly hideous.

"Tell you what," she murmured, backing up and climbing onto the love seat again. "You stay there. I'll stay here, and we'll both be happy as clams."

The cat didn't seem to understand.

If he did, he didn't care. He stalked the rest of the way across the room, jumped onto the love seat's armrest, and crouched right next to Charlotte's head.

"Please don't bite my face off," she whispered, trying really hard not to move her lips. Just in case.

The cat growled low in its throat, its body vibrating.

Maybe not a growl. A purr.

She turned her head slowly, looked into one golden-green eye and a face that only a mother cat could love. The cat meowed, butting his big head against her shoulder.

"What?"

He meowed again.

"Are you hungry?"

He jumped off the armrest and slithered into the kitchen. Charlotte would have ignored him, but she thought he really was hungry, and she hated to see anyone or anything go without food.

She dropped her book on the couch, left the cookies on the side table, and walked into the kitchen. The cat was there, batting at the cupboard under the sink. Sure enough, a plastic container of cat foot stood front and center there.

"Where's your dish?" she asked, as if the cat could answer.

He just stared at her, his one eye unblinking.

She lifted the cat food, found two shallow dishes behind it. One for food and one for water? Maybe Max had put them away when Zuzu arrived. Knowing her, she'd have probably eaten cat food and flung water all over the place.

"All right, guy. I'm going to feed you, and then you can go hide under the couch again." She filled a bowl with food, filled the other with water, and set them on the floor near the sink.

Good enough.

She settled back onto the love seat, opened the book, took a bite out of the raspberry-filled cookie. It tasted like heaven, the buttery shortbread melting in her mouth, the raspberry filling tart and just a little sweet.

"Perfect!" she murmured as she turned to the first page and met McAllister McDermott, the last of the McDermott clan. The guy had to find a spouse posthaste or lose his leadership position.

"Big problem," Charlotte muttered as she finished off the raspberry-filled cookie and took out the dark chocolate oatmeal.

"Meow!" the cat replied, jumping back up on the armrest.

"I thought we had an agreement." She stared at the beast's ugly face. Maybe it wasn't so much ugly as unfortunate in a kind of scruffily cute way. "Go back under the couch."

The cat settled onto its belly, stretching its paws out so they were within a millimeter of Charlotte's hair. She planned to push it off, but it started that growly purr again, and she didn't have the heart to do it.

She turned back to her cookie and book instead. Maybe she'd find out who the highland guy's love interest was before Max got home. Otherwise, it might be a year before she had time to pick up the book again.

Outside, the wind howled beneath the eaves. Cold air seeped through the window behind Charlotte. She slipped into her coat, shoving her hands in the pockets and frowning as she felt something soft. She pulled out the white feather, smoothed her fingers over it and returned it to her pocket. Tessa might want it back. Or Gertrude. She'd have to try to remember to ask.

The wind blew again, frigid air seeming to find its way through the old walls. She didn't dare walk down the hall to look for a blanket. She was afraid she'd wake Zuzu. She grabbed the jacket she'd draped on the back of a kitchen chair when she'd arrived, tucking leather around her thighs. It smelled like Max. Spicy and masculine with just a hint of the outdoors.

She shivered, told herself it was because of the cold, and tried to focus her attention on the book as she waited for Max to return.

Charlotte was going to kill him.

Max glanced at the dashboard clock for the tenth time. As if somehow looking at it could change the numbers. One in the morning.

Charlotte was definitely going to kill him.

Or at least take a piece out of his hide.

He pulled into the driveway in front of his apart-

ment. No sign of Morgan's car. He'd been half
hoping that she'd be there when he returned or that
she'd returned at some point and taken Zuzu with
her. Seeing as how Charlotte's station wagon was
there, it didn't seem likely that had happened.
Lights spilled out of the living room window. Charlotte was probably pacing the floor, ready to bolt.

He jogged up the stairs and walked into the apartment, expecting to be greeted by an angry woman.
Nothing. Not a sound. No screaming kid. No complaining baker. Even Pete didn't make an appearance.

He glanced around the living room, saw a mound
of fur on the love seat. No. Not the love seat. Pete
was lying on his leather jacket, which was lying on
Charlotte. Her head slumped forward, a book lax in
her hands. A cookie lay on the table beside her.

Pete looked up as he approached, glaring out of
his one good eye. "She fed you, didn't she?" Max
murmured, shooing the cat off of the jacket.

Charlotte shifted, the book falling onto the floor.
There was a guy on the cover. A guy dressed in a kilt,
carrying a sword and looking like some Scottish
he-man. No guy had muscles that big. Unless he
took steroids.

"Charlotte?" He nudged her shoulder, and she
sighed, shifting so that the jacket fell away. Her coat
had fallen open, her T-shirt twisting beneath her
and pulling up to reveal a pale taut abdomen.

Max's stomach clenched, heat roaring through
his veins at the sight. He wanted to run his finger
along the sliver of flesh, feel the silky warmth of her
stomach.

"Idiot," he admonished, nudging her shoulder with a little more force. "Charlotte! Wake up. I'm home."

She screamed. Not a little delicate squeak of surprise, either. A full-fledged, I'm scared out of my mind, scream of terror that made the hair stand up on the back of Max's neck.

"Charlotte?!" He touched her cheek, and her eyes flew open, her cheeks pink from sleep. God, she was beautiful.

"What's going on?" She jumped up, nearly ran him down trying to put some distance between them.

"You screamed."

"I did?" She frowned, snatched the book from the floor, and shoved it in her purse.

"Loudly. I'm surprised it didn't wake Zuzu."

"For your sake, I'm glad it didn't." She shoved her feet into shoes. "What time is it?"

"A little after one."

"Your shift ran late."

"I had to book a couple of teenage vandals. They spray painted the side of the school."

"They're in jail?" She took a plastic-covered plate out of the fridge. There was food on it. The kind that didn't come from a box or a fast-food joint. His stomach growled, and she smiled. "Hungry?"

"Just a little."

"Then I'm glad I brought you dinner." She put the plate into the microwave oven.

"What is it?"

"Meatloaf. Mashed potatoes. Peas. Zim wanted carrots, but I thought Zuzu might like to chase little green balls around her plate for a while."

"Did she?"

"Yes. She managed to get them all over my floor, in her hair, and on the ceiling while she was at it."

"The ceiling?"

"She has a good pitching arm."

He laughed, relaxing for the first time in what seemed like hours. He'd made a mess for himself, taken on a responsibility that he wasn't ready for, but Charlotte's easygoing attitude made him think that things might just work out okay. "I'm sure Morgan will be happy to hear it. Although, knowing her, she'd probably prefer it if someone told her that her daughter had model potential."

"Zuzu might. She's an awfully cute little girl."

"Morgan doesn't believe in cute. She believes in beauty. In her world, it gets people what they want."

"Interesting philosophy of life," Charlotte said on a yawn. "Speaking of Morgan. Zuzu gave me this." She walked into the living room and returned with a business card in hand. "I wasn't sure it belonged to your Morgan, but Zuzu insisted on speaking to her mother, so we called the number."

"She's not *my* anything, but that is her name." He studied the card. "She must have decided to try her hand at something new while she was in Miami. Did she answer when you called?"

"No, but Zuzu heard her voice on voicemail and thought that she did."

"That's something then." He tucked the card into his wallet. He'd call in the morning, in the afternoon, at night. He planned on calling incessantly until Morgan answered. He wanted to know when she was coming back for Zuzu, and he wanted to know it yesterday.

The microwave beeped, and Charlotte took out the plate. "Go ahead and sit down. You want a soda or anything?"

"I'm fine." And the food smelled great. His stomach growled again, and Charlotte smiled again.

"You'd better eat, and I'd better head home."

He grabbed her hand before she could go. "There's plenty here for two. Let's share."

"I don't think—"

"Scared?" he asked, his fingers sliding along her wrist, resting on the warm skin at the base of her palm.

"Of what? You?" She laughed, but the sound was shaky and uncertain.

"Maybe." He tugged her so close their knees touched. "You didn't tell me why you screamed."

She brushed invisible lint from her jeans, refusing to meet his eyes. "I was asleep. You woke me up. I screamed. Seems pretty straightforward to me."

"I've woken up plenty of people, and none of them screamed like Freddy Krueger was after them."

"Probably because most of them hadn't spent fifteen hours with a three-year-old and a crotchety old man," she said dryly, tugging away from his hand.

"That scary, huh?" he asked, even though he knew that wasn't the real reason she'd screamed. If he pushed too hard, she'd leave, and he wasn't ready for that.

There was something . . . nice about having Charlotte around. Pleasant. Easy.

And just a little exhilarating, too.

"Scary enough to give me nightmares, I guess."

She shrugged as if it didn't matter, but he had a feeling that it did.

"Where are you from, Charlotte?" he asked, because suddenly he wanted to know where she'd come from, what she'd left behind.

"Apple Valley. Same as you."

"You know that's not what I mean."

"Do I?" She tucked a strand of hair behind her ear and frowned.

"You're a smart woman, so yeah. I think you do." He took a bite of meatloaf and nearly groaned. It was *that* good. "Damn, you can cook!" he muttered, shoveling another bite into his mouth.

"That's what Brett said the first time I cooked for him," she said, and then pressed her lips together as if she'd said too much.

"Who's Brett?"

"He was my husband. He died a couple of years ago."

She was young to be a widow, but he'd known a few women who'd lost husbands at younger ages. "I'm sorry for your loss."

"Thanks," she responded with absolutely no emotion in her voice. "He was a Marine. Then a truck driver. He died of kidney cancer."

"Where'd you guys meet?"

"Why do you want to know?" she asked.

"Curiosity?"

"It's kind of late for an attack of curiosity, isn't it?" She hitched her purse up on her shoulder. "And I think we're both tired. I'd better head out."

"I'll walk you down." He stood, but she shook her head.

"And leave Zuzu up here by herself?"

"I'm offering to walk you down to your car, Charlotte. Not drive you home."

"I know, but trust me, that little girl can get into trouble in about five seconds flat. You'll both be better off if you stay up here." She smiled and walked out of the kitchen.

He didn't follow.

She had a point. Zuzu was a little kid, and kids knew how to get into big trouble. He'd been called out plenty of times to find a missing child or to help one who'd been hurt doing some stupid stunt or another. Sometimes things ended well. Sometimes they didn't. Knowing that was enough to keep him in the kitchen as the front door opened and closed.

He listened for her car engine, heard it rumble to life.

She'd be home in a few minutes and would probably be thrilled to have her house to herself again.

He settled into the chair again, dropping a piece of meatloaf on the floor as Pete slunk into the room. The cat batted it around for a minute before gobbling it up. Fun times!

After a double shift, he was just tired enough to appreciate being home alone.

Not alone. Zuzu was there.

And Pete.

He tossed the cat another piece of meatloaf.

The rest he was going to eat. After all, it wasn't often that he got a good home-cooked meal from a pretty young woman. He'd gotten his share from the older citizens of Apple Valley after Morgan had left him. Pity feeding. That's what Ida had called it. Max called it trolling. Every one of the ladies had brought a tidbit of information about a daughter, sister, granddaughter, or niece along with the meal.

A few were fair cooks. None of them had cooked like Charlotte. Even the peas tasted special, and in Max's estimation that was a damn hard thing to do.

He scooped up potatoes, walked to the fridge, and surveyed the nearly empty shelves. He needed to go to the grocery store. He might be able to live off fast food and coffee, but Zuzu couldn't.

He filled a glass with water, sat back down at the table.

He'd make a list of everything he needed. Make sure he took it with him when he went shopping. That was the only way that he'd remember that shopping for Zuzu was different than shopping for himself. Little kids needed good nutrition, right? Vegetables. Fruit. Whole grain bread. At least, that's what he thought a little girl like Zuzu should be eating.

He could call Charlotte. She seemed like the kind of person who would know. She'd probably babysat hundreds of times during her life. He opened his wallet and almost took out the business card he'd tucked in behind his driver's license.

Charlotte had already done enough for him, though.

For them.

He and Zuzu were going to have to find a way to make things work without calling in help.

Besides, he had other reasons for wanting to call

Charlotte, reasons that he doubted very much she'd appreciate.

He frowned.

He liked Charlotte. He had from the first day he'd met her. Quiet, hardworking, focused on her goals, she had no use for drama and she stayed far away from people who did. She went about her business and let everyone else go about theirs. In the time she'd been in town, there'd been plenty of speculation about her past but no gossip about her life in Apple Valley. No secret trysts that had been discovered. No stealing someone else's boyfriend or pilfering apples at the farmer's market. Nothing to talk about but how delicious her baked goods were and how hard she was working to make a go of her business. She'd made and maintained a reputation that was above reproach.

That was something in a small town, and he'd noticed it.

She had secrets, though. Max was sure of that. He wanted to know what they were. Wanted to know about the husband who must have been a decade older than Charlotte. A truck driver, she'd said. A Marine. A tyrant? It seemed like a good possibility. Charlotte had scars. The one on her temple was the most obvious, but he'd seen one on her arm, too, just peeking out from beneath her long-sleeved shirt.

He'd wanted to push the sleeve up and take a closer look, but he'd barely known her at the time. Had just been asking her out to dinner, because she was quieter than the women he usually dated, more subdued and introverted. He'd kind of liked that. Kind of wanted to know what it would be like to go out with someone who thought before she spoke, gave more than she demanded, wanted nothing more than a nice dinner out.

When she'd said no, he'd moved on to someone else. Just the way he always did.

Maybe he'd made a mistake in not trying to convince her. She was a stellar woman *and* she could cook. That was an impressive combination.

That didn't mean he had to pursue her, though. It just meant he could appreciate what she had to offer. He put away his wallet, found a pen and notebook, and started making his list.

Chapter Seven

She'd almost stayed, and she didn't know why.

Or maybe she did.

Max was a good-looking man and Charlotte was a woman who could appreciate that. It wasn't a crime to notice, but she wasn't fool enough to think that sticking around his house was a safe or good idea.

She'd heard all about Max and his many conquests. He'd dated just about every woman in Apple Valley, and if rumors were true, he'd started trolling downtown Spokane for fresher blood.

Not that any of the women who'd dated him complained. They'd all seemed to know the score before they'd gone on the first date. Good for Max letting them know how things were going to be.

Not that Charlotte cared one way or another.

If she hadn't been so tired, she probably wouldn't have been tempted at all to sit across the table from Max for a while. Tomorrow she'd probably think she'd been crazy. Right now, though, she had to admit her heart beat just a little faster when she thought about what it would have been like to spend a little more time with him.

"Idiot," she muttered as she pulled into her driveway.

Usually she left the porch light on when she was going to be out at night. She hated coming home to a dark house.

She got out of the station wagon, the wind chasing dead leaves across the pavement, the sound like dry bones rattling together. Not a good image after having the nightmare. Max had been right; most people didn't wake from a sound sleep screaming.

Charlotte did.

Not often, but every once in a while the distant past came for a visit. She shuddered. Compared to her father, Brett had been a saint. If there was a silver lining in the debacle that she'd called a marriage, that was it.

She made her way up the porch stairs, the cold biting at her cheeks. If it weren't so late, she'd make a pot of coffee.

Not late.

Early.

She unlocked the front door and walked into the house, expecting to be enveloped in warmth. It felt chillier than it should have, the air crisp and wintery. She exhaled, saw her breath hanging in the air.

"Great! A busted furnace." She flicked on the light, put her hand near the old radiator. Warmth seeped into her icy fingers.

Not a broken furnace. Good, because she didn't want to have to spend the money to replace the old one. Of course, the house was still cold, so the problem wasn't solved. She glanced around the living room. Everything looked just the way she'd left it. Windows closed tight. Zuzu's blanket lying on the floor. She'd have to bring it by Max's place.

The wind whistled in the eaves, icy rain splattered on the roof, and a door slammed, the sound so startling, Charlotte nearly jumped out of her skin.

She scurried back across the room, ran out of the house, and jumped into the station wagon. She didn't know where she was headed, but she knew for sure that she wasn't going back in the house. Not alone, anyway.

She grabbed her cell phone and dialed 911, her gaze glued to the front door of the house, her heart pounding so loudly in her ears that she almost didn't hear the operator's voice. At any moment the door might fly open and a specter might appear. A madman. A serial killer. Someone or something horrifying. Charlotte was sure of it.

She shoved the keys in the ignition, starting the engine and backing out onto the street. She didn't want to leave before the police arrived, but she didn't want to sit in the driveway waiting for whatever horror was in the house to appear, either.

A retreat seemed prudent and necessary, but she only retreated as far as the driveway for This-N-That Antiques. The shop was closed, of course, the lower level dark. Faint light shone from one of the upper-level windows. Maybe a light in the hallway outside of Alex's room. From what Tessa had said about her nephew, he didn't like the dark any more than Charlotte did.

She hunched over the steering wheel, her muscles tense and taut, her stomach churning with fear. Icy rain splattered on the pavement and yard, coating everything with a blanket of white. Christmas lights shone from the windows and doors of every house on the street. It should have been cheerful and comforting, but Charlotte was too busy being terrified to find any comfort in the charming scene.

Apple Valley was a beautiful little community, but that didn't mean bad things didn't happen there. Just last year Byron Sheffield shot out the window of Erma May Potts's brand-new Cadillac because she'd jilted him at the altar.

Thank God he hadn't proposed after eating one of Charlotte's double chocolate delights. He'd probably have come after her!

Sirens blared, police lights flashing on the ice-coated pavement as a cruiser sped into view. It turned into Charlotte's driveway and two police officers jumped out.

She climbed out of her station wagon, calling out to get their attention. "Over here!"

Both officers veered in her direction, their uniforms and jackets black against the darkness, their faces clearly visible in the streetlight. She recognized both of them. Elizabeth Duncan and Simon Baylor. They'd worked for Apple Valley Police Department for longer than Charlotte had been in town.

"What's going on, Charlotte?" Elizabeth asked. Tall and narrow with short-cropped blond hair, she worked part-time as a police officer and part-time as a high school teacher. The first job was probably a lot easier than the second.

"I walked into the house and heard a door slam."

"Not the one you'd just walked through? It's a windy night. Those kinds of things can happen," Simon commented. Coming from anyone else, it might have been an insult, but Simon oozed kindness. He was the sort of guy Charlotte had always wished she could be attracted to. Nice. Just . . . nice. He'd do anything for anyone anytime, and he wouldn't complain about it. He didn't gossip, didn't play the field, didn't kick dogs or steal candy from children. Apparently that was enough to keep the single and available women of Apple Valley far away from the guy. Which was strange, because he wasn't just nice, he was handsome, his ocean-green eyes and deeply tanned skin attractive enough to make most women take second and third looks. Plus he was a widower with twin daughters. A shoo-in for female attention in a place like Apple Valley.

"I'd already closed the front door. Another door closed. Maybe the back door. It was really cold in the house when I got home."

"It's an old house," Elizabeth pointed out. "We'll go check things out. See if there's anything to be worried about. Stay here. Come on, Si!"

Charlotte climbed back in the car and watched as Simon and Elizabeth crossed the street. She wasn't brave. She had no desire to pretend to be. As a matter of fact, if she'd had a choice, she'd be driving away from the house and whatever was inside of it.

Since Elizabeth had told her to wait, that's what she'd do.

Someone knocked on the back window of the car. She turned, her heart jumping as she looked at the pale specter that stood near the car's bumper. Wild orange hair. Pallid skin. Bright red mouth with an unlit cigarette dangling from between thin lips.

She unrolled the window and stuck her head out. "Gertrude! What are you doing out there?"

"What are you doing in my driveway? That's what I want to know, Charlie." Gertrude shuffled around the side of the car and bent so that they were eye to eye. "There I was, catching up on my beauty sleep, and suddenly I hear sirens and cars and doors slamming." She touched her hair and sniffed.

"I'm sorry the noise woke you."

"You should be. At my age, a lady needs all the help she can get." She tucked the cigarette behind her ear and yanked the door open. "Scoot over. It's colder than a witch's tit out here."

Her comment surprised a laugh out of Charlotte.

That was Gertrude. Completely unapologetic, uninhibited, and opinionated. Not someone that Charlotte would want to be on the wrong side of, but when Gertrude cared about someone, she'd do anything for that person.

"You have an interesting way of describing the world, Gertrude," she said as she slid across the bucket seat.

"Yeah. Well, when you've lived as many years as me, you have a more mature way of looking at things."

"More mature, huh?"

"What? You don't think I'm mature?" Gertrude sniffed, her nose in the air. "I'll have you know I'm the most mature person on our block."

"I think Zim would argue with that."

"What does he have to do with anything?" Gertrude demanded.

"He helped me out a lot today."

"Probably wanted you to cook for him."

"Maybe."

"That man does love a good home-cooked meal. Guess that wife of his spoiled him. Cooked every night. That's what he says, at least. I'm not sure that he isn't misremembering."

"You've been spending a lot of time with Zim lately, haven't you? Are you two dating?" She'd seen the two leaving This-N-That together, seen them at the diner, even noticed them sitting together at church on Easter Sunday.

"Me and that old fart? What a thought?!" Gertrude retorted, her eyes flashing with a little too much indignation.

"Yes. What a thought. You and a nice-looking older gentleman spending time together? Preposterous!"

"What do you know, Charlie? You're young and pretty. You could have any man in town. Instead of going after one, you lock yourself inside the house all day and bake cakes and cookies for other people."

"So?"

"So . . . you're wasting time." Gertrude crossed her arms over her scrawny chest, her eyes flashing.

"Trust me. My schedule is tight. I don't waste a second."

"Don't be obtuse. You know what I'm saying. At your age you probably think you have all the time in the world to find the perfect guy. I'm here to tell you that time just skips along while we're busy. Next thing a girl knows, she's an old woman, lying alone in bed at night, wishing that she'd spent a little more time looking for love and a little less time looking for success."

That sounded . . . horrible.

Sad.

Lonely.

But only if what a person wanted was to find someone to fill her life, heart, and bed.

"Is that what you do?" Charlotte asked. "Lie alone in bed at night wishing you'd spent more time looking for love?"

Gertrude laughed, the sound as rough and gritty as sandpaper. "Me? I'd rather sleep with an alligator than a man. Not that I'm opposed to a little hanky-panky. A long afternoon in the sack with—"

"How about we change the subject?" Charlotte cut in quickly. She did *not* want to know who Gertrude's lover was, and she really didn't want to hear about the two of them spending the afternoon together.

"Why? You think because I'm in my seventies I can't enjoy—"

"I *think* that if being single is good enough for you, it should be good enough for me."

"You're young. You don't want to spend the rest of your life alone."

Yes, she did.

Alone was a heck of a lot easier than together with someone who didn't love you.

"We'll see." That seemed like the best response, the only one that wouldn't bring on more conversation about her past.

Knowing Gertrude, she wouldn't let it drop.

Headlights flashed on the icy pavement and a car eased down Main Street. It slowed as it neared This-N-That, pulling up to the curb and stopping there. She knew the car. There weren't many people in Apple Valley who didn't. Max's vintage Corvette was easy to identify,

"What's he doing here?" Gertrude asked, craning her neck as she stared over the dashboard.

"He's a police officer."

"Not when he's driving that Corvette. He's off-duty, but he's here anyway, and if he's here, where's the kid everyone has been talking about?"

"Zuzu?"

"Who names her kid Zuzu? That's what I want to know," Gertrude griped.

"I don't . . ." She lost her train of thought as Max got out of his car.

God, he looked good.

Even in the dark, even with icy rain and howling wind, even though she could barely see his face in the streetlight, he was the most gorgeous guy she'd ever seen.

It was the way he moved—long easy stride, confident carriage—and the way his clothes clung to broad firm muscles. He oozed masculinity, and that was a difficult thing to ignore.

Even for a die-hard bachelorette widow like Charlotte.

"You were saying?" Gertrude prodded.

"Just that Zuzu's mother must have liked the name, since she gave it to her daughter."

"Humph. Liked it? She probably did it to be smart. Problem with that is she stuck her poor kid with a moniker that people are going to comment on for the rest of her life."

"I think it's cute."

"Cute when you're a child. What's going to happen when she's in high school? College? Has a career? Morgan wasn't thinking about that when she named her kid, I'll wager."

"I guess not."

"Guess? Of course not! Morgan Fairmont had a few screws loose. That's what I always thought, and naming her child Zuzu proves it," Gertrude said with a quiet huff.

"You knew her?"

"There's not many people in town who didn't. She lived with Max for a couple of years. Not a good match for him, though. She wanted too much, and he tends to be the kind of guy who's content with what he has."

"Is that why they broke up?"

"Don't know. Here he comes, though. Why don't we ask him?"

She was right. Max was heading straight for the car.

"I hope you're kidding?"

"Why should I be? I never really thought much about the breakup before, but now that you've asked, it's a curious thing. They moved here from Los Angeles together. Apparently Morgan grew up here. I can't say that I remember her. She was probably one of those preppy cheerleader types. Not the kind of girl Tessa would have hung out with."

"Curious or not, Gertrude, you shouldn't ask Max why they broke up. It's probably a sore subject."

"It's been years. I don't think it's that much of a sore subject anymore."

"Just—"

Max stepped up to Gertrude's window and looked into the car.

"You okay?" he asked as he met Charlotte's eyes.

"He asked if you're okay," Gertrude nearly shouted, as if speaking loudly would help her pass along the message.

Not that Charlotte needed any help interpreting what he was saying. She could hear him just fine. That might change if Gertrude kept shouting right next to her ear.

"I'm fine," she responded.

"Since you are, and since Max is here, I think I'll head back to bed and finish resting up for tomorrow. Tessa will be here around noon, and I don't want to be grumpy from lack of sleep."

Charlotte had the feeling that Tessa would say her aunt was always grumpy. She kept the thought to herself. "Thanks for sitting out here with me, Gertrude."

"Don't mention it, kid." Gertrude patted her arm and climbed out of the car. "That's what neighbors are for."

She walked to her house, offering a jaunty wave as she retreated.

"Is there room for one more?" Max poked his head in the car and smiled, the fine lines around his eyes deepening. Brett had had lines there, too, but they hadn't been from smiling. They'd been from squinting into the sun while he was driving his truck, the deep crevice between his brows from his nearly constant frown. By the time they'd been married a year, the ten-year age difference between them had seemed more like twenty.

Obviously trying to keep up with two wives and four kids was enough to age anyone.

Not a good place for her mind to be going.

She patted the seat Gertrude had abandoned. "I'm the only one here, so I guess there's plenty of room. Where's Zuzu?"

"I asked Ida to stay with her while I came over to check things out." Max slid into the car.

He took up a lot more room than Gertrude had, his arm bumping Charlotte's as he settled into place.

"You woke Ida so you could come over here?"

He shrugged. "She was as concerned as I was, so I don't think she minded. Want to tell me what's going on? I heard the sirens and turned on my scanner. Sounds like you had an intruder."

"I don't know if there was an intruder." She explained everything just the way she had before. By midafternoon, the entire town would be talking about how she'd entered the house, heard the door slam, and run for her life. More than a few people would probably be saying that she'd been chased out of the house by a chainsaw-wielding murderer. She made a mental note to drink copious amounts of coffee before she left on her first delivery. It was that or wine. Since she couldn't drink and drive, it was going to have to be coffee. Hopefully the caffeine would keep her brain sharp, because she'd probably be answering a lot of questions. She'd stash a few candy bars in the glove compartment, too. Just in case.

"Elizabeth and Simon are in there, right?" Max

asked, his gaze on her house. It looked like every light in the place had been turned on. "They'll take care of things."

"Then why are *you* here?"

"I'm glad you appreciate my presence," he said with a laugh.

"Sorry. I didn't mean that the way it sounded."

"Didn't you?" He raised one sandy eyebrow.

"Okay, maybe I did," she admitted. "I didn't really need you to come running to my rescue, Max. I'm perfectly capable of taking care of myself."

"I came out of morbid curiosity, Charlotte. There isn't a whole lot of action in Apple Valley. When there is, I like to be around."

"Oh. Well, then . . ." *I feel like a fool* didn't seem like the right thing to say, but she *did* feel like one.

"Of course, if it had been someone else's house," he continued, "I probably would have stayed home. It's windy and cold, and I have Zuzu to worry about. I wanted to make sure you were okay, though. You helped me out today, and I owe you."

"Owe me or want to make sure I stay healthy so I can watch Zuzu again?"

He laughed again, the sound rumbling through the car and landing right square in the center of Charlotte's heart.

Damn its fickleness.

She did not want to like Max's laugh.

She didn't want to go all melty when she looked in his eyes, either.

"No need to watch Zuzu. Ida is going to watch her tomorrow. Hopefully I'll be able to find a full-time sitter soon. Ida has her ear to the ground, and she said she'd let me know of anyone looking for a job."

"Anyone?"

"Not literally, Charlotte," he responded. "I'll be checking credentials before I hire anyone, but I work five or six days or nights a week, and I need someone reliable to be at the apartment when I can't be."

"It sounds like you're preparing to have Zuzu for a while."

"I'm hoping she'll be gone in a couple of days, but I *am* preparing. Just in case."

"Isn't that part of the Boy Scouts motto? Be prepared?"

"Beats me."

"You weren't a scout?"

"I was more of a gangster, but that's another story, and since it looks like Simon just walked out of your house, I think we'll skip it."

Charlotte looked across the street.

Sure enough, Simon was making his way down the stairs.

She was almost sorry to see him.

She wanted to hear more about Max and his gangster days. Looking at him now, all clean cut and neat, she'd have thought he'd been a jock in school. The kind of guy that any father would be happy to see his daughter go to prom with.

She shoved her door open, would have climbed out and gone to meet Simon, but Max snagged the back of her coat.

"Let's wait here," he murmured, tugging the coat so hard Charlotte tumbled back.

"Hey!"

"Sorry, but I don't want you out of this car until Simon gives us the all-clear."

"Clear of what?"

"If someone was in the house waiting for you to arrive—"

"He wouldn't have slammed a door to let me know he was there the minute I got home," she said, cutting him off because she really did *not* want to imagine someone hiding in her house, waiting for her to come home.

"Stranger things have happened, Charlotte. You wouldn't believe what I saw when I worked in L.A."

She thought she probably could believe it. She'd spent most of her childhood on the outskirts of one of Chicago's roughest neighborhoods. By the time she graduated high school, she'd seen more than any kid should, and she'd seen most of it in her own home.

She shivered.

"Cold?" he asked, and started shrugging out of his jacket.

No way was she going *there* again. To that place where she was wrapped in his coat, his scent, his warmth.

"Not at all," she lied. She *was* cold actually, the icy wind seeming to blast right through the station wagon's old windows. The tired heater pumped out warmth as quickly as it could, but it couldn't keep up with the frigid storm.

"Liar," he murmured.

She didn't have time to respond, because Simon finally reached the car and knocked on her window.

She scrambled out, pulling her coat closed tight against the wind and ice.

"Did you find anything?" she asked.

"Your back storm door wasn't latched. It was blowing open and closed in the wind. You probably heard it slamming against the back of the house."

That didn't sound right.

She'd heard a door. Not something slamming against the back of the house.

Before she could say that, Simon took her arm. "Let's go over to the house. You can listen to the storm door slam and tell me what you think."

"Alright."

He leaned into the car. "You want to drive this across the street for her, Max? The road is an ice slick."

"I can—"

"No problem. Mind if I come in and look around when I get over there?" Max asked.

"It's not a problem for me. You may have to check with Elizabeth. You know how she is." He shut the door and led Charlotte across the street.

Chapter Eight

Max waited until Charlotte and Simon made it across the street before he pulled out. The old station wagon chugged across the road, the tires spinning on the thick sheet of ice.

Not good.

They'd have worse weather before they had better, and Charlotte made a lot of deliveries. Not that it was his business, but he hated to think of her driving around on bald tires.

He checked them when he got out, cringing at just how bare they were. She needed new snow tires. Preferably ones that were studded or chained. He doubted she'd want to hear it from him, but he'd probably say something anyway. He owed her, and he planned to pay her back. One way or another.

She and Simon were already inside, so he jogged up the porch stairs and walked in. He didn't bother ringing the doorbell or knocking. He knew *exactly* how Elizabeth was. Protective of her jurisdictions. Not that there really were such things in Apple

Valley. The police force was small enough that one person's case was just as much someone else's. They worked together on things. That was part of what Max loved about working for Apple Valley PD.

Charlotte's living room was empty, a blanket lying in a heap on the floor. Zuzu's from the look of it. He didn't touch it. Just in case Elizabeth decided to process the house as a crime scene.

Voices drifted from the kitchen, and he followed the sound, the old wooden floor creaking under his feet. He'd never thought much about houses. He'd lived in dive motels and roach-infested apartments for most of his youth. When he'd moved to his grandparents' two-bedroom rancher on the outskirts of L.A., he'd thought he'd died and gone to heaven. Morgan's house had been even bigger. Three bedrooms, two baths, a large recreation room in the basement, and an attic that had been converted to a bedroom. He'd liked it, but he'd known he could live in something smaller and dirtier and still be fine. The apartment was much smaller, but it was clean and nice. He liked his landlady, liked the little piece of property the apartment sat on. He was content, but he'd learned to be that a long time ago.

Still, if he were going to choose any place to live, he'd probably want to be in a house like Charlotte's. Not too big or too small. Old wooden floors and trim. Old single-pane windows that let the sound of the wind seep in. He even liked the radiators, painted white sometime in the distant past.

Elizabeth peered out of the kitchen. "What are you doing here, Max?" she snapped, her dark brown eyes flashing with irritation.

"I heard there was trouble. I thought I'd check things out."

"Because you didn't trust us to do the job ourselves?" she demanded, her hands on her narrow hips.

"Because Charlotte is a friend of mine." Sort of. "And I wanted to make sure she was okay."

"Hmph!" Elizabeth responded, obviously not convinced. That was fine. He hadn't come to step on toes, and he didn't plan to. If he did, Cade would hear about it when he got back in. Not that Max was concerned about what his friend and boss would say. It was more that he didn't want Cade to have to deal with in-fighting the minute he stepped back into the office.

"Would you prefer that I wait outside while you finish up in here?" he asked, making sure that his voice was pleasant and his smile at least halfway real.

"As a matter of fact—"

A muffled thump interrupted her words. She glanced back over her shoulder. "That was it, Charlotte, right? The banging door?"

It didn't sound like any banging door Max had ever heard, but he decided not to mention that.

He followed her as she walked into the kitchen.

Unlike the rest of the house, this room had been updated with modern appliances and some fancy type of countertop. At the far end of the room, a door opened into what looked to be a pantry lined with food and equipment. Charlotte and Simon stood beside it, their heads cocked to the side.

Thud!

The storm door slammed against the siding again.

"Well?!" Elizabeth demanded. "Isn't that what you heard?"

Talk about leading a witness!

"I don't think so," Charlotte said with a frown. She walked into the pantry and opened the door, snagging the storm door as the wind blew it closed again. "Besides, I keep this locked because it does bang open when it's windy out."

"Is it possible you forgot to do that today?" Simon asked. A good question. Especially because Charlotte had had Zuzu at the house.

"It's possible. I had a couple of people here. They were out in the backyard for a while." Her gaze shifted to Max, but she didn't mention Zuzu.

He wasn't surprised. Charlotte wasn't the kind to gossip. He *was* pleased, though, glad that his assessment of her had been correct.

"And you didn't check the lock on either door when you left this evening?" Elizabeth asked, her fingers drumming against her thigh. She had a wedding ring and an engagement ring, but she wore them on her right hand. Max had never figured out why. Some people in town said that she'd been married to a Marine and that he'd gone missing in Iraq several years before. Others said that she hadn't ever been married and wore the rings to make people think she was a widow. She had two teenagers, but Max didn't think she'd care one way or another what people in town thought about her being a single parent.

"No, I didn't." Charlotte blushed. "But I can tell you for sure that I heard a door slamming, and the house was icy cold when I got home."

"Hmmm." Simon pulled the door so that it was not quite closed, then stepped away. The wind sucked it open a couple of inches, then slammed it closed. "Is that what you heard?"

"I think so," Charlotte admitted.

"It looks like someone left the door cracked open. When you walked into the house, it might have created just enough of a vacuum to slam the door closed." Elizabeth nodded, obviously satisfied with what they'd found.

"I'm sorry for calling you out for nothing." Charlotte touched the door, her hand resting against white paint. She had faint white scars on her knuckles that Max had never noticed before.

"We were glad to come and check things out for you." Simon smiled gently, and Charlotte returned it with a smile of her own.

Max liked Simon. He was a nice guy who'd apparently had a great marriage until his wife's death from a prescription drug overdose. Charlotte was a young widow. She understood about relationships and grief and all the stuff they'd both lived through. They'd be perfect for each other.

For some reason that annoyed Max.

"It's always better to be safe than sorry," Elizabeth intoned, but she looked irritated, her short-cropped blond hair shoved under her uniform hat. "If you have any more trouble, give us a call. You ready, Simon?"

She was out the door before Simon had a chance to answer. Typical Elizabeth. She was a good cop, but she wasn't all that pleasant to be around.

"I guess that's that, then." Simon's gaze lingered

on Charlotte for a few seconds longer than Max thought was necessary. "Take this." He pulled a business card from his wallet and handed it to her. "If anything comes up, give me a call."

Charlotte took the card and followed Simon as he walked out of the kitchen.

Nice guy.

Nice girl.

The perfect couple.

And that really pissed Max off.

He'd never been nice, didn't plan to be nice. He tried to be fair, tried to play by rules that others could live with. Especially when it came to relationships. His father had been a bastard. Every man who'd ever been in his mother's life had been the same. Users who'd taken what they wanted and left. He'd sworn that he'd never be that. He'd been a lot of other things, but he'd never treated a woman with anything other than respect. Even women like Morgan.

He opened the fridge, listening as Simon murmured something to Charlotte. She chuckled, and it was all he could do to not go into the living room. It wasn't his business if the two got chummy.

But damn if he didn't want to make it his business.

He scowled, closed the fridge, and stalked to a cookie jar that sat on the counter. Shaped like a pig with shiny pink cheeks and a round body, it had chips and scratches and looked like it had come from the junk shop Tessa's sister and brother-in-law had run before they were killed in a car accident.

The shop had been failing miserably when Tessa arrived to take care of her nephew Alex. Now it was thriving.

The floorboards creaked as he peered into the chunky pig. It was empty.

Damn it!

"Looking for something?" Charlotte asked, walking into the kitchen, her dark hair bouncing, her face soft. She looked beautiful and young and just a little too naive for someone like Max.

"Cookies," he growled, because he'd been spending way too much time thinking about Charlotte. There were plenty of other women he could think about, and most of them would be very happy to have him thinking about them.

"Sorry. I don't usually keep cookies around the house. Too tempting. I have some chocolate bars in the freezer in the pantry if you want one."

He snagged her hand as she walked by. "Candy bars can't compare to your cookies. And what's wrong with being tempted?"

"Nothing. Until I look in the mirror and find out I'm fifty pounds heavier." She laughed.

He loved the sound of her laughter and the way her eyes sparkled when she was amused. He loved standing in her kitchen, his fingers around her wrist, silky skin beneath his palm.

"You'd make fifty extra pounds look good," he said, knowing he was flirting.

Her eyes widened, her cheeks flushed pink. "I bet you say that to every baker you know."

"Only the ones that feed me meatloaf and mashed potatoes."

"I fed the same thing to Zim and Zuzu," she pointed out, but she didn't pull away. She could have. He kept his grip loose, slid his thumb along the heel of her hand. "I'm sure they'd both flirt with you, if they knew how to flirt."

She laughed nervously and slid her wrist away.

"It's the strangest thing," she said, walking into the pantry and opening the back door again. "Zim doesn't seem like the kind of guy to leave a door open. He's probably the only one in Apple Valley besides me who locks his windows and doors religiously."

She had a point. Zim was one of the least trusting people Max knew. If rumors were true, he kept his money on his property because he worried that banks would run away with his hard-earned cash. Max didn't know what he'd done as a young man, but now that he was older, Zim dabbled in real estate. He owned several properties in town and rented them to local businesses for a fair price. They were the only businesses on Main Street with security cameras on the premises.

Yeah. Zim definitely wasn't the kind of guy who'd forget to close a door.

"Is the door hard to close?" He pulled it shut. It fit like a glove, snapping into place and staying solidly there. "It's definitely a tight fit. If he shut it, it wouldn't have opened."

"That's what I was thinking." She brushed back her bangs, and he caught a quick glimpse of her scar. He almost ran his finger on the ragged edge, just to see how far into her hair it went. "But Zim was carrying Zuzu when he came in. He probably did just forget to pull the door closed all the way."

"You don't sound convinced."

"I am. It's a perfectly reasonable explanation, right?"

"Right." But if she was worried, he was worried, too. Not that his coworkers hadn't done a thorough job of searching for an intruder, but he didn't think it would hurt to go through the house one more time. "How about we do a walk-through? Just to make sure the windows are locked."

"I . . ." She sighed. "Won't sleep a wink if we don't, so I guess I'm going to agree."

"That makes things a lot easier. Lead the way, Charlotte."

"The house isn't all that big. Just the rooms down here and the attic bedroom upstairs. It was converted after the house was built, I think. There's a second bathroom up there, too."

"Do you use the attic as your bedroom?"

"No!"

"That's a pretty strong reaction, Charlotte," he commented as he followed her into the living room.

"I've never been that keen on attics," she responded.

"Why's that?"

"Too many horror movies, I guess." She shrugged as if it didn't matter, but he had a feeling there was a story there just begging to be told.

"You watch horror movies?"

She hesitated, and then shook her head. "No. I hate watching hapless victims walk into danger. Plus the music is always as scary as the dark creepy basement or box-cluttered attic. How about you? Are you a horror movie fan?"

She was changing the subject. That was fine. He'd

figure out why she was afraid of her attic eventually, because he found himself wanting to know that and a lot more about Charlotte. "I'm more a romantic comedy kind of guy."

"No way!" She eyed him suspiciously.

"It's true. I'm a big fan of anything that will make my dates happy and weepy all at the same time."

"Now *that* I believe!" she said.

He didn't bother asking what she meant. He knew his reputation.

They checked the living room and dining room windows, the wind buffeting the single-pane glass. Everything was locked up tight in the main living areas. The bedrooms were smaller than bedrooms in modern houses. One was empty but for a large dresser that looked like it had been there for as long as the house had been around.

Charlotte hurried to the lone window and checked the lock.

"This one is locked too," she said as she sidled past him and walked back out into the hall. She seemed to be getting more nervous by the minute, her shoulders tense, her movements quick and stiff. "I feel really silly about this, Max. Why don't you go ahead home? I'm sure that Ida wants to get back to bed."

"What's to feel silly about?"

"Us. Going through my house checking all the locks even though two police officers just told me that no one was in the house when I got home."

"We could check under the beds, too, if you want," he suggested.

Charlotte wanted to. She really did. She wanted

to check under the beds, in the closets, under the couch, and in the cupboards, because no matter what Elizabeth and Simon thought, she couldn't imagine Zim leaving the back door open.

"That would be even sillier," she said, doing her best not to notice the breadth of Max's shoulders as he pushed open the door to her room. She really didn't want him in there. It was too . . . old-fashioned. Too much of what she didn't want to be anymore—sweet and unassuming, traditional and boring.

She'd tried to give that up after she left Montana. She'd made sure to decorate the kitchen with modern appliances and state-of-the-art equipment. She'd used most of her savings to create what she imagined most chefs would love. She *did* love it, but when she was honest with herself, she'd admit that she'd have been just as happy with cherrywood cabinets and a 1950s stove.

She'd pulled up 1970s carpet in the living room and left the old wooden floors because they were more her style than the modern sofa she'd bought. The fact was no matter how much she tried to be different, she really was an old-fashioned kind of girl.

"Nice room," he murmured as she walked past.

She didn't dare look at his face. If he was mocking her, she didn't want to know it. "Thanks."

"You have good taste in furniture." He ran a hand over the antique headboard she'd bought after Brett died. It wasn't the kind of thing he'd have appreciated, but she'd loved the carved Victorian piece. "This is Victorian, right?"

"Yes." She checked the window. Locked tight. Just as she'd known it would be.

"And how about this?" He lifted an old Foley from the shelf above the bed. It was part of her secret passion. No knickknacks. No expensive jewelry. No shoe closet full of shoes or clothes. She collected old kitchen equipment.

"It's a Foley."

"Okay," he said, setting it back on the shelf. "That helped me not at all."

"A Foley is a masher. You can put cooked apples or potatoes in it." She lifted it, loving the feel of the old metal and the wooden edge of the handle. "It attaches to a bowl, and you just spin this handle and the food comes out the holes. It makes great applesauce."

"You've used it?"

"Just once. I wanted to see how it worked."

"I bet you were imagining the first owner, right? Hanging out in her hot kitchen, excited to use her brand-new, state-of-the-art potato masher."

He was right.

That's exactly what she'd done.

"There's just one more lower-level window. It's in the bathroom," she said, because they were stepping into personal territory, and that was a place she tried hard not to go.

"Charlotte." Max stepped between her and the door, his expression soft and easy, his eyes deep midnight blue. He shouldn't have been a nice guy. Not with his looks and his reputation, but she was starting to think he was one, and that could prove a very dangerous thing.

"It's late, Max. You need to get back to Zuzu." She tried to get him moving, but he didn't seem eager to step out of the way.

"What are you running from, Charlotte?" he asked.

"I'm not running."

"Could have fooled me." He tucked a strand of hair behind her ear, traced a line from there to her temple and the scar she'd had for so many years, she'd almost forgotten how she'd gotten it.

Almost.

But it was hard to forget something that haunted her dreams.

"You took a pretty hard hit," Max murmured, following the scar with his finger. It felt so good to be touched, and it had been so long since anyone had bothered, that she let herself stay right where she was, his fingers moving along her scalp, his free hand cupping her upper arm. "What happened?"

"I fractured my skull. I was in the hospital for nearly two weeks." Because it hadn't just been her skull that had been fractured. She'd also cracked a vertebra in her back and fractured her arm.

"Car accident?"

"I fell down the stairs." At least that's what the ER doctor had been told. It's what the police had been told. It's what Charlotte's mother had told herself so many times that she'd started believing it.

That was the thing about lies. If you told them enough, they became their own version of the truth.

"Must have been some steep stairs."

"Attic stairs in an old Chicago apartment. They were very steep with a wooden floor at the bottom."

"That explains it, then."

"Explains what?"

"Your unreasonable fear of attics."

"I am not unreasonably afraid. Even if I was, it

wouldn't have anything to do with my fall," she protested, but he was right. She'd always been afraid of the attic in that old house. After she'd been shoved down the stairs, the fear had blown itself completely out of proportion.

Not every attic had a monster living in it.

"Good, because we need to check that bathroom window and then check the attic before I leave." He sauntered into the bathroom, checked the lock on the window, and made his way to the end of the hall. The attic door was there. She kept it locked. For obvious reasons. If her bastard of a father could come back to haunt her, he'd do it from the cavernous room at the top of those attic stairs.

Max turned the old-fashioned glass knob. "Where's the key?"

"In my room."

"Want to get it?"

Not really. But she'd look like a fool if she told him that, so she grabbed the skeleton key from the jewelry box on her dresser and handed it to him. She wasn't even sure the key would work. It had been in the door when she'd moved in. She'd taken it out, put it in her jewelry box, and she'd left it there for the past two years. She only knew that there was a bedroom and bathroom upstairs because a Realtor had tried to convince her to sell the property. She would have made a tidy sum off the sale, but she'd liked the peaceful town, loved looking out her windows and seeing distant mountains and deep green pine forests. She also loved not having a mortgage.

The skeleton key slid into the lock easily.

Max turned it and the door swung open on creaky, squeaky hinges.

"You need to oil the hinges," Max commented as he flipped a switch and turned on the light. He glanced over his shoulder and frowned. "Coming up?"

"Sure," she responded, because walking up into the attic with Max was the reasonable thing to do, the mature thing.

But God! She didn't want to do it.

The stairs creaked under her feet. Of course. That's the way it always happened in horror movies. Doors squeaked. Stairs creaked. Dark shadows hid danger. In her nightmare, she was always right at the top of the stairs when the monster lunged.

Not the best time to be thinking about *that*.

Max reached the top of the stairs and disappeared into the room beyond, his footsteps padding on hardwood floor. She could just let him search the room, but that would be the coward's way of doing things.

She might have spent a lot of years being a fool, but she'd never been a coward. She walked up the last few stairs, her heart galloping like a racehorse.

"Someone spent a lot of money on renovating this," Max called from the doorway of what must have been the bathroom.

Really?

She hadn't noticed. She'd been too busy trying to keep herself from running right back down the stairs.

"Hey"—he crossed the room, put a hand on her shoulder—"don't look so scared."

"I'm not scared," she managed to say. "I'm terrified."

"Too bad. This is a beautiful room. If you got over your unreasonable fear—"

"I already told you, I do not have an unreasonable fear of attics! My fear is completely rational and normal," she snapped, anger chasing away a little of the fear. It must have cleared her vision, too, because she could suddenly see just how beautiful the room was. Muted yellow paint and white wainscoting on the walls, a four-poster bed and antique dresser with a warped mirror, bookcases covered with old books. Dormer windows looked out onto Main Street and two more windows looked into the backyard.

"Sure, it is."

"It is, and even if it wasn't reasonable, being afraid of attics doesn't mean I have a phobia."

"But isn't that's what a phobia is? An unreasonable fear?" His hand slid from her shoulder to her hand, his fingers curling around hers.

"I do not have a phobia of attics," she protested again, but he was probably right. She probably did.

Which was really a shame, because the room was dusty but gorgeous. She could see the previous owner in every detail of it. The silver brush and mirror sitting on the dresser, the pictures of angels hanging from the walls. The renters must have left the attic alone and untouched. A miracle, really. Although anyone in his right mind could see that the room was a special place.

Too bad it was an *attic*.

"Sure you do, but you know what they say."

"Who's they?"

"Whoever says things." He tugged her deeper into the room, his fingers woven through hers. "The best way to get over a phobia is to face it head-on. Replace all those old fears with pleasant experiences."

"I hate to break the news to you, Max, but standing in an old attic is never going to be a pleasant experience." Ever. Not in a million years. But she had to admit, the space felt more like a room than an attic, the narrow planks of the wooden floor scratched and dull but lovely. Someone had hung a huge crystal chandelier from the cathedral ceiling. It would have been gaudy in another room, but it fit there, the old crystal sparkling like snow on a winter morning.

"Are you sure about that?" he murmured, his free hand sliding around her waist, his fingers finding their way under her T-shirt and settling right at the base of her spine.

She should have backed away. Really. She should have, but he smelled like thick forest and late-summer sunshine, and she couldn't make herself move.

"Sure about what?" she managed to ask, her voice breathy and light.

Walk away! her brain whispered.

But Max leaned down, his face so close, she could see silver flecks in his dark blue eyes. "Sure that we can't replace those old memories with some new much more pleasant ones?"

She was going to tell him that she was sure, but his lips skimmed hers, tentative, light. Questioning and questing, looking for something she wasn't sure she should want to give.

"What do you say, Charlotte?" he murmured, his

lips grazing her jaw. "Want to make some pleasant memories?"

No. God, no!

Because once those memories were made, she'd never be able to unmake them.

"Thanks, but I think I'll pass."

He nodded, but his gaze dropped to her lips. It lingered there, and she could swear that she still felt the light tentative touch of his lips brushing against hers.

"The room is clear. Looks like you're good to go, so I'd better head out," Max finally said. Then he walked down the stairs and out the front door without another word.

It was for the best.

There was nothing either of them could say about that moment of weakness, that sweet tentative touch of lips.

Except . . . *let's do that again.*

That would probably get them both into more trouble than either wanted to be in. Better to say good night and forget the whole thing, because Max was a player, and Charlotte didn't need someone like that in her life ever again.

Chapter Nine

Max called the number on the business card three times before eight A.M. Morgan didn't answer. He hadn't really expected her to. She'd always been the kind to do things in her own time and in her own way. The only obligation she'd ever seemed to feel was toward her skin and her hair. When they'd lived together, she'd had a tight schedule for that kind of stuff. Everything else happened when it happened.

He hadn't cared. He had his own issues, and he wasn't big on criticizing others for theirs. If Morgan hadn't had the opposite philosophy, they might still be together. She'd been a nitpicker, a micromanager. A cheat. He'd seen that one coming a mile away, but he hadn't cared all that much about that, either.

Which had been as much of the problem as everything else.

He should have cared, right?

He picked up the phone, dialed one more time. Voicemail picked up immediately. He left a fourth message. "Morgan, I'm assuming you're not dead, so how about you check in and see how your kid is doing? If I don't hear from you by this evening, I'm going to put you into the system as a missing person and issue an APB on your car."

He would, too. He didn't have time for Morgan's crap. He had a job, a life, things he wanted to do besides care for a little girl.

Although, he had to admit, Zuzu was a cute kid. The kind of kid Max had probably been. Full of energy and mischief.

Speaking of which . . .

He glanced into the living room. Zuzu was parked in front of the TV, watching a cartoon about guinea pigs. Or maybe they were rats. Either way, he wasn't sure it was the best show for a little kid.

"What are you watching, Zuzu?" he asked, tucking the business card into his wallet.

"TV."

"Smarta—" Nope. Not the right thing to say to a three-year-old. "What is it about?"

"Monkeys."

The things didn't look like monkeys to him, but he wasn't going to argue with a little kid. "Cool. Are you hungry?"

"I want cookies," she said, scrambling up from the floor and running over.

"Not for breakfast."

"I want pizza."

"You can't have that, either," he responded, scooping her up. She wrapped her arms around his neck and planted a kiss on his cheek.

"Please?" she begged.

He laughed, surprised and just a little pleased by her mischief. She was a cute kid, a sweet kid, and if she was *his* kid, he'd do everything in his power to make sure that she had the kind of childhood that he'd missed out on.

He grabbed crackers and the last piece of cheese from the fridge. He had to find the grocery list he'd made the previous night, because he was going to have to stop at the store.

"I'm going to make you a cracker sandwich, and then I have to go to work. You're going to be good for Ms. Ida today, right?"

She put her hands on his cheeks, looked him straight in the eyes, and said, "I don't think so."

"*I* think so. If Ms. Ida says she can't watch you any-more, we're going to be sunk. You know what that means?"

She shook her head solemnly.

"It means big trouble." He set her down and dragged a bowl from the cupboard. He had one fry pan, two or three plates, and a few cups. Every one of them in the tiny dishwasher. Still dirty. He needed dish detergent.

"I'm not gettin' trouble." Zuzu's fists rested on her hips and she stuck out her lower lip.

"Not if you're good for Ms. Ida, you aren't." He layered cheese on four crackers, covered each with another saltine. "There you are, kid."

He lifted her into a chair, and let her go to town. Ida would be there any minute, and he needed to clean the living room before she arrived. There were dolls on the floor, piles of clothes on the sofa. Every-thing he'd brought home from the office was spread over every surface in the room. Ida would have heart failure if she saw it.

He scooped up an armload of clothes, headed for the guest room, and heard someone knock on the door.

"Damn!" he muttered. He tossed the stuff on the bed and ran to the door. Zuzu was already there, doing everything in her power to open it. That would have been fine, except that he didn't want her opening doors when she didn't know who was standing on the other side.

Plus she was holding a handful of crumbled cracker and smooshed cheese.

"You have to let me open the door, Zuzu. You don't even know who's out there."

"It's Ida!" she squealed.

"You still have to let me open the door."

He'd have to remember to bolt it next time.

He moved her out of the way and opened the door himself.

"Good morning," Ida said cheerfully, her slacks crisp and neat, her coat pristine, her shoes practical.

"You're a little early," he responded.

As was Ida's way, she didn't take offense. "Fifteen minutes." She glanced at Zuzu and the handful of food that was spilling onto the floor. "But I can see that I'm not a moment too soon. Come on, dear, into the kitchen with your food."

She took Zuzu's hand and walked her into the kitchen.

She'd probably cataloged every piece of clothing, every doll, every blanket that needed to be picked up on her way there.

"I'm sorry about the mess, Ida," he started to explain, but she raised a hand and shook her head.

"No need to apologize. Parenting is hard work. Let me tell you, when I had children this age, there were always baskets of dirty laundry and a sink full of dirty dishes. I blessed the day my husband bought me a dishwasher, I can tell you that!" She grabbed a dishcloth and wiped Zuzu's hand. "Of course, the days when children are this age pass too quickly, so I'm glad I didn't waste too much time trying to keep up with the mess."

She helped Zuzu back into her seat and kissed her head. "There you are, darling. You finish at the table, and when you're done, we'll go over to my house."

"Are you sure about that, Ida? Zuzu is a little . . ." He was going to say hellion, but he didn't think his landlady would appreciate the language. ". . . bit of trouble."

"Have you forgotten that I have several great-grandchildren? One of them is close to Zuzu's age. I know how to keep a toddler occupied. Besides, I'm having the ladies' auxiliary over this morning. We're having some of Charlotte's delicious scones. Pumpkin. Raisin. Lemon. Blueberry." She sighed in apparent bliss.

Max didn't sigh but he did start thinking of reasons to stop by Ida's place after Charlotte delivered the goods. She made fantastic scones. The kind a man could eat every day and never get tired of. She also made good cookies, good meatloaf, good mashed potatoes. As a matter of fact, after last night's kiss, he was beginning to wonder if the rumors about

Charlotte's cooking were true. Maybe there really was something magical in things she baked.

He frowned, turning his thoughts away from Charlotte, because he'd been spending way too much time thinking about her. "Sounds great, but won't it be difficult to watch Zuzu and have a meeting?"

"Are you kidding me? The ladies are dying to meet your little girl. They'll all help out." She picked up a blanket and folded it into a neat little square.

"Ida, I already told you, she's not my—"

"Hush! Do you want the poor little thing hearing you deny her paternity?" she whispered.

He didn't suppose that he did.

"I don't think she understands a word we're saying."

"She's a very bright little girl, Max. Even if she wasn't, it can't be good for a child's psychological well-being to be denied by someone."

"I'm not denying her. I'm just saying—"

"Here's what I think, for what it's worth. Wait until you've had a paternity test. Then let everyone know the truth. One way or another."

"That's what I was planning to do."

"You were planning well. You just forgot that Zuzu is perfectly capable of understanding a lot of what you're talking about. And, really, Max, the fact is, no birth control is a hundred percent effective. Unless you and Morgan weren't having—"

"Ida, I really don't want to have this conversation with you."

"Do you think I don't know where children come from?" She laughed.

He tried to smile, but he figured it looked more

like a scowl, because Ida patted his cheek. "Go to work. As mayor, I'd hate to write you up a citation for being late to your job."

"Yes, ma'am." He shrugged into his coat, grabbed his hat, and shoved it on his head. He didn't have to leave for another fifteen minutes, but if Ida was sending him on his way, he'd happily go.

"Bye, Daddy!" Zuzu called.

His blood ran so cold, he was surprised it didn't solidify in his veins.

He wanted to say, *I'm not your dad*, but he didn't have the heart to correct the kid. Besides, what if he *was* her dad?

God! Wouldn't that be a mess?

"Bye, Zuzu," he said.

She blew a kiss, and he had no choice but to reach out and catch it. He had to blow one back too, because kids had sensitive feelings.

The previous night's storm had blown over, and the air was dry and still, the frigid cold slicing through his coat as he made his way to the Corvette. He'd thrown salt down on the steps, but he grabbed a bag from the garage and layered some more down. He didn't want Ida or Zuzu to fall.

He was setting the bag in the garage when Charlotte pulled into the driveway, her station wagon chugging fitfully, white exhaust trailing along behind it.

She had the scones with her, but that wasn't why he opened her door and offered her a hand out.

Dear heaven above, did the man have to be in Ida's driveway just as Charlotte was pulling in? And

did he have to look so refreshed and wide-awake
and happy when Charlotte felt tired and crappy and
all-around frumpy?

"Good morning, Charlotte," he drawled as he
tugged her out of the car, the heat of his palm sear-
ing through her skin.

Her toes curled in her boots and her insides
threatened to melt.

She yanked her hand away.

"Pretty day, isn't it?" he asked with a smile.

"If you say so," she muttered, wishing that she'd at
least taken the time to dry her hair. All the creaks
and groans of the old house, the howling of the
wind, the splattering ice against the windows had
kept her awake way too late. She'd pressed snooze
three times before she'd finally dragged herself from
bed and started baking. That had been four hours
ago. Which meant she'd gotten about an hour of
sleep. She scowled and stalked to the back of the car.

"Not a morning person, huh?" Max followed her
and took the first box of scones as she dragged it
from the car.

"I can manage this, Max. If you need to go to
work, go right ahead and leave."

"In other words, you'd rather I weren't here?"

"In other words, I'm not in the mood for conversation."

"Tough night?"

"You could say that." She took the second box of
scones. Lemon and blueberry. Still warm from the
oven. She could smell the fruit and vanilla, and her
stomach growled.

"Any more slamming doors?"

"No." But she'd imagined all sorts of other noises. Creaking floorboards. Heavy breathing. Curtains swishing when they shouldn't have been. It seemed silly in the bright light of day, but if she hadn't walked through every room with Max, she'd have been absolutely convinced someone was in the house with her.

"But you were scared, huh?" He touched her waist, leading her along the cobblestone path to Ida's house.

"Not enough to call in the cavalry," she replied.

"I'm not surprised."

"What's that supposed to mean?"

"Just that you don't seem like the kind of person who ever feels the need to call for help."

"I called yesterday."

"Because you thought you were in imminent danger."

"Is there any other reason for calling in the cavalry?"

"Ask Zim. He calls every hour on the hour."

"Zim is a law unto himself, but he's a good guy. Underneath all the gruff and gristle."

"Gristle?"

"You know . . . the chewy fatty part of the beef that no one can stomach?"

"That's a perfect description of Zim's personality." He chuckled as they walked into Ida's huge foyer.

Marble tiles, gorgeous oil paintings, and a basket of shoes left behind by Ida's great-grandchildren. Fancy mixed with homey. Charlotte had been in the house quite a few times, and she'd always been secretly pleased at the little bits of childish clutter she found there. This was the kind of place every child should have in his life—a nice place to come for a visit or to stay for a while. No need for the marble floors, of course. Or the oil paintings. It didn't need to be a big place or a fancy one. It just needed to be a place where children were welcome and wanted, where they could be nurtured and loved. That's what Charlotte would have wanted for her children if she'd had any.

The dining room jutted off to the left of the foyer, and Charlotte set the scones on the cherrywood table there. She hadn't bothered bringing anything but the scones and some plastic wrap. Ida liked to serve everything on the tiny silver plates that she kept in her antique buffet.

Charlotte opened the cupboard beneath it and took out what she needed.

"Those are some fancy plates," Max commented as he took one from her hand and set it on the table.

"They're family heirlooms. Ida says that her great-great-grandmother received them as a wedding gift." She took out the silver teapot that Ida would fill with hot water and use to serve tea. The only thing Charlotte had from *her* family were scars, but she tried not to be bitter about it.

"These look good," Max said as he peered into a box of scones. "They smell good, too."

"Is that a hint?" she joked, trying to keep the conversation light and easy and free from any of the tension that had been between them the night before.

It had been late. They'd both been tired. The room had been romantic and sweet. She'd come up with plenty of reasons for that momentary lapse of judgment, but she hadn't been able to forget it no matter how much she tried. And God knew she *had* tried.

"I'm not much for hinting. When I want something, I make it known." His gaze dropped to her lips, and she could swear she felt his kiss again.

She looked away, cleared her throat. "Good to know."

"So since I'm not much for hinting, I'm going to make it very clear that I would love to have a scone. Zuzu kept me busy this morning, and I haven't had time to eat."

"What kind do you want?"

"What kind do you have?" He leaned over the box, his hand flat on the table, all tan and large and masculine. Just thinking about the way that hand felt against her skin made her muscles weak with longing.

She sighed inwardly because there was no way she was going to sigh out loud.

The fact was, Max was a very attractive man, and she was a woman who'd spent too many hours working lately and not enough hours pursuing friendships and fun. She needed to loosen up a little, let her schedule go once in a while. That way her head wouldn't be turned by handsome faces and big muscles.

A handsome face.

Max's handsome face.

"Should I just guess at what kind of scones they are?" he pressed.

What kind of scones had she brought?

That should be easy enough to answer. She'd been up since five baking them.

"Pumpkin?" Maybe. "Lemon."

"Ida said you were making blueberry." He helped her along, and she nodded.

"Right. Blueberry."

"I'll take one of those. If you don't mind."

She didn't mind.

But she'd have to figure out which scone was blueberry before she handed it to him. Usually that wasn't a problem. She knew her scones. She'd made hundreds of them.

For some reason her brain didn't want to work, her thoughts muddled and scattered. Not because of Max. That was for sure. She'd blame it on a sleepless night, the old creaking house, and the attic above her bed.

She looked into the box, grabbed the scone most likely to be blueberry, and handed it to Max. "Sorry I don't have napkins. Ida is providing them."

"Bet they're going to be cloth and as fancy as those silver plates." He bit into the scone and closed his eyes. "God, this is good, Charlotte."

"Thanks." She busied herself placing scones on silver trays she found in the hutch, because watching Max enjoy his scone felt a little too intimate.

Strange, because she watched people eat her baked goods all the time. Old, young, in between— she'd fed just about everyone in Apple Valley, and she'd never felt the need to turn away when someone was enjoying one of her products.

Until now.

She covered the trays with plastic wrap she'd brought from home. There wasn't anything else to do. Ida was easy that way. She provided napkins, centerpieces, plates. She'd probably have provided her own scones if she hadn't wanted to support Charlotte's business.

She was that kind of mayor. When someone started a business, Ida did everything she could to make sure that it was successful.

"Finished?" Max asked as she grabbed the empty boxes.

"Yes. I've got to head out to my next delivery."

"Who's on your schedule?" He took the boxes.

"I can get that myself, Max."

"I know, but why should you?"

"Because . . ." She couldn't think of a reasonable answer. At least not one that didn't include mention of Brett.

He waited a few seconds, eyeing her dispassionately. "Can't think of a reason, can you?"

"I can."

"But?"

"It's not one I want to share."

"You know what the problem is with telling me something like that?" he asked as he led the way out of the dining room and shouldered open the front door.

"What?"

"It makes me want to know exactly what it is you don't want to share."

"Nothing exciting," she murmured, hoping that he'd drop the subject.

She should have known that he wouldn't.

Max had a reputation for being doggedly determined when it came to getting what he wanted. That worked out well when it came to his job. She wasn't sure how it was going to work out if he decided he wanted to know about her past. He had the means and the know-how to find out anything he wanted to.

"Nothing exciting, huh?" He walked to the car and slid the boxes into the back of the station wagon. Bright winter sunlight gleamed in his hair, turning dark blond to burnished gold. He had a clean-cut and polished look that should have been preppy and a little bland, but it came off as sexy and terribly appealing instead.

She really had to stop noticing.

If she couldn't manage that, she had to stop spending time around him.

How hard could avoiding him be?

All she had to do was make sure she didn't hang around Ida's place, Main Street, Riley Park. She should probably avoid the grocery store, too. She'd run into him there a time or two. Basically, as long as she stayed home, she'd be just fine.

He closed the back hatch of the station wagon and turned to face her, his arms crossed over his chest, his eyes midnight blue. "Is that another way of telling me to mind my own business?"

"Yes."

"And you actually think I'm going to?"

"Why wouldn't you?" She slid behind the driver's seat, determined to end the conversation.

"Because I'm a police officer. It's my job to be

curious, to dig for answers, to figure out what people are doing, why they're doing it, and what kind of trouble it might cause."

"If I were a criminal that would make sense." She shoved the keys into the ignition and the engine roared to life. "But I'm not. I've been in town for a while, and I haven't caused any trouble."

"Except for the frenzy over your dark chocolate cupcakes," he said with a grin. "I haven't tasted them yet, but I heard they were great."

"I'm surprised that one of your girlfriends didn't try to ply you with one."

"Actually, a lady I dated did try to feed me one a few months ago. I'd already eaten, though, so I didn't take it."

"That must have been before I stopped baking them."

"Why'd you stop? From the way women were talking, you could have made a fortune off those things." His eyes sparkled with amusement, and Charlotte wanted to be amused too. She wanted to grin and act like her double chocolate delights were a big joke.

But she just didn't have it in her. Not so close to the twenty-seventh, and not after a very long day and night.

"I don't believe in making money off of other people's foolishness," she replied.

"Foolishness? Is that what you think it is?"

"Of course. There's no magic formula for love, and there's no secret ingredient that can make it last." She smoothed her still-damp hair, irritated that her hand was trembling. She hated talking about this kind of stuff. She always ended up sounding jaded and bitter.

"There's a formula, alright," he argued. "And several ingredients."

"Like what?"

"Commitment plus friendship plus shared interests. Toss in some passion and admiration and you've got yourself a winning recipe for success in love."

"If it were that easy, everyone would have it."

"It isn't easy, but it *is* simple. My grandparents were married for nearly seventy years. Ida was married for sixty. It's our generation that has problems. Most people are just too selfish and self-absorbed to offer the first two things for more than a couple years."

"I probably shouldn't point out that you're single, Max."

"And yet you did," he responded.

She laughed, some of her tension easing away. "You're right. Sorry."

"Hey, it's the truth. I'm just as selfish and self-absorbed as the next person." He leaned down so they were face-to-face and smiled. "Of course, you're single, too."

"I'm too busy for the kind of commitment you're talking about." Too old. Too scarred. Too . . . everything that mattered when it came to love.

"Are you too busy for dinner with a friend Friday night?"

"I always make time for my friends," she assured

him, because she didn't want to him to think that she was completely pitiful.

"Good. I'll pick you up at six."

She shoved her hand against the door as he tried to close it. "What are you talking about?"

"For dinner."

"I can't go to dinner with you!"

"Why not?"

"I don't date."

"It's not a date."

"Then what is it?"

"Just dinner between friends. My thank-you for helping out with Zuzu."

"I don't think—"

"You know what?" He made a show of glancing at his watch. "I'm going to be late if I don't get out of here. See you Friday."

"I'm not having dinner with you Friday!" she shouted, but he was already getting in his car and pulling out of the driveway.

He was going to show up at her place Friday.

She was sure of it.

She didn't have to be there.

She could be out with other friends or off at the movies. There had to be something playing at the old movie theater in town.

The thing was, she hadn't been out to dinner with friends in a while. She'd been too busy trying to make and save money for her storefront. That probably explained the mood she'd been in lately.

Dinner out would be good for her.

Plus spending a little time really getting to know Max was exactly what she needed to get him out of her head.

She nodded to herself, because there was no one else around, and headed to the next delivery.

Chapter Ten

Morgan finally called at five-thirty in the morning, three days after she'd left. Max was dead asleep when the phone rang, but he still recognized her number when he opened his eyes and saw it. He'd memorized it around the twelfth time he'd dialed it. In the fifty or so times he'd called since then, he hadn't even had to look at the business card.

He snatched his cell phone from the nightstand and pressed it to his ear.

"It's about damn time," he growled.

"I called as soon as I could," Morgan responded.

"You've got a kid, Morgan. As soon as you could isn't good enough." He grabbed his jeans from the chair beside the bed and tugged them on. Just in case Zuzu heard him talking and decided to come for a visit.

"How dare you judge me!" Morgan went on the defensive immediately.

"How dare *you* not care enough to call your kid.

She's been asking for you every night. She left messages on your voicemail at least five times."

"I didn't get them until today. My car broke down, and I had to stay in some Podunk little town while it was being fixed."

"What does that have to do with you calling Zuzu?"

"Just everything," she said with sigh. She'd decided to change strategies. He'd forgotten how good she was at that. "My cell phone battery died, and I didn't have my charger. It's probably in Zuzu's suitcase."

"It's not, and I'm pretty sure you know it."

"Then I left it at home," she continued as if he hadn't just accused her of lying. She must want something. "And the tiny little town I've been stuck in didn't have one in any of the stores."

"You could have called from the hotel."

"Hotel? Do you really think I have that kind of money? I barely had enough to pay for my car to be fixed. I haven't eaten in two days, because I don't have cash to pay for food. Things are tough, Max. Tougher than they've ever been. Some old lady put me up in her trailer home for the night so I wouldn't have to sleep on the street."

"Uh-huh." It probably made him a bad person that he thought she was telling him her story from a fancy Las Vegas hotel with a tray of hot food beside her. "Give me a second to wake Zuzu, and then you can tell her all about it."

"Don't wake her. She needs her sleep."

"She needs to talk to you, too."

"I'll call again at a more reasonable time. It's just that once I got my cell phone charged, I wasn't thinking about the time. I just wanted to check in with you."

"I thought you said you didn't have a charger."

"I don't. Some guy from the garage that's fixing my car loaned me his. I'll probably run out of battery soon."

"Then I'd better hurry and get Zuzu so you can talk to her before it does."

"Max, I don't want you to do that. She gets grumpy when she's overtired."

"She hasn't been grumpy for me." She'd been ornery, but that was a different thing altogether.

"Because you're perfect. Because you've become a better parent in three days than I've learned to be in nearly four years," she snapped.

"Sarcasm suits you, Morgan."

"Ass."

"I've been called worse." He walked into the guest room, determined to wake Zuzu. He'd probably regret it in about ten minutes when she refused to go back to sleep, but he didn't want her to miss out on a phone call from her mother.

Morgan sighed again. "I'm sorry, Max. It's just been a long trip. My interview is tomorrow morning, and I have to be there for it. I really need this job. Without it, I don't know how I'm going to keep feeding Zuzu."

You're not feeding her. I am, he almost said, but he wanted to hear where she was headed, figure out exactly what she wanted. It certainly wasn't to check up on Zuzu. She hadn't even asked about the kid. "Yeah? Sounds like things are desperate."

"More than you know. I was thinking that maybe you could lend me a couple of hundred. Just until I get my new job."

"Sorry. That's not going to happen."

"Why not?"

"Because I don't believe you really need the money, Morgan." He nudged Zuzu's shoulder and the little girl turned over, her eyes opening slowly. "It's your mommy. Want to say hi?"

"I told you not to wake her up!" Morgan barked

"Since I'm the one taking care of her and I'm the one who's going to deal with her later, I decided that I got to choose whether to wake her or not."

He handed the phone to Zuzu, helped her hold it to her ear. She was still half-asleep, her eyelids drooping.

"Say hi to your mom," he said.

"Mommy?" She sat up and took the phone from his hand, her hair a tangled mess. He shouldn't have put her to bed before it was dry. "Where are you?"

He leaned close, trying to hear Morgan's response. All he could hear was a few mumbled words. Something about Vegas and money.

"Okay," Zuzu responded, shoving her thumb in her mouth as Morgan continued to speak.

She went on for about thirty seconds while Zuzu sucked her thumb and listened.

"Bye!"

Max heard that clear as a bell.

He grabbed the phone from Zuzu.

"Don't hang up!"

But of course she already had.

"Da . . ." He looked at Zuzu. She was watching him with big blue eyes and about the most pitiful expression he'd ever seen on a kid's face. "Doggone it!"

"Doggone it!" she repeated, and then her chin started wobbling and her thumb dropped away from her mouth, and she started wailing like she had the night they'd met.

Only now, he wasn't just hearing a little girl crying for her mother, he was hearing Zuzu, and that was about a thousand times worse.

"Don't cry, Zu," he said, watching as big tears rolled down her cheeks. He picked her up, and she wrapped her arms around his neck, but she didn't stop crying.

"It's okay." He patted her back, feeling awkward and unsure. He wasn't used to that. He knew what to do in emergencies, knew how to take down a criminal, how to deliver a baby, how to offer first-aid to people with any number of injuries. What he didn't know, because he'd never *wanted* to know, was what to do with a distraught child.

Zuzu hiccupped, and he wondered if she was about to lose the macaroni and apples he'd fed her for dinner.

"Shhhh." He patted her back a little more gently. It pissed him off royally that Morgan had spent less time talking to her than she had trying to wheedle money out of Max. "Don't worry, Zuzu. Your mom will be back soon."

"She going to Vegas, and she's not taking me," Zuzu cried.

"That's okay, sweetie." That was what Ida always called her. If it was good enough for her, it was good enough for Max. "We'll have more fun here."

"But there's castles there. And princesses," she explained, as if it would make all the difference.

"Are you sure you're not thinking about Disney World?" he asked.

"I'm not going to Disney. I'm going to Vegas. With Mommy." She patted his cheek as if he were just a little too dumb to understand what she wanted. "You come, too."

"I have to work. Remember?"

"No, you don't."

"I do."

Her face fell, more tears streaming down her cheeks. Poor kid. She deserved a hell of a lot better than a thirty-second conversation with her mother.

"We can't go to Vegas?" she asked.

"Not today."

"Tomorrow?"

"I have to work then, too." He had Friday off, but he wasn't planning to make the trip then, either. He and Zuzu had an appointment to get DNA testing. He had to know the truth. One way or another. It was the right thing to do and the fair thing. Once he had the proof of her paternity, he could figure out the next step in her care. He couldn't keep her forever, that was for sure, but the more he thought about sending her back to her mother, the worse the idea seemed. "But I can take you to the park on Friday. You can swing and go down the slide."

"And eat ice cream?"

"It's too cold for ice cream."

"Cookies?"

"We'll see." He set her on the bed, and she curled into a little ball and pulled the covers over her head. She probably hoped that when she crawled out from her cocoon her mother would be there.

He flicked off the light, had his foot in the hallway when she sniffed. "You're not crying, are you, Zuzu?"

"Yes!" she wailed.

He rubbed the back of his neck, told himself that he could tell her to go to sleep and walk out of the room. Kids were resilient. They could go through hell and come out with barely a scratch.

He couldn't make himself do it.

"Why are you crying?"

"I needs a cookie, Maxi. I needs a cookie right now!"

He thought that what she probably really needed was Morgan. Maybe she'd already learned that her mother wasn't always available. A disheartening thought, but probably a true one. Morgan hadn't wanted kids any more than Max had. She'd made that abundantly clear when they'd met, and he'd been very happy to oblige her in that area.

"I don't have any cookies." If he did, he'd have given her an entire box.

"Charlotte's got cookies," Zuzu sobbed. "I needs Charlotte."

"Charlotte is in bed. Sleeping. Like every other

normal person in town," he muttered, but he flicked the light back on. He couldn't leave her crying in bed.

"She's not sleeping. She's baking."

The kid had a point. If the last few days were indicative of her habits, Charlotte rose before dawn, made her morning deliveries before most people had their first cup of coffee. He could picture her, puttering around in her kitchen, her hair pulled up in a high ponytail, the end just brushing the nape of her neck. She'd be wearing one of her frilly aprons, humming something under her breath while cookies or muffins or scones baked in the oven.

If he'd been there, he'd have been tempted to slide his hands around her waist, bury his nose in her hair. It probably smelled like cinnamon and sugar. That's what her lips had tasted like. Cinnamon, sugar, and some exotic spice that he wanted to taste again and again.

"It's still dark out, Zuzu."

"It's not dark," she argued.

"Look." He carried her to the window that looked out over Main Street. The sky was pitch-black, thousands of stars sparkling in the darkness. In the distance, Apple Valley Community Church stood on a hill that overlooked Riley Park, a lone spotlight shining on the nativity that the church set up after Thanksgiving every year. He couldn't see the nativity, but the light was like a golden beacon, pointing the way to some universal truth, some deep mystery.

"What's that?" Zuzu whispered, pointing to the light. "Is it an angel?"

"No. It's a nativity. For Christmas. You know. Baby

Jesus and Mary." He wasn't sure if Morgan had ever taken the kid to church. They'd gone together on holidays when they'd lived together, but neither had been much for religion.

"And Joseph and the shepherds and the angels?" Zuzu asked.

Obviously she was familiar with the story.

"That's right."

"Can we go see?"

He planned to say no, but she had a rapturous look on her face and her tears had stopped. She wasn't asking for cookies or ice cream or visits with her mother. She was asking him for something he could actually give her. Even if it was dark and cold and too early for any normal human being to be awake, Max couldn't see any reason to deny her. His shift didn't start for a few hours. It wasn't like he didn't have the time.

"Sure, but we'd better dress warm. It's cold as a witch's—" He cut himself off. He had to watch his language around Zuzu. She copied everything he said.

"Witch's hat?" she suggested.

"Yeah." He opened the dresser drawer and looked through the clothes that Ida had carefully sorted and folded, pulling out pants and a pink sweater and setting them on Zuzu's bed. Zuzu loved pink. "Cold as a witch's hat. You put these on while I get dressed. Put on socks, too." He tossed a pair of balled-up socks in her direction, and she giggled as she tried to catch them.

Pete chose that moment to slink out from under

Zuzu's bed. No screaming from Zuzu this time. She'd decided she loved the old cat almost as much as she loved pink. Max wasn't so sure how the cat felt about her. He was a good old tom, though. No scratching or clawing or biting. He'd even let Zuzu put him in one of the hats the historical society had brought over.

"Pete!" Zuzu cried. "We are going to see the nate-ivy. You can come. He can come, right, Maxi?"

No. The damn cat couldn't come. He'd yowl the whole way.

"He doesn't like car rides, Zuzu."

"He does! You do!" She lay on her belly and looked into Pete's ugly face. "Right, Pete?"

The cat meowed and butted his giant head against hers.

"Tell you what," Max said, too tired to keep arguing. He needed coffee. Lots of it. "You two work it out while I get dressed."

"Okay," Zuzu agreed solemnly.

"And make sure you're dressed and ready to go when I come back."

"Okay," she said again, reaching for her clothes.

At least she could dress herself, use the bathroom by herself, brush her teeth mostly by herself. All in all, she wasn't quite as much trouble as he'd thought she would be.

He closed her door and walked into his room. He'd grab coffee and a couple of doughnuts at the coffee shop. Zuzu would probably like some hot chocolate with a little whipped cream on the top. Not the best choice of breakfast for a growing girl, but it was about all Max had the energy for. With any luck, she'd fall asleep in the car on the way to see the nativity. If she did, he might just be tempted to take a little nap himself.

She was going to die. On the way to church, in the middle of the icy street, her face planted in the boxes of coffee cakes she was carrying. Her body would probably be discovered right around the time the women's mission team was scheduled to meet. Some hapless woman would swerve to avoid Charlotte's frozen body and drive into the copse of trees to the left of the road. Or worse, swerve to the right and head down the steep hill that led to Riley Park.

Either way, the accident and Charlotte's frozen carcass would be the talk of Apple Valley for the next century or two.

Not a pleasant thought, but she couldn't avoid thinking it.

She hadn't realized just how steep the road to Apple Valley Community Church was until she started walking it. She hadn't realized how cold she was going to get until she'd been out in the wind for about ten minutes. She glanced back at her good-for-nothing station wagon and its good-for-nothing tires. It would take longer to get back to the car than to get to the church, so she'd just have to keep walking forward.

"If I survive this, I'm joining a gym," she vowed, her breath forming a cloud in front of her face. "And I'm working out every day, so that the next time the stupid car won't make it up the stupid hill, I can jog the mile and a half to the church and avoid freezing to death."

Of course, if she had a heart attack from over-exertion, she wouldn't have to worry about freezing.

She readjusted the pile of boxes. Six coffee cakes for the ladies' mission meeting that was going to be at the parsonage at eight.

The parsonage that was at least another tenth of a mile past the church.

A tenth of a mile that she was going to have to walk in the freezing cold on the slick road.

She groaned and kept walking, the distant sky tinged pink with dawn, the mountains gray-blue. Ice coated the trees and grass, sparkling in the faint morning light. If she hadn't been near dead from cold and exertion, Charlotte might have stopped and admired the view.

Since she was both, she trudged forward, the boxes getting heavier with every step. An engine broke the silence, purring up behind her. She stepped to the side but didn't stop walking. If she did, she didn't think she'd start again.

Max's Corvette rolled past, stopped a few feet away.

Perfect. Just the person she wanted to see at seven in the morning when she was ice cold, out of breath, and about to die.

The driver's window unrolled and Max stuck his head out. "Need a ride?"

"Yes."

"Hold on." He jumped out of the car, keys jingling in his hand as he jogged to her side. He took the boxes. "It's ten degrees, Charlotte. You should have stayed in your wagon and called for help."

"Called who? Everyone I know is retired. I didn't want to wake them up this early in the morning."

"So you'd rather freeze to death?"

"Not particularly."

He laughed quietly and opened the passenger door. "Go ahead and turn the engine back on while I put these in the backseat."

He tossed the keys into her lap and closed the door. She didn't even try to put the keys in the ignition. Her fingers had frozen about five minutes into her walk.

"Charlotte!" Zuzu squealed from behind her. "You going to see the nat-ivy with us?"

"The nativity?" Charlotte asked, smiling at the little girl. "Is that where you're going?"

Zuzu nodded and held out a takeout cup. "I have chocolate."

"Is it good?"

"It would be better if I had cookies," Zuzu responded as Max got into the car.

"Zu, I told you that you weren't having cookies." He took the keys and started the engine. "Besides, you already had a doughnut."

"Mommy gives me cookies," Zuzu claimed.

"Mommy isn't here," Max responded, and Charlotte was pretty sure he added *damn her* under his breath.

"Charlotte will give me cookies."

"Max said no. Besides, I don't have any cookies with me. Just coffee cake."

"Were you heading to the church?"

"The parsonage."

"Mission meeting this morning, right? Ida said she couldn't watch Zuzu until it was over."

"You haven't found a babysitter yet?"

"It's been a little harder than I thought it would be. I'm going to interview a couple of people Friday when I have the day off."

She wanted to ask if he thought he'd still have Zuzu after the weekend, wanted to ask if he'd heard from Morgan, but Zuzu was in the backseat, and she wasn't sure how she was feeling about her mother being gone. "Have you contacted any of the local daycares?"

"There's one in town, and it's full. Besides, I don't know how long she's going to be here." He turned up the heat and handed her a disposable cup. "Have some coffee."

"I'll wait until I get home."

"Charlotte, your teeth are still chattering. You need to warm up. Drink the coffee."

"Drink it!" Zuzu chimed in.

The cup *did* feel warm, and she *was* freezing. She took a sip. It was nice and hot, black and bitter. Not her normal morning drink, but the heat wound its way down her throat and settled in her stomach. "Thanks. That was nice and warm."

She tried to hand it back, but Max shook his head. "Drink the rest. I've had so much coffee, I'm getting jittery."

"Long night?"

"Early morning. My phone rang at five-thirty." He glanced in the rearview mirror, and she knew without asking that Morgan had called.

"That was good, right?"

"Wrong. Some people don't deserve . . ." He glanced in the review mirror again. "Now's not the time. We can talk about it at dinner Friday night."

Dinner. Yeah. She'd been trying to forget about that.

Sure, she'd convinced herself that it would be a good thing, but she could already hear the gossip. She really didn't want to be the center of that.

He pulled up in front of a small clapboard house that had served as the parsonage for as long as the Apple Valley Community Church had existed. At least that's what Ida said. According to her, the first pastor of the church had wanted to give his wife a home of her own, and he'd asked the congregation if he could build on the church property. They'd wanted to build the place for him and had planned a huge house with fancy everything. Before construction could begin, the pastor made it clear that he and his wife didn't need anything big. Just a two-bedroom cottage that would be warm in the winter and cool in the summer.

Charlotte had been in the house during both seasons, and she'd say that the builders had fulfilled the pastor's request. Over a hundred years later, the cute little bungalow was perfect for Natalie and Jethro Fisher.

"Stay here," Max said. "I'll bring the coffee cakes to the house."

"That's okay. I can manage." She jumped out of the car and ran around to the back, nearly slipping on ice in her haste.

She needed to slow down.

She did *not* want to fall on her butt in full view of Max. He lifted the boxes from the backseat and handed them to her. They didn't seem as heavy now that she didn't have to cart them up a hill.

The front door opened before she reached it, and Natalie Fisher appeared in the doorway. "Charlotte! I was hoping that was you! Where's your station wagon?"

"At the bottom of the hill. It decided it didn't want to make the drive."

"That hill is a bear to walk up, isn't it? But it looks like a hunky hero drove to your rescue, so I guess things worked out just fine," Natalie said, smiling and waving in the direction of Max's Corvette.

Hunky hero?

Is that the way pastors' wives always talked?

"Yes, I guess they did," she mumbled in response. "Where would you like me to set up the coffee cakes?"

"I'll take care of that." Natalie took the boxes. "Since you didn't charge me a dime, I wouldn't feel right having you do any more work."

"I was happy to donate the cakes, and I enjoy setting things up when I deliver a product." She liked the tables to look a certain way, have a certain feel. She wanted her customers to enjoy every part of the experience. The look, the taste, the smell of the food she'd delivered.

"I'll make sure it looks very pretty," Natalie said. "But I can't take advantage of you by asking for more than you've already given our mission committee.

Besides, I wouldn't want to keep Max waiting for his damsel in distress."

"I'm not a—"

"Just a joke, Charlie. Thank you so much for these." Natalie hefted the boxes. "Will we see you Sunday morning? Alex Riley is going to play special music in honor of Tessa and Cade's wedding."

Probably not, but Charlotte didn't feel all that comfortable admitting that she'd rather sleep in than attend service. "I'll have to look at my schedule."

Natalie laughed, and Charlotte smiled. "Sorry. I didn't mean to sound like I was rebuffing a dinner invitation from a loser."

"At least you didn't lie. You know Isaac Millwood?"

"The guy who owns a farm on the east end of town?"

"That would be the one. I saw him in the park and asked if we'd be seeing him Sunday. He said he'd love to come to church, but his cows get lonely if he leaves for more than twenty minutes."

"It could be true."

"It could be. If he *had* any cows. Now I really had better let you go. Doesn't Max have a little girl he's taking care of for a while?"

"Zuzu. She's in the car."

"Is she?" Natalie glanced toward the Corvette, something lonely and sad flashing across her face. She and Jethro didn't have children, but if the rumors were correct, they wanted them.

Charlotte knew exactly how it felt to long for a baby, to want to parent and not be able to.

She touched Natalie's arm. "Why don't you go say hello?"

"Not this morning. I have too much to do." Natalie offered a brittle smile. "Thanks again, Charlotte. The committee is going to enjoy these!"

She walked into the house and closed the door with a firm snap that echoed on the still morning air.

Chapter Eleven

He should have finished his coffee.

That's what Max was thinking as Charlotte walked back to the car. He was also thinking that Charlotte had a decidedly sexy way of moving. Smooth. Elegant. Just a hint of hips beneath her frilly apron and short winter coat.

"Charlotte!" Zuzu called from the backseat. "Let's go see the nat-ivy!"

"I think Charlotte is just going to want to go back to her car, Zu," he cautioned.

"Why?"

"Because she's busy."

"A girl is never too busy to haves fun," Zuzu intoned.

"Where'd you hear that?"

"Mommy."

Of course. That had been Morgan's philosophy when they'd met—have fun, do what makes you feel good, enjoy life because you only live it once. Those had been the reasons why she'd moved to L.A. in the first place, why she'd moved back to Apple Valley, why she'd finally sold her parents' home and left town for good.

He wasn't there to judge, but he sure as hell didn't agree. Especially when it came to parenting. Pursuing fun for the sake of fun was fine and dandy when you had no one to worry about but yourself. Once a kid entered the picture, things were supposed to change. Priorities were supposed to change.

"Charlotte is not a girl," he said as Charlotte climbed into the car. "She's a woman."

"*Who* is a woman?" Charlotte asked.

"You."

"Uhm. Thanks?" She reached for her seat belt, the scent of vanilla and cinnamon filling the air as she moved.

"God, you smell good," he said.

Yep. He should have had the rest of the coffee.

She raised an eyebrow, her mouth curving into a half smile. "Okay."

"What I mean is . . . you smell like cookies. Or scones. Or something equally delicious." She tasted that way too.

His gaze dropped to her lips.

He wouldn't mind tasting them again. He wouldn't mind at all. He leaned toward her, and he was pretty sure she leaned toward him. They were a hairsbreadth away from each other, staring into one another's eyes.

"This is a really bad idea," Charlotte whispered, but she didn't back away.

"Why?" he asked, because he couldn't think of one reason.

"I don't date."

"And?"

"You date lots of women."

"I *used* to date lots of women. I haven't been out with anyone in a couple of months." He lifted a strand of her hair, let it slide through his fingers. It felt like spun silk, smooth and cool to the touch. "You have beautiful hair, Charlotte."

"And you are a flirt."

She was probably right about that. He did flirt with women. He *liked* women. All women. Older, younger, thin, round, pretty, plain. He appreciated good mothers and good teachers and good cops, and he enjoyed letting women know that they were admired, because there weren't enough men in the world who did that.

"It's not flirtation if it's true," he said. "And you do have beautiful hair, and you do smell like something delicious. Something that I would very much like to—"

"*I* would very much like to go to the nat-ivy," Zuzu cut in.

Charlotte laughed nervously, scooting away so that she was nearly pressed against the car door. "That's a good idea. We should probably do it."

He'd planned to take her to her car, but if she wanted to see the nativity, he wouldn't complain.

The church sat a ways back from the road, its white siding gleaming in the rising sun. Behind it, a cemetery stretched along the hillside, gray headstones poking up from the lush, well-manicured lawn. Reverend Fisher worked hard to keep up with the church and grounds, but it was a big job. One that Max had helped with on a few occasions. He loved the community spirit that held Apple Valley together. It reminded him of family. Or what family should be.

The nativity sat in the center of the church's front yard, a lone spotlight shining on the carved wooden scene. It wasn't at all magical up close. Just a back-drop made of plywood and an old manger. Max had helped Jethro Fisher drag it out of storage and had perched the carved angel on top of a rickety frame. He'd done a little stabilizing when Jethro wasn't look-ing, because he'd been afraid the figure would crash down onto some unsuspecting parishioner's head.

"There it is!" Zuzu squealed as he parked the car. "The nat-ivy."

"Nativity," he corrected her, just like he had about ten dozen times since she'd seen it from his window.

"Yep! There it is. Let's go." She unsnapped her car seat straps and tried to squeeze into the front seat.

"Hold on, kid. Let us get out first," Max ordered, more amused by her enthusiasm than annoyed.

"Can you hurry up?" she asked. "Please?"

Charlotte laughed. "At least she has manners."

"She needs to have patience," he replied.

"That's kind of hard when you're three."

"I'm going to be four on Christmas," Zuzu inter-rupted, half her body hanging over Charlotte's seat. "I'm going to have a big party with a thousand balloons."

"Are you?"

Zuzu nodded, her tangled hair flopping over her face. He probably should have brushed it before he brought her out.

"Yes!" she said with one last emphatic nod. "And we're going to go to church, too, and we're going to sing happy birthday to the baby Jesus, and we're going to give him a balloon. So let's go see him and tell him."

"We probably should," Charlotte said solemnly. She opened her door and got out, taking Zuzu's hand and helping her exit the car.

"You know what, Charlotte?" Zuzu continued as they walked to the nativity.

"What?"

"I was thinking something portant."

"Important?" Charlotte asked, still holding on to Zuzu's hand, the icy grass crunching under their feet, their arms swinging a little. They looked . . . right together. Connected. As if they'd known each other a long time.

Max felt like an interloper, not quite in sync with their steps or their conversation. He crossed the yard with them, the sun nudging the horizon, Apple Valley sleeping snug and peaceful below. Christmas lights sparkled, streetlights burned bright, a few cars meandered along Main Street, their headlights muted in the purplish predawn light.

"Yes. Important," Zuzu repeated perfectly.

"Are you going to tell me what?" Charlotte asked.

"I was thinking you would make my cake for my birthday. I was thinking it could be a big huge giant cake with pink flowers and—"

"Zu!" Max cut her off. "Charlotte is way too busy at Christmastime to bake a cake for you."

Zuzu's face fell, and he felt like the worst kind of scum for stealing her dream of a big cake.

"The thing is—" he started to explain.

"Of course I have time to bake you a cake, Zuz," Charlotte cut in.

"Really?"

"Yes, really." Charlotte scooped her up and walked the last several feet to the nativity, whispering something to Zuzu as they went. Whatever it was, it made the little girl happy. She squealed with delight when Charlotte set her down in front of the carved figures.

He hated to burst either of their bubbles, but it didn't seem fair to offer Zuzu something she wasn't going to get. No way was a big cake from Charlotte in the cards. Zuzu would be back with her mother soon, and they'd all go on with their separate lives.

Somehow that didn't sound quite as great as it had a couple of days ago.

"You shouldn't have told her that," he murmured in Charlotte's ear. "She's going to be disappointed when it doesn't happen."

"Who says it won't?" she whispered, her gaze on Zuzu, her face soft with longing.

He wanted to ask her what had happened with her husband, how long they'd been married, why they hadn't had children. He knew she wouldn't answer any more than he'd answer a question about why he'd stayed single. "Christmas is five weeks away. She's not going to be here that long."

"If she isn't here, I'll bring the cake to her."

"You'd drive a cake to Las Vegas for a kid you barely know?"

She finally met his eyes, her hair gleaming in the rising sun, her eyes dark and so filled with sadness, his heart lurched and the air just kind of caught in his chest.

"I know Zuzu," she said. "I took care of her for sixteen hours, remember?"

"Sixteen hours doesn't make for a lifetime commitment."

"No, but it's enough to make someone a cake."

"Not when they're a thousand miles away. It would take days to get to Las Vegas and back. You have a business to run."

She shrugged. "I usually have all my orders filled by the twenty-third. If Zuzu is back with her mom, I'll make sure I finish on the twenty-second. I can leave that evening and easily be in Vegas by Christmas."

"What if she goes back to Miami? That's the kind of thing Morgan does. She hops from one place to the next, trying to find whatever it is she's looking for." For all Max knew, Morgan would decide to take Zuzu on a trip to Europe.

"Then I'll take a plane and have the cake shipped."

"It's really sweet of you to want to do that, Charlotte, but I still think it isn't a good idea to get Zuzu's hopes up." He glanced at the little girl and frowned. "Besides, you don't want to spend Christmas away from home."

Charlotte couldn't see any reason why she *wouldn't* want to spend Christmas away. As far as she was concerned, Christmas was just another day on the calendar.

"Why not? It's not like I have family to spend the day with. I don't even have a cat to worry about," she said without thinking.

Oh, God.

That sounded pitiful, and from the look on Max's face, he thought it *was* pitiful. Which was the absolute *last* thing Charlotte wanted. She didn't need anyone's pity. Living alone was a heck of a lot easier than living with someone else.

"What I mean," she said quickly, "is that I'm not tied down. I'm free to go do what I want and be where I want. If I want to spend Christmas in Vegas, I can. Maybe I'll go to the Strip, do a little gambling."

"Maybe you will, but the way I see things happening," he said, his voice low and just a little rough, "you'll make this huge cake for Zuzu and deliver it to whatever hotel Morgan is staying in. She may or may not thank you, and she may or may not let Zuzu eat it. Then you'll check into a motel for the night and drive back home the next day."

That sounded about right.

Except she'd probably sleep in her car. It would be warm enough in Las Vegas, and it would save her money.

No way would she admit that to Max. He probably had tons of plans for Christmas. Breakfast with someone, lunch with someone else, dinner with a third person. Charlotte could have had the same. She'd been invited by just about everyone she knew, but spending time with happy families, happy kids, and happy couples on Christmas Day wasn't exactly her idea of a good time. She preferred her quiet undecorated house and her romance novels. Neither of those things ever disappointed.

The fact that she felt that way probably did make her pitiful, but she didn't care. She'd decided to be herself after Brett's death, to enjoy the things she enjoyed and to not apologize for them.

"I take it from your silence that my description is pretty much how things are going to pan out. Which is a shame. *If* you go to Vegas, you should live it up a little."

"I've been to Las Vegas, and I lived it up plenty while I was there," she murmured, not really wanting to go into the reason *why* she'd been there.

"What'd you do? Slots? Blackjack?"

Got married to a guy who was already married.

"We went to a couple of casinos, but I don't remember much about what we did there." Mostly she'd watched her new husband lose about a thousand dollars of the money she'd saved for their wedding and honeymoon. She hadn't been all that offended at the time. She'd wanted him to have fun. It had taken her a couple of years to realize that he should have wanted her to have fun, too.

"So you were with friends?"

"You could say that."

"I could but you won't?"

"Something like that."

"You're a mystery, Charlotte. You know that." He brushed the hair away from her temple, uncovering the scar that she'd had for nearly two decades. The pad of his finger slid across the raised edges of the old wound, and her pulse jumped, every nerve leaping to attention.

"There's nothing mysterious about me," she said, her mouth so dry she was surprised she got the words out.

She wanted to feel hard muscle and warm skin

and the heady touch of callused hands against her flesh, but that would be a huge mistake.

Wouldn't it?

She wasn't so sure. Not when the sun was peeking over the mountains and the grass was sparkling with frost. Not when the air held winter's chill and a hint of Max's spicy cologne. Not when she thought about another Christmas sitting in her house alone with a book while the world celebrated miracles and love.

She was a fool for even entertaining the idea of throwing herself into Max's arms.

Not that he was asking her to.

She walked to the carving of Mary. Whoever had made the nativity had whittled a face into hardwood and created something that was both beautiful and haunting. Even with the paint fading from time, and the carving shallow from years of Decembers spent out in the winter weather, the visage was beautiful.

"What's mysterious," she said, desperate to change the subject, "is how this thing has stayed in such good condition for so many years. Ida told me it's been around since the church was built."

"That's what Jethro said. He thinks the first mayor of Apple Valley commissioned a local artist to make it for his wife. She wanted a nativity to display in their yard. When she died, Daniel donated it to the church. It's been here ever since."

"Incredible," she breathed.

"I agree," he responded, but he wasn't looking at the carving, he was looking at her.

That was her cue to go, because she kind of liked

the way he was looking at her, and she sort of didn't want him to stop.

She made a production of looking at her watch and checking the time. "I need to get going. I have another delivery to make, and I don't want to be late."

He took her hand as she walked past, pulling her to a stop, his thumb running across the underside of her wrist. "I think you're forgetting something."

"What's that?"

"Your car is at the bottom of the hill."

"I didn't forget."

"Then you forgot that you were nearly frozen from the walk when Zuzu and I found you."

"The sun is up. It's warmer now." And she'd be walking downhill, so she wouldn't be dying from overexertion.

"If it's warmer, I can't feel it." He glanced at Zuzu who was busy trying to crawl into the manger. "Zu! No! You'll break it."

"Baby Jesus can't break," Zuzu said, looking like she had every intention of continuing her efforts.

"Sure it can, and even if it couldn't, that's not the point. The manger the baby is in is delicate." He lifted her, muttering something under his breath as he did so.

"What?" Charlotte asked.

"I said I should have had a couple more coffees. I need all the caffeine I can get to keep up with this one." He tickled Zuzu's belly and set her on his shoulders. "Come on. Let's get you back to your car."

"I don't want you to have to rush because of me. Stay and let Zuzu enjoy the nativity."

"She enjoyed it for about as long as I can take.

Besides, I'm working in a couple of hours, and it's freezing out here. It'll be hard to work if I'm frozen solid." He used one hand to keep Zuzu balanced. His other hand rested on her waist. If anyone saw them together, they'd think they were a couple, heading to the car with their child.

"I'm surprised." She gave up the fight to walk back to her car and got into the Corvette.

"About what?" He snapped Zuzu into her seat.

"You're a weather wimp. I thought you said that you were used to Inland Northwest cold."

"I am. I just use my thin blood as an excuse to get women to do what I want." He grinned as he got behind the wheel. "Where's your next delivery?"

"Town Hall. There's a poetry reading. You know Alma Wilkins?"

"That weird old lady who lives on the corner of Morris and Lambert?"

"She's not weird. She's just . . ."

"Weird."

"I was going to say shy." Charlotte had met Alma at a picnic hosted by one of Ida's many clubs. The woman had been a little different, her cat shirt, cat skirt, and cat earrings a bit over the top for a picnic. Charlotte had figured her to be the resident cat lady. Alma had been nice enough though, talking about her pets as if they were family. Charlotte had taken her for a lonely older woman who had either never been married or whose husband had died when he was very young.

It turned out that Alma had been married five times. Six if you counted the fact that she'd married her second husband twice. Alma did, and she seemed quite proud of the accomplishment when she talked about it. That happened almost every time she saw Charlotte.

"Shy? The last time I saw Alma, she described her ingrown toenail surgery in excruciating detail." Max shuddered as he pulled out of the parking lot.

"She *is* shy, but once she's comfortable around a person, she *does* like to talk."

"Wish I'd known that before I'd made her comfortable around me."

"At least she doesn't talk to you about her pets."

"Let me guess, she has six dozen cats."

"Try a dozen rats." Charlotte hated rats almost as much as she hated attics.

Max shook his head. "I'd like to say I'm surprised, but I'm not."

"She said her first rat was a birthday gift from her second husband. She got rid of the husband and kept the rat."

"I want a rat!" Zuzu called from the backseat.

"No," Max responded firmly.

"For my birthday."

"Pete would eat him."

"Pete won't eat my rat. He won't!" Zuzu's voice wobbled and Max raked his hand over his hair. "This is what happens when a kid's mother calls at five-thirty in the morning."

"How did it go?" Charlotte asked quietly, because she really wanted to know.

"About like I expected it would. She called to ask me for money," he bit out, anger seeping through every word.

"I'm sorry."

"Don't be sorry for me. I was over her before she sent me packing." He glanced in the rearview mirror, and she knew he was looking at Zuzu. She was the one who was missing out. Poor little thing. She loved her mother, but it didn't seem like her mother was quite as attached to her.

"Did she talk to Zuzu?"

"For about thirty seconds."

"Nice."

"She isn't. She never was."

"And yet you were dating her," she felt obligated to point out.

"I was young and stupid. I wanted a relationship without the commitment that goes with it. Morgan wanted the same." He shrugged. "You could probably say that we deserved each other."

"What happened?"

"Now who's the curious one?" He glanced her way, his lips curved in an easy smile. He had nice lips, the bottom just a little fuller than the top. Soft lips, too.

She shouldn't have known that, and she wished she didn't.

"Sorry," she mumbled, looking away.

"No need to apologize. I don't mind talking about it. Morgan and I were good for each other for a while. Then we weren't. I moved out. She moved on. I thought that was the end of things."

"But she didn't?"

"I think she did until her husband died. Now she needs someone. I was as good an option as any."

Poor Zuzu. She'd become a pawn that her mother could use to get what she wanted. It seemed what

Morgan wanted was Max. At least, she wanted what Max represented—security, help, support. He pulled up next to her car, and she knew it was time to get out and go on with her day. There was nothing more to say. At least nothing that was going to do Max and Zuzu any good, but she felt bad for both of them, tossed into a situation neither had any responsibility for.

"You're doing a good job, Max," she said as she got out of the car.

"Being chauffeur?" he responded with a smile.

"Being Zuzu's father."

His smile fell away. "How about we not talk about that right now?"

She'd touched a nerve.

She hadn't meant to.

Whether or not Zuzu was his, he was doing a good job of caring for her. She should have just said that.

"Sure. No problem. Thanks for your help this morning."

He nodded, his eyes shadowed, his expression hard. "No problem."

She wanted to say something else. Maybe tell him that she was sorry for bringing up Zuzu's paternity. Maybe explain that whether or not he was Zuzu's father didn't matter to her.

She kept her mouth shut and closed the door.

Max waited until she was in the station wagon before he drove off. When he was finally gone, she pulled away from the curb and headed back to Main Street. She still had cupcakes to frost for the poetry reading. That should only take fifteen minutes.

She'd pack them up, bring them to Town Hall, and head back for the next delivery.

What she would not do was spend another minute thinking about Max and Zuzu. She *would* make that cake though. A giant pink cake for Zuzu's birthday. Every little girl deserved at least one special cake.

She dragged keys from her purse and unlocked the front door, memories of the last time she'd returned to the house making her hesitate on the front porch. If she walked in and the house was freezing, she was walking right back out and calling the police again.

The house was warm. Thank God. She waited near the door anyway, listening to the quiet house. No door slammed. No feet tapped on the attic floor. No one came rushing out of the closet or jumped out from behind the couch. The house felt empty. Just the way it should be.

That never used to bother her, but lately, coming home to no one had become a chore, walking into the silent house a reminder of all the dreams she'd had when she was a kid. She'd planned to do so much better than her mother had. She'd thought for sure she knew just the kind of guy to look for. She'd written it all out in her diary when she was twelve. She still had the thing in a box somewhere, all the attributes of the perfect guy scrawled in pink ink on the inside of the front cover.

Once she got her storefront, she needed to get a puppy to fill the emptiness, because she sure as heck wasn't going to get a man.

Yes, a pet would be nice. Some furry little creature to greet her when she got home from deliveries would make the house seem so much more like a home. Just as long as she didn't decide to add a dozen rats to her life, she'd be just fine.

She shoved her hands into her coat pockets and frowned, pulling out the white feather. It was in remarkably good shape for having been crammed into her pocket for several days. Funny that Gertrude was so superstitious about the thing. An angel's feather that would bring love and good luck?

Charlotte snorted. She didn't believe in luck or love. She believed in hard work.

She found a vase and put the feather in it, then set it on the fireplace mantel. Hopefully that would be enough of a reminder that she needed to return it. If not, Gertrude or Tessa would visit eventually. They'd see it and take it home if they wanted to.

Four and a half dozen cupcakes sat on the kitchen counter. She'd counted carefully. Twice. Because Alma had been specific about the flavors of cupcakes and the number. It had to be exactly fifty-four. Alma's age. Plus one for happiness.

Six of the cupcakes had to be apple spice with no frosting. Charlotte had the strange feeling those six were going to be rat food. It didn't matter to her. As long as she got paid.

She pulled java buttercream frosting from the fridge and let it warm up while she beat together room temperature butter and powdered sugar, added melted semi-sweet chocolate, and beat it all to a light creamy texture.

It looked good. It *smelled* even better.

She filled a pastry bag and got to work, piping chocolate frosting onto half the remaining cupcakes and java onto the other half. She loved the easy rhythm of the work, the quick results. One minute, a dozen cupcakes were bare. The next, they were covered with beautiful swirls of frosting.

If only life were as easy as cooking!

She set the newly frosted cupcakes into a box, careful not to wreck the frosting top. They looked beautiful and delicious. Exactly the way Charlotte wanted them. The spiced pumpkin cupcakes were already frosted, their rich aroma making her stomach growl. She should have made a couple of extra, but she'd been in a hurry to finish baking cupcakes and get on to the next order. She'd made an appointment to do a walk-through with the owner of the storefront she wanted to rent.

Just thinking about it made her happy.

Maybe Nick Simon would be desperate enough to re-rent the building to give her a discount. A hundred dollars less a month, and she'd snatch the storefront up in a heartbeat.

She reached for the last two cupcakes, set them in the box, and blinked. Ten cupcakes. There should have been twelve. She looked at the banana peanut butter Elvis cupcakes, their frosting sprinkled with bacon. No pumpkin mixed in with those. She quickly filled a box with Elvis cupcakes. Or should have filled it. There were only eleven.

"What in the world?!" She checked the fridge, checked the floor, checked everywhere she could think of for the missing cupcakes.

Nothing. Not even a crumb.

"This is so *not* good."

She was being paid to deliver fifty-four cupcakes.

She couldn't walk in with fifty-two. Okay. She'd just have to mix things up a little. She had a variety of cupcakes in the freezer, kept there for last-minute orders and walk-ins. Two or three times a week, someone came looking for a sweet snack, and Charlotte was always happy to make a sale.

She'd have to restock later.

She took a plastic container from the very back of the side-by-side freezer and pulled out three vanilla bean. She didn't pull out the lone double chocolate delight cupcake that she'd mixed in with the rest. She saved those for special friends. Married friends or single friends who had absolutely no ulterior motive for eating or serving someone a double chocolate delight. She set the container on the counter. She'd bake more cupcakes later and refill it before returning it to the freezer.

She frosted the cupcakes quickly, piping on chocolate frosting and setting them in the empty spots in the boxes. If Alma complained, she'd apologize, but she was banking on the woman not paying any attention to anything but the poetry she was reading.

She checked each box, made sure it was filled and that the cupcakes were in good shape, their domed tops and swirled frosting perfect. Everything looked good. Crisis averted, and she could move on, but she couldn't quite shake her unease. She'd been selling cupcakes for nearly two years, and she'd never miscounted an order before.

So how had she come up short on the cupcakes?

She checked the back door. Just to make sure it was locked.

It was.

The front door had been locked, too. Obviously no one had walked into the house and snagged a few cupcakes.

So she'd made a mistake when she'd counted. Somehow.

Or Zim had come for a visit and decided to take a couple of snacks with him. It didn't seem like his style, but there was a first time for everything.

She covered all the boxes and packed napkins, plates, and a tablecloth. Alma planned to provide the decorations. Hopefully that didn't mean rat figurines.

Charlotte glanced around the kitchen. She'd cleaned before she went on her first delivery. Aside from the frosting bags and the thawing cupcakes, she was done. With time to spare. That was the way she liked to do things. She hurried into the bathroom, ran a brush through her hair, and put a little makeup on. Alma had very particular taste, and she liked things a particular way. She believed people at work should dress professionally. Which, Charlotte guessed, did not include faded jeans.

She should change. Put on a skirt and a blouse or a dress. Something a little more polished.

She rushed into her room and scrounged through the closet, pulling out the first dress she found, a dark blue A-line that she'd bought at a vintage clothing store. She'd never had an occasion to wear it. It seemed fitting for a poetry reading, so she tugged it on, her mind circling around the problem she'd had with the cupcakes. She had to be more careful. This time she'd had extra. What if she didn't next time?

Alma didn't seem like the kind to forgive and forget, and she certainly wasn't the kind to keep her mouth shut if she wasn't happy.

She hurried into the hall, remembered that she was going to the storefront after her delivery, and skidded to a stop. She wanted to bring a camera, take a few pictures to show Zim. He'd flipped a few houses, and he'd said he could help her paint and put down new flooring in the building.

She wasn't sure if he'd be more help or hindrance, but she'd promised to take photos for him. Even though she was pretty sure he'd been inside the building on more than one occasion.

She sighed and turned back toward the room. Something lay on the floor at the end of the hall, right near the attic door. She stepped closer, her heart nearly jumping out of her chest when she saw the old skeleton key. It had been in the attic lock when she'd left.

Hadn't it?

Lately she didn't seem to know if she was coming or going, but that didn't mean she'd been wrong about hearing the door slam. Despite what the police had said, she wasn't convinced that she'd been alone in her house that night. She *wanted* to believe it, but no amount of wanting something could make it true.

Could someone be in the house now, lurking in the attic bedroom? She cocked her head to the side. As if that would help the situation.

She didn't hear anything. Not a creak or groan. Not a breath.

The house felt empty.

Just like always.

She could call the police, but she'd already called them out on a false alarm once. She didn't want to do it again.

There was someone she could call, though. Someone who would probably be willing to check the house out while she was making her delivery. Max had said she should call if she needed anything.

Don't do it.

Do not *pick up the phone and call Max.*

She didn't need him. She could do it herself. Just walk up the stairs and take a look around, make sure the room was as empty as she thought it was going to be.

Who was she kidding?

She might be *able* to do it, but she wasn't *going* to.

She was too much of a chicken.

Max wasn't.

He'd be able to handle her attic dilemma, and he wouldn't tell everyone he'd done it.

She slid the skeleton key into the lock and turned it, sealing whatever trouble there might be behind the thick wooden door. When she was done, she took the boxes of cupcakes to her car and did exactly the one thing she knew she shouldn't do.

She called Max.

Chapter Twelve

Charlotte's house looked just like it always did. Curtains opened wide in the living room so that Max could see straight into the house, front door closed tight, porch light on. If someone had been inside, it wasn't obvious. No sign of any of the windows being jimmied. The front and back doors were both still intact, their locks functioning properly.

If anyone else had called to say she'd found a key on the floor and thought someone might be hiding in her attic, Max probably would have assumed an overly wild imagination was at work. He'd taken Charlotte seriously. He hadn't even bothered going to the office after dropping Zuzu off at Ida's. He'd thrown on his uniform and headed to Charlotte's house.

He stood on the sidewalk in front of the house and looked up at the second-floor dormer window. Nothing moved. No one peered out from behind the gauzy curtain. Not that he'd thought anyone would. If he were hiding in some unsuspecting woman's house, he wouldn't be peering out at the world while he was doing it.

He wouldn't have left a key in the middle of the floor, either.

"What are you doing, copper? Thinking about searching Charlotte's house without a warrant?" someone called from across the street.

He didn't even bother looking. He knew Gertrude McKenzie's husky voice.

"Thinking about becoming a Peeping Tom," he responded.

"Should have waited until the sun went down. People are going to talk."

"That's what I'm hoping for. Some good old-fashioned gossip." He turned around, scanning the old Riley place until he spotted Gertrude in an open downstairs window. He crossed the street, smiling at the older woman. "A little cold to have the windows open, isn't it?"

"Tessa is back."

"And?"

"She's running a class on refinishing old furniture. Every one of those damn old ladies who's taking it is wearing a boatload of flowery perfume. Place smells like a funeral parlor."

"So you thought you'd freeze them all out?"

"Nah. Tessa makes good money on the classes. I've got to give the girl credit. She's got business sense. I'm just trying to air the place out before they all come in from the refinishing shed and stink it up again. So what are *you* doing over *there*?"

"Just looking around."

"That much is obvious. How about giving me a little more? Some juicy little tidbit that I can pass along?"

"If there was anything juicy, you'd be the first to know." Unless he didn't want it spread around. In which case, Gertrude would probably be one of the last to know. She was a great lady—funny, outspoken to the point of rudeness, but absolutely devoted to her family and the people she cared about. What she was not was quiet. Ever.

"Liar."

"True."

She let out a bark of laughter. "Good to know. Since you don't want to tell me what you're doing, how about you just tell me if I should be worried about Charlie. She's not in trouble or anything, is she?"

"Charlotte? When has she ever been in trouble?" he asked, curious despite himself.

"Not legal trouble," Gertrude said with a deep exasperated sigh. "*Man* trouble."

Man trouble?

He hadn't known there was a man, and he didn't think he liked the idea that there was one.

Scratch that.

He *knew* he didn't like the idea.

"What man?" he asked, the question a little gruffer than he'd intended.

"You're the cop. It's your job to figure it out," Gertrude huffed, her face nearly pressed against the window screen, her orange hair slipping out from between the mesh.

"It would help," he said with exaggerated patience, because Gertrude loved to talk, but getting helpful information out of her could be like plucking a flower out of the brambles. "If you told me exactly what I'm supposed to figure out."

"Can't say that I know. Charlotte is pretty tight-lipped about her past. If you haven't noticed."

"I have."

"Well, there you go," Gertrude said with just a hint of sarcasm. "You're on your way to becoming deputy of the year."

"No such thing. If there were, I'd have already won it," he responded lightly. He'd spent enough time around Gertrude to know that she loved to push people's buttons. Sometimes he pushed back, because she also loved a good verbal sparring.

Today he wanted to get back to the subject.

Charlotte and man trouble.

"That's what I like about you, Max." Gertrude chuckled. "You know how to take it and you know how to dish it out."

"I'm glad to know you appreciate one of my finer qualities. So *is* there a man in Charlotte's life?" he asked bluntly. No sense beating around the bush with Gertrude. She hated that almost as much as Max did.

"Don't know if there *is* one, but I can tell you there *was* one, and I don't think he was very good to her."

"What makes you say that?"

"She's a widow, right? Young, right? How many young widows do you know that never ever talk about their husbands?"

"I don't know a whole lot of young widows." But he *had* noticed how reluctant Charlotte was to talk about Brett. The husband who'd been a Marine and truck driver.

"Then use your imagination," she snapped, her eyes blazing from behind the mesh screen, her finger poking right at his face. "A woman gets married, and she's pinning all her hopes and dreams on this one guy. Over the years, she's bound to get a little jaded and realize that her Prince Charming is just another guy. But if the prince dies before he has a chance to annoy the hell out of his princess, she's going to spend the next decade waxing poetic about what a paragon he was."

"Interesting theory."

"*Theory?* I've been alive for four decades longer than you. I know a thing or two about women that you only wish you knew."

He wasn't going to argue *that* point.

"No doubt about that, Ms. Gertrude. But what does all this have to do with Charlotte?"

"She doesn't talk about her husband. Not at all. Not a word. Ever. Even when she's asked, she just kind of meanders around the subject and gives vague answers that could mean anything."

"I've noticed."

"Give the man a prize and call him a genius," she muttered.

"Ms. Gertrude, I'd love to stay and chat all day, but I don't think my boss would appreciate that, so how about you just tell me exactly what you think about Charlotte's husband."

"I think he was a bastard, that's what I think."

"Way to be blunt."

"You asked."

True. "I did, and I've been thinking the same."

"Of course, you were. You're smart. You've got your head screwed on straight. You're also handsome as sin, and if I were a couple of decades younger, I'd be—"

"How about you save that for another day?" He cut her off, because he really didn't want to hear what Gertrude would be doing if she were a couple of decades younger.

"My point is this, Max . . ." She pressed her forehead to the screen, her eyes blazing green fire. "Charlotte is a pretty young woman. She's hardworking and sweet and just about the kindest lady I've ever met. She should be out there looking for someone, but she's got her head in cookbooks and romance novels and spends most of her days and nights in the kitchen."

"There's nothing wrong with that."

"Did I say there was? I'm just pointing out that there are plenty of guys in this town who'd be thrilled to spend time with her. More than a couple of them would stick a ring on her finger tomorrow if she were willing. But she's not even looking." She shook her head sadly. "Her bastard of a husband ruined it for her. She doesn't have to say one word about it for me to know it. It's a damn shame."

If it were true, Max had to agree.

Charlotte was too young to put herself on a shelf.

"You're right about that, Ms. Gertrude. Now if

you'll excuse me, I've got to get back to what I was doing."

"Which was? You still haven't told me squat!"

"I know." He grinned. "See you around, Ms. Gertrude."

He walked away, her curses ringing in his ears.

That was Gertrude. A heart like an angel and a mouth like a drunken sailor.

Charlotte had left her front door unlocked, and he walked into the quiet house. The hardwood floor glowed in the light shining through the front windows, the furniture polished to a high sheen. A narrow vase stood on the fireplace mantel, a single white feather jutting out of it. Before Charlotte moved in, the place had been empty, the last family that had rented it gone for a few months. They'd moved to a farm outside of town, because the little cottage had been too small for seven kids and the baby that had been on the way.

"Eight kids," he mumbled as he walked through the house. "That's a hell of a lot."

One was a lot.

Zuzu had spent the entire morning asking questions.

Where are we going?

What are we going to do there?

Why is it cold? Why is the sky blue? Why is the cat named Pete? Can I call him Sparkle?

No. She could not call the cat Sparkle.

She couldn't call him Glitter either.

That had been her second choice.

He eyed the attic door. The key was in the lock, and

he couldn't see any easy way for it to be dislodged. He used a gloved hand to pull it out and push it back in again. It was a little tricky, but fit smoothly once he got it into the lock. If it had been put in properly, it would be almost impossible for it to fall out.

The old cut-glass handle would be the perfect conduit for fingerprints. Even though Charlotte wasn't sure anyone had been in the house, he'd dust it. Make sure that he did things right. Just in case.

That would have to wait until he had the patrol car and his fingerprint kit. He couldn't touch the knob until he dusted it, so he headed out, leaving the front door unlocked and driving over to the station. He didn't bother going into the office. Just got in the patrol car and drove back to Charlotte's place.

Her old station wagon was parked in the driveway, so he pulled up to the curb, got out, and grabbed the fingerprint kit from the back of the car.

Charlotte met him halfway to the house, her hair loose around her shoulders, her simple blue dress falling to just above her knee. She hadn't buttoned her coat, and he caught a glimpse of narrow waist and full breasts beneath the body-hugging bodice of her dress. God, she looked good.

"Looks like I beat you here," she said.

"Actually, I was here a few minutes ago. I had to run to the office to get my patrol car."

She frowned, shoving her hand into the pockets of her coat. She needed to button up in this kind of weather, wear gloves and maybe a hat, but he doubted she'd appreciate him telling her that. "Did you find anything?"

"I haven't been up in the attic yet. I wanted to dust for prints on the knob first."

"I really appreciate you doing this, Max. I probably should have just phoned the sheriff's office—"

"No need for thanks, Charlotte. I owe you big-time for taking care of Zuzu the other day. Besides"—he touched her back, urging her into the house ahead of him—"I never mind spending time with you."

"You're flirting again."

"Telling the truth again," he corrected her, smiling when she scowled.

"Well, cut it out."

"Why?"

"Because I'm not into flirting anymore."

"That means that you were into flirting at one time or another," he pointed out.

"Isn't everyone? When we're kids and we have a whole lifetime of dreams ahead of us, it's easy to get caught up in games. The problem with games is that someone always ends up being the loser." Her voice was light, but the look in her eyes was anything but.

It angered him more than he wanted to admit.

No woman should ever be left scarred by a relationship, and no guy should ever leave shadows in a woman's eyes.

"I wouldn't know," he responded, making sure to match her tone. Light. Easy. No emotion in his voice. "I don't play games any more than I make hints. If I want a woman, I let her know. I don't flirt with her."

She glanced over her shoulder as she led the way

down the hall, her eyes still filled with shadows. "So you just flirt as a matter of course?"

"I *tell the truth*, because everyone needs a pick-me-up every once in a while," he corrected. "A kind word doesn't cost a whole lot. And for the record, I compliment men, too. Unless they're assholes. In which case, I tell them so to their faces."

"Oh," Charlotte murmured, surprised and a little pleased by his honesty. "Good to know."

Good to know?

What kind of idiotic thing was that to say?

Charlotte would have taken the words back if she could have, but they'd already been said and Max already had a hint of a smile at the corner of his mouth.

"What I mean," she added, knowing that she was heading into even lamer territory by attempting to explain, "is that I'm glad you aren't the kind of guy who plays games, because I hate when people do that. I always have. I'm more an up-front kind of person. Just tell it like it is. Say what you mean. Be who . . ." *Shut up already!*

"Be who you want to be?" He finished the thought. It sounded just as lame when he said it as it would have coming out of her mouth.

"Something like that."

"Too bad that's not nearly as easy as we think it should be." He opened the fingerprint kit and looked like he was ready to get down to official business. That was as good an excuse as any to put some distance between them.

"Want some coffee?"

"If I drink any more, I might end up with caffeine poisoning," he responded, looking up from the contents of the kit. He had beautiful eyes. Such a dark deep blue that they almost looked black in certain lights.

"I can make decaf."

"No, thanks."

"Orange juice?"

"I'm fine."

"How about a couple of cookies?"

"Charlotte"—he laughed—"you don't have to feed and water me every time I cross the threshold."

He had the best kind of laugh. The kind that could fill a room, a house, a heart if someone let it.

"Sorry. I know you're not livestock. It's just a habit."

"No need to apologize. I just don't want you to feel obligated." He took powder and a brush from the kit. "Want to help me with this?"

"You've been a police officer for a lot of years. I doubt you need my help dusting for prints."

"Just because I don't need it, doesn't mean I don't want it. Like I said before, I enjoy spending time with you." He dusted the doorknob carefully, his attention completely focused on the task.

She had the strangest feeling, though, that he was aware of her, tuned in to her, reading her reactions and responses despite the fact that he wasn't looking her way.

Her insides quivered in response, her body just begging her to move a couple steps closer. She could pretend that she wanted to help with fingerprinting, lean in close, and inhale the heady masculine scent that clung to him. She could put her hand on his broad shoulder, feel the hard muscles and warm flesh beneath his shirt.

Or she could run for her life.

She chose that option, nearly tripping over her own feet in her haste to retreat. She skidded to a stop in the kitchen, her heart pounding way too fast for the amount of effort she'd put into the run.

She needed to pull herself together.

Max was just a guy who happened to smell really good, look really good, taste really good.

"Stop it!" she hissed.

"Did you say something?" Max called from the hallway.

"No," she lied.

"You sure?"

"Yes."

"Okay. Good news! I found a couple of prints on the knob."

"You did?" She peeked into the hall, watching as Max carefully pulled a section of tape off the doorknob. "Who do you think they belong to?"

"Who's been in your house?"

"Me, you, Zim, Zuzu."

"We already have my prints. Zim's are on file. Thanks to his little indiscretion last year."

"He returned the angel to the Rileys." The figurine had been made by the wife of the first mayor of Apple Valley. Zim had been feuding with Gertrude and had taken it out of spite.

"We still have his prints. I'll take yours when I'm

done. We can rule out Zuzu. The prints are definitely too big."

"What if none of the prints match the ones you found?"

"Good question." He pressed another piece of tape to the knob. "Is anything missing from your house?"

Nothing except the cupcakes, but they didn't count. Did they? "Not really."

"Not really? Or no?"

"Remember the delivery I was making to Alma?"

"The crazy rat lady? Yeah. I remember."

"I baked the cupcakes this morning. I didn't finish frosting them, so I left them on the counter. When I got home from the Fishers, I was missing a few."

He looked up from the doorknob, his expression neutral. "So you're saying someone came into your house and took some cupcakes?"

"I'm saying that I thought I counted accurately, but I came up short. I've never had that happen before."

"Did you leave the front door unlocked when you left this morning?"

"No. The back door was locked, too. I double-checked."

"Anyone have the key?"

"Zim has one. Gertrude and Tessa do, too."

"Hmmmm." He gently removed another piece of tape from the doorknob, pressed it to what looked like an index card, and closed the fingerprint kit. "Wonder if Alex was over here. He likes sweets, and he's smart enough to find a key and take it if he decided he wanted to."

True, but she couldn't believe that he'd enter her house without permission or take something that didn't belong to him. "Alex is a good kid. He wouldn't come into my house and steal cupcakes."

"He's a good kid, but he *is* a kid. They make mistakes and do stupid things all the time."

"I guess I can talk to Gertrude or Tessa. Just kind of feel around and make sure they know where the key is and are sure it hasn't been used by anyone else."

"If something is missing from your house, this is police business. I'll take care of things with the McKenzies," Max said.

Take care of things?

As in . . . march over there and tell them their nephew was a thief?

Good God! Max was about to start a war over cupcakes!

"You can't go over there in your uniform and accuse—"

"Hold on." He held up a hand. "I never said I was going over there or making any accusations. I just said I'll take care of it."

"How are you planning to do that without starting an all-out battle with Gertrude? You know how protective she is of Alex. She'll be offended, and she'll hate me forever."

"I'm not going to talk to Gertrude. I'm going to mention it to Cade. He's more diplomatic than I am, and he'll know exactly how to handle the investigation."

"Investigation! It's a couple of missing cupcakes, Max. Not grand theft auto."

"It's theft. No matter how small the item," he said dispassionately. "Besides, I'm not planning to take the kid to jail. If he came in your house and took a couple of cupcakes, he can pay restitution, and we'll call it a day."

"How about we just call it a day now? These are my neighbors. I don't want to spend the next twenty years avoiding them."

"Tell you what," he responded. "How about you hold off worrying until we have more information? It's possible Alex didn't have anything to do with your missing cupcakes. Come on. Let's go check out the attic."

He opened the door and walked up the stairs.

She followed, because she didn't want him to comment on her irrational fear of attics again. Plus she really thought she should get over it. Maybe if she called the room something other than attic. Upstairs room? Sanctuary?

"Shit," Max muttered under his breath, stopping short a half foot in front of her.

"Wha . . ." Her voice trailed off as she caught sight of the room. Every drawer in the dresser had been pulled out, the mattress on the bed flipped onto the floor. "Good God! What happened?"

"I'm going to take your reaction to mean that you had no idea the room looked like this?"

"None."

"I need to call this in and get someone over here to help me process it. You want to go downstairs and wait for me there?"

Did she?

Not if some cupcake-stealing maniac was down there.

"I'm fine here."

"Charlotte, I don't think you understood me." Max spoke slowly and enunciated every word. "I want you to wait for me downstairs."

"But—"

"Go on," he prodded, giving her a gentle nudge toward the stairs. "You hate attics, anyway. Remember?"

Of course she remembered.

"And I have to do a little work up here."

"What kind of work?"

"Normal police stuff. Dusting for prints. Looking for evidence." He glanced around the room and frowned. "The place is ransacked, but nothing looks damaged."

"Are you going to call in CSI?"

"Not in a town this size, and not for a crime that seems fairly petty. I am going to call Cade, though."

"Maybe—"

"You know what? I need to get a couple things from my squad car. I'll walk you down." He took her arm, his fingers curving around her elbow. She hadn't removed her coat, but she felt his touch all the way to the depth of her churning stomach.

He was a solid mass of masculinity. Not a bit of panic in his voice as he called Cade and reported what had happened. No hurry, no rush as he walked her into the kitchen. He glanced around the room, his gaze lighting on the container of cupcakes she'd pulled from the freezer.

"Those look good enough to eat."

"Have one." She grabbed the container.

"I like frosting. Lots of it. Chocolate. Just pile it up on one while I check things out in the attic." He handed her the bag of chocolate frosting. "Cade will be here in a minute. Can you let him in when he gets here?"

"Sure, but didn't you have to get something out of your squad car?"

"I changed my mind." He walked from the room, left her with the bag of frosting in her hand and the feeling that he'd take care of everything if she let him.

"You're not going to let him, darn it," she muttered, snagging a cupcake and layering it three inches high with frosting. She did the same to all the rest, placing them on a plate and setting them on the counter. When she finished, she took out the ingredients for the lemon bars and oatmeal squares Emmett Lawrence had ordered for his wife's birthday party. Charlotte hadn't planned to make them until after she met with Nick. She'd had to cancel that to come home and see what was going on in her attic.

A sucky turn in an otherwise pretty good day, but she'd deal with it.

An hour and a half later, the bars were baked and cooling, their sweet scent filling the room. She glanced at the clock, wandered into the hallway. Cade and Max had been in the attic for a long time. Maybe they'd found something worse than fingerprints.

Bloody handprints on the wall or a threatening note?

A headless doll? A body?

There were a heck of a lot of things that could be

hidden in an attic. Even an attic that was bright, clean, and pretty.

She stood in the attic doorway, looking up into the well-lit room. "How's it going up there?"

Cade appeared at the top of the stairs. "We're just about done."

"Find anything?"

"Nothing to write home about." He walked down downstairs, inhaling deeply as he stepped into the hall. "Smells good in here."

"I was baking."

"And here I thought you were shellacking furniture." He smiled, his eyes crinkling at the corners. "You doing okay?"

"Right as rain."

"No, you're not." He gave her a quick hug, patted her shoulder the way he had a dozen times before. He was a good guy. The kind that existed in a few little corners of the universe and that some deserving woman always snagged up and held on to forever.

"Okay. Maybe I'm not," she admitted. "Someone was in my house, Cade. I'm not happy about it."

"We've collected a few fingerprints. We'll see if there's a match in the system. Max said all the doors were locked."

"They were."

"From the look of things, the locks weren't jimmied. Anyone besides Tessa have the key to your house?"

"Just Zim, and I don't think he'd be interested in going through my stuff."

"He's been known to skirt the law on occasion," Cade said, walking to the back door and studying the lock. "But I think after he took Miriam's angel last year, he's repented. No more pilfering things that don't belong to him. This lock isn't very sturdy. I bet I could open it with a credit card. Hold on."

He stepped outside and closed the door.

"Go ahead and lock it," he called.

She did.

Ten seconds later the door swung open.

"See?" Cade said. "Easy as could be."

"What was easy?" Max walked into the room, his blond hair a little ruffled. She wanted to smooth it down, rub the tension from his neck, feed him lunch and dinner and maybe breakfast.

God, she was a mess.

"Getting inside." Cade gestured to the back door. "Charlotte needs a new lock. A bolt would be best."

"Yeah." Max leaned in to take a closer look, the subtle scent of his cologne mixing with the homey scent of lemon and sugar. "I see what you mean. I'll stop by the hardware store when I finish my shift. It'll be late, but I can install it for you tonight."

"I'll figure it out." Because there was no way she wanted to start relying on Max. He was the kind of guy who'd mean well but break her heart anyway. One broken heart in a lifetime was plenty.

"Thanks for the offer, though," she added.

"You sure?" He eyed the cupcakes on the counter. "Because it wouldn't be a favor. I'd want a few cupcakes as payment."

"I was already planning on giving you a cupcake," she reminded him. The last thing she wanted was Max hanging around her house late at night when she was loneliest and the most likely to notice just how nice it was to have a man around.

"Right." He snagged a cupcake from the plate. "But what about Zuzu? She loves your cooking."

"Who doesn't?" Cade asked, grabbing a chocolate frosted vanilla cupcake and biting into it. "You need to give Tessa the recipe for these."

"Would she make them if I did?" As far as Charlotte knew, Tessa wasn't a cook.

"No, but she might buy a few dozen from you and tell me that she made them. Just to impress me."

"I think Tessa impresses you without even trying, and I think she knows it." Charlotte laughed and handed Cade the entire plate. She could make more, and she loved knowing that people enjoyed her food. That had been one of the nice things about working at a convalescent center: The people there had been so thankful for every dish she served. "Why don't you take these home? You can come back for more anytime."

"You know I will. Now that I live across the street, there's nothing stopping me from pilfering cupcakes anytime I want."

"Nothing but the law," Max muttered.

Surprised, Charlotte met his eyes. He looked pissed off, but she wasn't sure why. "It's not stealing if I said he could have them. Which I did."

"Right." He peeled the paper off his cupcake.

Oh, dear God!

What had she done?

The man had a double chocolate cupcake with chocolate butter cream frosting. Double chocolate delight. She'd stopped making them months ago, but there it was. Right in his hand.

She wanted to snatch it back, but she didn't know how to do that without looking like a lunatic.

Besides, it was just a cupcake.

No magic power. No secret love potion.

Nothing but lots of good quality chocolate.

Intellectually, she knew it, but she still wanted to snatch the thing back and toss it into the garbage.

Chapter Thirteen

Max was being petty.

He knew it.

But it irritated him to see how relaxed Charlotte was with Cade. For whatever reason, Max resented that.

Probably because he wanted to be the one that Charlotte was comfortable with. He wanted to get the full force of her relaxed smile.

Right at the moment he was getting the full force of Cade's curious gaze. "She's right, Max. I was joking. I'm not planning to walk into her house anytime I please and take whatever sweet treat I'm craving."

Max nodded, biting into the cupcake to keep from making more of an ass of himself. Dark decadent chocolate melted on his tongue and exploded through his senses. He had tasted a lot of chocolate and a lot of cupcakes, but he'd never tasted anything as good as *that* chocolate and *that* cupcake.

"What the hell is this?" he asked, taking another bite.

"Is something wrong with it?" Charlotte leaned close, and he caught a whiff of vanilla and sugar and something so sweet and lovely he wanted to take a deeper breath of it.

"Maybe you shouldn't eat it," she murmured, her cheeks deep pink, her eyes bright.

"I'm already eating it, so it's a little too late to be worrying about that." He polished it off, licked rich chocolate frosting off his fingers. "Besides, if it was poisoned, I'd die a happy man. That was the best damn cupcake I've ever eaten."

"Good to know," she responded, her gaze on the floor, the counter, the ceiling. It seemed she wanted to look at anything but him.

"Do I have one here?" Cade glanced at the plate of cupcakes.

"No!" Charlotte almost shouted. "What I mean is that I don't actually make that kind of cupcake anymore."

"Why not?" Max asked at the same time that Cade started laughing. Not just a quiet laugh either. An obnoxiously loud laugh that made him want to plant a fist right in his good friend's mouth. "What's so funny?"

"Absolutely nothing," Charlotte said, shooting Cade a look that might have killed if she'd had the power to do that with her eyes.

"Nothing?" Cade snorted. "He just ate one of your double chocolate delights, didn't he?"

"So what?" she demanded, her cheeks cherry red. "They're just cupcakes."

She was wrong about that. What he'd eaten hadn't *just* been a cupcake. It had been a little slice of heaven, and if he had ten more sitting in front of him, he'd have probably eaten every single one of them.

Damn!

He hadn't just eaten a cupcake. He'd eaten one of *those* cupcakes. The ones that every woman in town wanted to feed the man of her dreams. The one that Carla Mae Rhinefield had tried to pawn off on him a couple of months ago. He hadn't believed the hype. As matter of fact, he'd laughed at more than one man who'd told him that the cupcakes were the work of the devil.

He'd still laugh at that kind of talk, but damn if that one cupcake hadn't made him want a hell of a lot more. And he wasn't just talking about cupcakes!

"Double chocolate delight, huh?" he asked, looking at the empty wrapper and wondering what Charlotte put in them.

"I'm afraid so. If I'd thought about it, I'd have left the double chocolate in the freezer, but I didn't, so . . ." Charlotte shrugged and offered a wry smile.

"We're destined to be together forever?" he joked.

It didn't feel quite like a joke, though.

And if he were going to be totally honest with himself, he'd have to say that forever with someone like Charlotte didn't seem like as much of a bad thing as it probably should have.

Sure, he'd made a decision to never get married,

never have kids, never pass along the piss-poor
people skills his parents had had. Life wasn't about
absolutes, though. He'd lived long enough to know
that. People changed. Things changed. Goals and
dreams and thoughts changed.

"It was just a cupcake, Max," Charlotte responded
easily, still not meeting his gaze. He wanted to tilt
her chin, make her look into his eyes so that he
could see what was going on in her head, but Cade
was watching them both with a look that was both
amused and worried.

"I think we're done here," he said. "Let's head over
to the office and get those fingerprints processed,
Max."

Cade wasn't the kind to give orders, but that was
pretty close to one. It didn't bother Max. He was on
the clock, working for the town, and he'd do what
he was told when he was told.

On his own time, though . . .

That was a different story.

He walked outside, ignoring Cade's hard look
as he got into his cruiser. It was impossible to ignore
Cade's entire upper body leaning into the car,
though.

"It's going to be hard for me to get to the office
with you hanging out of the door," Max said calmly.
No sense getting upset. Charlotte and Cade had
been friends for a couple of years, and Cade was the
kind of guy who looked out for the people he cared
about.

"What's going on with you and Charlotte?" Cade

didn't beat around the bush, and Max wasn't going to sidestep the question.

"Nothing. Yet."

"What's that supposed to mean?"

"It means that maybe I want something to happen."

"You could have any woman in town, Max. How about you leave Charlotte alone and go find one of them?"

"How about you worry about my work ethic and my job and leave my personal life alone?" Max suggested, keeping his tone as even as Cade's had been. They were friends, and they'd never let women get in the way of that. When Cade had gone after Tessa, Max had stepped back and watched him do it.

Not that Tessa had ever paid Max more than five seconds of attention. She'd had eyes for no one but Cade. That had been obvious from the beginning. Still, Max *had* stayed away and kept his nose out of Cade's relationship.

Cade's jaw tightened, his eyes flashing with frustration. "Charlotte is a friend of mine, and I don't want to see her hurt."

"Since when do I hurt women?" he demanded, finally getting about as pissed off as Cade seemed to be.

"Since when have you ever wanted a woman who needs more than a few nights out and a couple of compliments to make her happy?"

"I haven't decided what I want. When I do, I'll be sure to let you know," he responded, every word dripping with sarcasm. He needed this discussion about as much as he needed to chase cows along the interstate again.

"Yeah? Just be aware, that I don't want Charlotte hurt. If she is, I'm going to take it damn personally."

"I am, too, so how about we both drop the subject until there's some reason to bring it up again?" Max suggested.

Cade eyed him for a moment, and then nodded. "As long as we're both clear on where we stand, there's no reason to keep hashing things out. I'll see you at the office."

He stepped back, shoving his hands in his pockets and watching as Max backed out of the driveway.

Knowing Cade, he wouldn't mention the subject again. Unless Max did hurt Charlotte. Which was a distinct possibility. He wouldn't mean to. He wouldn't want to. He'd have absolutely no intention of it, but Charlotte was the kind of woman who'd want the white picket fence and the kids and the little dog yapping in the yard. She'd want to make dinners every night and sit down as a family to eat them. She'd probably give shoulder massages and pep talks and spend her days trying to think up ways to make the people she loved happy.

Max just wasn't that kind of guy. The kind that could appreciate a woman like that. The kind that could give her what she wanted and make her happy.

Not that he didn't want to be. He just . . . wasn't. Simple as that.

He flicked on the radio, ran a hand over his hair, catching a quick whiff of dark chocolate. Must be on his hand. He was tempted to lick his fingers, just to get another taste of the cupcake.

"Damn!" he muttered, because he wanted to turn around and go back and ask for a couple more of the things.

He wouldn't, but he was still going to take Charlotte out to dinner Friday night. As a thank-you for her help, and maybe to get to know her a little better.

One dinner wouldn't hurt either of them.

He just wasn't sure it would be enough.

Maybe, like the damn chocolate cupcakes, he'd end up wanting more.

There were a few of reasons why Charlotte was wandering down Main Street at midnight. First, she couldn't sleep. Second, she had no idea how to replace the lock on her back door. She hadn't even been able to figure out what kind of lock to buy. She really didn't want to sit around at home imagining someone sliding a credit card between the old lock and the door and walking inside. Plus, she just . . .

Well, she was lonely.

Simple as that.

She wanted a house filled with noise. Not the empty silent shell of a home she lived in.

Especially with Christmas looming.

All the things she wanted for so many years, all the things she'd thought that she'd have after she married, they were like the Christmas carol drifting from the upstairs apartment of one of the businesses— faded reminders of a million hopes that had come to nothing.

She stopped in front of the storefront she'd been

drooling over for months. A two-story brownstone with a huge picture window in the front, it had office space and storage upstairs. Downstairs, the place had everything she'd need to run a bakery.

That's what she should be thinking about. Not old dead dreams.

She pressed her nose to the glass, trying to see into the interior.

Hers.

That's what it felt like, what she wanted it to be, but even a storefront couldn't fill the emptiness.

She shoved her hands deep into her pockets and turned away. She needed to shake off the funk that she'd been feeling since the twenty-seventh, let go of the niggling unhappiness. Or figure out what was causing it. Certainly not some sudden desire to jump back into the dating game, find another not-so-perfect match, and try the whole happily ever after thing again.

"That would be the definition of insanity. Doing the same thing over and over again and expecting different results," she muttered.

"But talking to yourself *isn't* the definition of insanity?"

She jumped, whirling to face Max.

"Where did you come from?" she demanded, irritated because her heart was racing. Not because he'd scared her, either. Because he was one fine example of male beauty.

"Your place. I'm replacing your lock. Remember?"

"I thought we agreed that I didn't need you to do that."

"My memory is fuzzy. Lack of sleep does that to

me." He grinned, and her stupid heart just about jumped out of her chest.

She had to pull herself together, keep the conversation on neutral ground so that she didn't find herself looking deep into Max's eyes, thinking about things she shouldn't.

Like what it would feel like to step into his arms, rest her head against his chest, listen to the quiet thud of his heart.

She was such a loser.

"Zuzu has been keeping you awake?" she asked, turning back to look at the storefront again.

Just keep your goals in mind and everything will be fine, she mentally reminded herself as Max stepped up beside her and peered into the dark store.

"No. She sleeps pretty well. I've just been working odd hours since the wedding. Now that Cade is back, things will get back to normal."

Good.

They were talking about something neutral.

She could handle that. Could just kind of keep the conversation going without making a fool of herself.

She hoped.

"How normal can they be when you have a little girl living with you?" she asked. He hadn't complained about having Zuzu dropped into his life, but Charlotte couldn't imagine that it had been easy to adjust to a toddler. Especially not one as precocious as Zuzu.

"Zuzu and I are kind of coming up with a new normal. Neither of us is all that happy about it, but we're getting used to it." He turned away from

Nick's store. She could feel the weight of his gaze, but she tried really hard to just keep looking at the large picture window.

Unfortunately she could see herself in the glass.

She could see Max, too.

She focused on the Christmas lights reflected in the glass. Red, blue, green, and white. The colors of the holiday painted across the wide window of the store she hoped would be hers soon.

There.

She'd refocused.

"Has Morgan given you any idea of when she'll be back?" she asked, finally ready to turn away from the window and look Max straight in the eye.

The real thing was much more impressive than the reflection. Not that she was noticing.

Much.

He shrugged broad shoulders beneath a dark wool coat.

Why was it that good-looking police officers always seemed to wear coats that emphasize their muscles? There should be some sort of law against that.

"So far I'm getting a lot of excuses for why she can't come get Zuzu and why I can't bring Zuzu to her. No definitive date, though," he said.

"You have the doctor's appointment Friday, right?"

"That's right."

"What if Zuzu *is* your daughter? Will you want her to go back to Mor—"

"You know, Charlotte"—he cut her off, his tone gentle with a just a hint of steel beneath it—"I'd rather not discuss my problems while I'm standing in the moonlight with a beautiful woman."

Her cheeks blazed, but she was not going to act like a simpering fool because he'd called her beautiful. "The moon is covered by clouds. Even if it wasn't, I'm not beautiful."

"Who told you that?" he asked, his hand sliding up her arm and coming to rest on her shoulder, his thumb just brushing the exposed skin of her neck. Her pulse thrummed in response, every nerve cell humming.

"Told me what?"

"That you're not beautiful. Because whoever it was," he murmured, bending down so that they were eye to eye, nose to nose, breath to breath, "was either blind or lying."

"Max—"

His lips brushed hers just like they had in the attic. Only this time, she couldn't seem to stop herself. She stepped right into his arms, her hands sliding inside his unbuttoned coat and settling on his firm waist.

He tasted like mint and coffee with just a touch of something dark and exotic and absolutely addicting. She could make a cupcake with those flavor profiles, and every woman in town would beg her for them. She moved closer, intoxicated with the moment and with Max.

He broke away, rested his forehead against hers. His eyes were the deepest blue of a dusky summer sky. Looking in them made her long for the time when she'd been young enough and naïve enough to believe in heroes and in happily-ever-afters. If she could go back to those times, she'd let herself relax into whatever spending time with Max might bring.

"You hooked me with that cupcake, didn't you, Charlotte?" he murmured.

She laughed shakily and stepped back because she sure as heck couldn't keep staring into his eyes. "Why? Are you about to propose?"

"Not quite," he muttered, raking a hand over his hair and scowling. "But I can't seem to stop thinking about you. That's got to mean something."

"It means we've spent too much time together lately."

"Maybe so." His gaze swept from her head to her toes and back again.

"*Absolutely* so. You and I are *not* a good match, Max. No cupcake in the world can change that."

"Really?" He raised an eyebrow and smiled, cupping her elbow and leading her back toward home. "I don't suppose you'd like to explain your reasons for saying that."

"You're adventurous. I'm a homebody."

"I'd be a homebody too, if I had the right person to go home to."

"No, you wouldn't. You'd get bored and head off into the wilderness to hunt or fish or whatever macho guys do when they're tired of the routine."

"I don't know what other guys do when they get bored, but I can tell you what I'd *like* to do." His hand slipped from her elbow to her hand, his finger twining through hers. There was something really comfortable about walking up Main Street with Max. Something homey and warm and delicious about the Christmas lights and the darkness and the man walking beside her. "I'd like go into the wilderness with a woman I cared deeply about. I'd like to build a fire and make a bed out of sleeping bags and lie under the stars with her. We wouldn't even have to talk if we didn't want to. We'd just listen to the world and watch the night together."

That sounded nice.

It sounded like the best romance novel she'd ever read, the best story she'd ever been told. It sounded like Christmas cookies and hot chocolate and marsh-mallows roasted over a fire. "If that's true, whatever woman you decide to care about is going to be very lucky."

"Why wouldn't it be true?" His thumb slid across the tender flesh on the inside of her wrist, and she shivered.

"People say all kinds of things that aren't, Max. You've been a police officer for long enough to know that." She kept her tone light even though her heart was beating frantically.

"True," he responded. "Speaking of which, I'd be remiss if I didn't ask why you were staring into Nick's shop in the middle of the night. You're not planning to turn to a life of crime, are you?"

His question surprised a laugh out of her. "Not unless renting a storefront on Main Street is against the law."

"A storefront, huh? I hadn't heard about that."

"No one has. Only Nick knows that I'm consider-ing it." At first the idea had been too new to share. Then she'd been afraid to say it for fear that she wouldn't be able to make the dream come true. "I figured there was no sense in mentioning it until I was certain it was going to happen."

"Are you certain now? Because news like you opening a store on Main Street is going to make a lot of people happy. If I start spreading it, and it turns out to be false, I'll have to explain myself to a lot of people."

"You can save yourself the hassle and not tell anyone."

"What fun would that be?" he asked with a grin.

She shook her head, but returned the smile. "You're an interesting guy, Max."

"Glad you think so." He led her up the front walk to her porch, waiting as she shoved keys into the lock, and opened the door. "I bought a lock for your back door. It's in the Corvette. How about you get it for me and lock yourself into the car while I check out the house?"

"Why would I do that?"

"Just in case." He handed her keys.

"In case of what, Max? I was home until an hour ago."

"A lot can happen in an hour. You saw how quickly Cade opened your back door."

True. She had.

He nudged her toward his Corvette. She went because she figured he was a lot more capable of handling an unwanted visitor than she was. Not that she thought anyone was going to be inside the house.

She *hoped* no one would be in there.

She grabbed the lock from the Corvette, glancing at Zuzu's car seat squeezed into the back of the vehicle. The little girl loved cookies. Charlotte would make her some in the morning. Sugar, because every child she'd ever known loved sugar cookies. Maybe she could even have her over and let her help decorate them. Max could bring her to the house, and they could spend the morning . . .

No! They could not spend the morning decorating cookies with Zuzu.

Not tomorrow. Not the next day. Not ever.

It was hard enough keeping *Max* at arm's length. No way would she ever be able to do that if she spent more time with Zuzu.

She scowled.

No more spending time with either of them.

No dinner Friday night. No walks along Main Street when the sun was down. No trips into the wilderness to lie under the stars and listen to the night.

What was the point of putting herself in temptation's way? She'd just avoid it until she got over whatever bee was buzzing around in her bonnet. Probably just Christmas depression. There had to be a clinical name for it. Holiday blues or something.

Whatever the case, she wasn't going to wrap herself in the warm strong arms of the best-looking guy in town just to make herself feel better.

She slammed the door to emphasize her decision and stalked across the yard. Frozen grass crunched under her feet, the frigid air stinging her cheeks. She'd always loved winter, and in Apple Valley it seemed even more wonderful. The fresh air, the decorated houses, the distant mountain peaks white with snow. She had never felt more at home than she did there. If things worked out the way she wanted, she'd spend the rest of her life there in her little house.

She wasn't going to let anyone steal away the sense of security she had there. Whoever had broken into her house and gone through her things had another thing coming if he thought Charlotte was going to be scared away. Not that the break-ins seemed particularly threatening.

She walked inside, hung her coat in the closet near the front door. Max's footsteps tapped on the attic floor, the old boards creaking beneath his weight. In another house at another time, the sounds might have been creepy, but right then they were comforting.

When Max walked down the stairs, she tried really hard to keep her focus on the lock she was still holding. She managed to do that for about thirty seconds before she met his eyes.

He smiled the kind of easy smile that she had only ever seen a few times, and her heart did the same silly little flip and jump it did every time she looked at the man.

She was a mess.

Pure and simple.

When it came to Max, all bets were off, every promise she'd made to herself just kind of floating away.

"Didn't I tell you to wait in the car?" he asked mildly.

"You won't be here every time I come home, Max.

I figured I had to get used to checking the place out myself."

"I see," he responded, taking the lock from her hand.

"What?"

"You're more scared of me than you are of who-ever has been breaking into your house."

"That's not true!" she protested, even though he was absolutely right.

"Sure it is, but Ida just called and she's wondering if I'm ever getting back. I need to install the new lock and head home." He walked into the kitchen and tore open the package.

"I can figure the lock out," she offered. Of course, she didn't have one tool to speak of, and she was fairly confident that she'd need a few to do the job.

"This won't take long. Want to get me a screw-driver?"

"I would if I had one."

"Do you have *any* tools?"

She shook her head, and Max sighed.

"What am I going to do with you, Charlotte?" he murmured, running his knuckles along the ridge of her cheekbone. His hand drifted down the side of her neck, his fingers tangling in the ends of her hair.

Right at that moment she could think of a dozen things he could do with her, and not one of them had anything to do with tools or locks. They were *that* close to kissing again, and she could honestly say that she wanted that more than she'd wanted anything in a very long time.

He dropped his hand, fisted it. "I'll get my toolbox from the car," he muttered and left the room.

Thank God.

Right?

Right!

She'd just make her way up to the attic while he got his tools. She'd clean up the mess the intruder had left while Max installed the new lock. She'd been too chicken to do it earlier, but with Max in the house, she felt ready to face the job. Once he left, she'd crawl into bed and get a good night's sleep. Tomorrow she'd have a clearer perspective and a little more self-control.

She hoped, because if she didn't, she might end up doing something she'd regret.

Probably regret.

Maybe regret?

Darn it all!

She'd had everything figured out until Max walked into the kitchen.

She'd just have to figure it out again.

That was all there was to it.

First though, she had to go up into the attic and face her demons.

Chapter Fourteen

It took less than twenty minutes to install the new lock.

As soon as he finished, Max packed up his tools and headed for the front door. Ida hadn't been upset when she'd called, but she'd sounded tired. At her age, she couldn't afford to be worn out by daily childcare.

He had to find a caregiver for Zuzu, and he had to do it soon. There was no other solution to the problem except for bringing her to Las Vegas and handing her over to her mother.

He knew intellectually that he should do it as soon as he took Zuzu in for the paternity test. As a matter of fact, he woke up every morning telling himself that he'd reserve seats on a weekend flight to Las Vegas. By his second cup of coffee, he'd usually forgotten all about it.

The odds were high that Zuzu wasn't his. If he handed her over to Morgan, the kid would be some-one else's problem, and he could go on with his life.

That was what he wanted, but somehow he kept letting the days slip by without making arrangements.

"Charlotte?" he called from the front door. "I'm heading out."

"Hold on!" Her voice drifted down from the attic stairway, and her feet pounded on the wooden steps. She rushed into the living room, her hair coated with a layer of dust, her shirt speckled with it.

"What have you been doing?" he asked, brushing the powdery stuff from the crown of her head, his mind-of-their-own-fingers lingering in the silky waves.

Her cheeks flushed, her gaze dropping for a fraction of a second before she met his eyes again. "Once I got started cleaning, I couldn't stop. I was under the bed, pulling out boxes that were stored there."

"What's in them?"

"It looked like clothes and photos."

"From the old owner?"

"It could be. Mary once told me that she'd left a lot of family things in the attic."

"Mary?"

"The former owner. It's been decades since she lived here, though. It would be a miracle if there were anything of hers left."

"You'll have to let me know when I see you Friday."

"About that . . ." She paused, her steady gaze suddenly jumping away. "I was thinking—"

"It's too late at night for thinking, Charlotte." He cut her off because he didn't have time to listen to all the reasons why they shouldn't go to dinner. He knew them all. He'd thought of every one of them. He still wanted to go. He thought Charlotte did too. She was scared, though. He could see the fear in her eyes and the tension in her shoulders. No woman should have to feel that way because she was going to have dinner with a man. No man should ever make a woman nervous about going out and enjoying herself.

Some guy had done that to Charlotte.

It had probably been her husband. If he'd been another kind of guy, he would have done a background check on the deceased just to see what kind of guy Brett had been.

"It's morning, Max," she reminded him. "And it's never too late to use our brains. As a matter of fact, there's no time like the present to make sure we're doing it."

He brushed the dust from her nose and her cheek, watching as her eyes widened. He could see her pulse racing in the hollow of her throat, and he touched his finger to the spot.

"What are you afraid of?" he asked.

"I'm not afraid. I'm cautious," she corrected.

"Because your husband was a bastard? What'd he do? Beat you? Is that where you got this?" He traced the scar that ran along her temple, following it into her thick hair.

She stiffened, her eyes flashing. "Brett never laid a hand on me. I would have had him thrown in jail and divorced his butt the first time he did."

"He *was* a bastard, though, right?" he prodded, because he wanted to know. Maybe he even needed to know.

"Why does it matter?"

"He *was*," he concluded, and she scowled.

"You want to know the truth, Max? The scar is from my father. He beat my mother from the day they married until the day he died. When he couldn't take whatever pissed him off out on her, he took it out on me. Brett was nothing like him, and he was everything like him. They were both self-centered egotistical men who cared more about themselves than they could ever care for anyone else." She nearly spat the words, her cheeks red, her eyes blazing. "My father was a bastard. My husband was a bastard. My track record with men is abysmal, and the last thing I want to do is throw myself into a relationship and then find out that I've made another mistake."

"Sounds like you're carrying a boatload of shit around, Charlotte," he responded.

"I'm not." She took a deep breath, brushed her hand over her hair, her fingers touching the scar he'd just traced. He didn't think she even realized what she'd done. "But I'd be a crazy if I didn't learn from my mistakes."

"I get it," he said.

He did, but he wasn't going to let Charlotte spend the rest of her life in the safety of her kitchen, baking cakes and cookies for Apple Valley while life passed her by. She deserved a lot better than that. She deserved a man who could teach her what it meant to be loved completely and to love completely. No holds barred. No reservations.

"Thanks." She smiled.

"No problem. I'll see you Friday."

"I thought we just agreed—"

He bent his head intent on shutting her up in the most enjoyable way possible.

He meant the kiss to be as light as the last two had been, but she moaned softly as his lips brushed hers, her hands skimming across his abdomen and settling on his waist. Fire raced through his blood, and he pulled her closer, his hands burrowing in her hair as he angled her head, tasted strawberries and chocolate and sunshine. Lost every thought in the sweetness of her lips, the feel of soft curves pressed close.

God, she felt good.

He wanted to back her into the house, lower her onto the couch . . .

He broke away, his breath heaving, his pulse thundering.

Charlotte looked dazed, her lips pink and lush from the kiss.

"I'll see you Friday," he repeated before he turned away and jogged to his car.

Charlotte had already closed her front door by the time he got in the Vette and shoved the key in the ignition. The living room light went out as he prepared to back out of the driveway. Knowing Charlotte, she was probably already in the kitchen starting her baking for the day.

He didn't call her and tell her to go to bed.

He considered doing it, though.

The fact was, it wasn't his business what she did, but he thought he might want it to be. That was a little surprising. Even with Morgan, he hadn't much cared what she did with her free time. When they were together, they were together. When they weren't, they were free to do what they wanted. As long as they were faithful to each other.

He had been, but he could have done a lot more to make their relationship work. He could admit that. He could also admit that he hadn't wanted to. He'd wanted Morgan from the moment he'd laid eyes on her. They'd been happy together. Until they weren't.

Then they'd been happy apart.

Easy in the relationship. Easy out.

He backed out of Charlotte's driveway, frowning as he neared Zim's house. A car was parked at the curb. He pulled up beside it, peering through his window and looking straight into Daisy Forester's face. He motioned for her to roll down her window as he rolled down his.

If her car hadn't been completely dark, he'd probably be seeing cheeks flushed deep red. As it was, he could only make out her dark eyes and pursed lips. "Hello, Max!" she said. "You're out and about late."

"I could say the same about you."

"We got new inventory today. That always takes a while to organize and put away." Her gaze skittered away, then darted back. "Once or twice a year I spend hours and hours shelving things."

"Good to know," he responded. "Of course, that doesn't explain why you're sitting outside Zim's house at nearly one in the morning."

"I saw your car in Charlotte's driveway." She paused.

She'd probably seen plenty more, too, and she'd

probably already made a list of every person she wanted to share the information with.

Let her do it.

The gossips would always talk, and he'd given up caring about three minutes after he'd arrived in town.

He waited for Daisy to continue.

And waited and waited.

Finally he ran out of patience. "I have to get back home, Daisy. If there's something you needed to talk to me about, how about you go ahead and do it?"

"Oh. Right." She smiled, but she looked anything but happy. As a matter of fact, he'd venture to say that she looked decidedly *un*happy. "I did want to ask you something."

"Okay," he prodded, biting back impatience. Daisy was the kind of mousy, easily intimidated woman that he tried to be careful around. He didn't want to scare the life out of her. On the other hand, he couldn't wait forever. "Go ahead. What do you want to know?"

"Umm. Well, Charlotte's house. I heard someone broke into it. Is that true?"

"Yes."

"Is she okay? She wasn't hurt by the monster who robbed her, was she?"

"She wasn't robbed, and she's fine."

"If she wasn't robbed, what was the purpose of someone breaking in?"

"That's a good question, Daisy. I don't have an answer."

"Is that why you were at her place? Were you looking for evidence? Fingerprints? DNA? Did you call in a team to search for clues?"

Obviously, she'd been watching too much *CSI.* Or maybe she'd just been reading too many murder mysteries. "This is a petty crime, Daisy. Nothing to call in backup for."

"But you did find something, right? You have some way of tracing the fiend."

Fiend?

Did anyone besides Daisy use that word?

"I'm not at liberty to say."

"Why not?" she demanded. "I'm a citizen of this town, and I have every right to know what's going on in it."

"Sorry, Daisy, but that doesn't include knowing every bit of information about the cases we're working on."

"I still think—"

"I need to head out. If you have any more questions, call the station and speak to Emma."

"She's a dispatcher. What's she going to be able to tell me?"

"You can leave a message with her, and either Cade or I will get back to you."

"But you're here right now. Why not just—"

"I really do have to go, Daisy. I'll see you later." He closed his window and drove away. He knew Daisy well enough to know that she'd hound him for hours if he let her.

He didn't have time for that. Not any day of the week at any time, but especially not in the wee hours of the morning when Ida was waiting for him to return.

He glanced in his rearview mirror to make sure

that Daisy hadn't decided to follow him. Her car was still sitting at the curb. No headlights. No interior light. It didn't look like she planned to drive away anytime soon.

Odd.

Daisy was a creature of habit. She worked six days a week, spent evenings watching TV with her boyfriend, and was in bed by ten on weeknights. That information came from Ida who thought Daisy could do a lot better in the man department.

Max hadn't spent a lot of time contemplating the situation, but the fact that the librarian was parked at the curb outside Zim's house was suspicious enough to get him wondering. She'd been awfully curious about the break-in at Charlotte's house and very pushy about getting answers to her questions.

Criminals often returned to the scenes of their crimes, and Charlotte's house sat catty-corner to Zim's. Daisy had a perfect view of the place from her car.

Not that Max was ready to make any accusation, but he *was* going to call Cade in the morning, see what he thought of the situation. Daisy out in the wee hours of the morning was *not* normal. That was for sure.

Not that much of life had been normal since Morgan had popped back into his life and thrust Zuzu into his arms.

He glanced at the dashboard clock. The kid would be up in about five hours. She'd be raring to go, too. There was no slow speed with Zuzu. Everything was full steam ahead. Maybe that's the way all kids were. He didn't have enough experience with them to know.

He pulled up to Ida's garage. A light shone from the living room window in the apartment, splashing out onto the driveway and gleaming on a little pink tricycle. It hadn't been there earlier in the day. Ida must have been shopping. She really needed to stop buying stuff for Zuzu. There was no way they'd ever be able to get it all on the plane to Las Vegas.

He could ship it there, but he had a feeling that once he handed Zuzu back to Morgan, the two would disappear from his life again, leave whatever hotel Morgan had been staying in without bothering to give him a forwarding address. He shouldn't care. He wasn't a kid kind of guy. He never had been.

But Zuzu wasn't just any kid.

She was kind of growing on him, and he'd worry about her when she was gone.

He ran up the apartment stairs and opened the front door.

Ida sat on the sofa, old Pete in her lap, his body flopped across her narrow thighs.

"There you are!" Ida said cheerfully. "Pete and I were just discussing whether or not I should call you again."

"What was Pete's opinion?" He lifted the old tom and set him on the floor. Pete gave him a disgusted look and meandered into the kitchen. He was probably hoping for a refill in his food dish, but knowing Ida, she'd fed the cat at least twice already.

"He said we should."

"And yours?" He helped her to her feet. She barely

reached his shoulder. For some reason that always surprised him. Ida had energy to spare, her personality always making her seem larger than life.

"If you wanted to spend more time with Charlotte, I saw no reason to interrupt you." Her eyes sparkled mischievously, her white hair neatly styled despite the hours she'd spent chasing after Zuzu.

"No matchmaking, Ida," he warned, taking her coat from the back of a chair and helping her into it.

"I would never—"

"You have. Too many times to count."

"Well," she murmured, patting her hair and adjusting her collar, "I'm quite good at it, you know."

"Ida, you set me up with your best friend's daughter," he reminded her. Though *he'd* tried really hard to forget that disaster of a first and last date.

"Samantha is a lovely woman. You two would have been wonderful together."

"She's sixty!"

"I felt that you needed someone older and more mature." She brushed lint off her coat and smiled demurely.

"When I picked her up she was wearing a tutu and angel wings. I don't think that counts as mature." She'd also been sporting a pink sequined tank top and bunny ears.

"Samantha is a unique person. She needs a man who can appreciate that."

"I'm not that man."

"Obviously," she huffed. "And I don't blame you one bit. You *do* need someone mature and settled, but that person also needs to have her head screwed on straight. Am I right?"

He wasn't sure. He was still trying to wrap his mind around the fact that Ida had used the word *screwed.*

"Of course, I am," she continued blithely. "What better person than Charlotte to fill that role."

"I don't need anyone—"

"Of course you do, dear. You have a little girl to take care of now, and you need a woman to help you do it."

"First of all, Ida, Zuzu is not my daughter."

"You keep right on telling yourself that."

"What's that supposed to mean?"

"Come now, Max. You're an officer of the law. You have keen observational skills. You can't tell me that you haven't noticed how much that child looks like you."

"Yeah. I can. She looks like her mother." Although she had blue eyes. Like Max. And like forty percent of the population.

"Do you have baby pictures of yourself?"

"Ida, enough."

"What?" she asked with an innocent smile.

"You're trying to distract me from the real issue."

"Which is?"

"Your matchmaking. I don't need your help finding someone. If I want a woman in my life, I'll pursue her."

"You told me that after the Samantha incident, and I've stayed out of your love affairs, haven't I?"

"Yes. Until now."

"I haven't even mentioned your name to Charlotte." She sniffed delicately and walked outside. "Yet."

"Ida!"

"Relax, Max. Charlotte is much too smart to be manipulated into your arms" She laughed and headed down the stairs.

He kept an eye on her until she was inside her house.

He loved Ida. She reminded him of his grandmother, but was sharper. In the best possible way. She did tend to meddle in people's business. He supposed that went with the job of mayor.

He closed the door, took off his coat, and yanked off his uniform tie. Cade didn't require it, but Max usually wore one. Because he could, and because he knew it made people think he was a little too polished, a little too city for small-town life. It always surprised people when they realized he enjoyed hunting, fishing, and four-wheeling. That he could pitch a tent or camp in a sleeping bag or even sleep on a bed of pine needles, really blew their minds.

He enjoyed that. He liked disproving stereotypes almost as much as he enjoyed small-town life. He flicked off the light, walking through the apartment. He could have eaten something, but his fatigue seemed to be outweighing hunger in terms of importance.

"Maxi?" Zuzu whispered from the doorway of her room as he walked into the dark hallway. "Is that you?"

"Who else would it be?" He flicked on the hall light, his heart jerking a little as he looked into

Zuzu's face. She had a crease on her cheek from her pillow and two little braids sticking out from the sides of her head.

"Some bad man," she replied, shoving her thumb in her mouth.

"Not in this house." He scooped her into his arms and carried her into the bedroom. It was starting to look like a girl's room. Pink blankets on the bed. Pink pillowcases. Dolls on the chair in the corner.

"How do you know?" she asked as he tucked her back into bed.

"Pete wouldn't let them in."

"Pete is nice." She folded her hands on her chest.

"He's nice to nice people, but he eats bad guys."

"No, he doesn't," she said with a frown.

"You're right. He doesn't, but if any bad guys came, he *would* scare them away."

"I think you would scare them away. Not Pete." She seemed really worried, her big blue eyes wary.

"You okay, Zuzu?" he asked.

"I'm scared," she responded, shoving her thumb in her mouth again.

"About what?"

"The bad man."

"I promise there isn't a bad man."

Even *he* thought it was a lame response.

Zuzu pulled the covers over her head and started crying. Not the loud wild sobs of the first night. These were quiet little sniffles that he wouldn't have heard if he'd been in another room.

"Don't cry." He patted the blanket.

"I have to cry, Maxi. But maybe I can stop if you

stay in here with me tonight." She peeked out, her eyes filled with tears. She was playing him. No doubt about it, but she really was scared, and he couldn't stomach the thought of leaving her alone to cry.

"Okay. Fine. Give me a second to get my blanket and pillow."

"I'll help." She hopped out of bed and took his hand.

It took a few minutes longer with her along, but he finally managed to grab what he needed and return to her room. He tucked her into bed for a second time, spread a blanket on the floor, and stripped off his shirt.

"Are you getting naked?" Zuzu piped up, and damn if he didn't blush.

"No! I am not getting naked." He lay down. The floor was hard, but he'd slept on worse.

"Mommy gets naked when she sleeps sometimes."

"Too much information, kid. Now go to sleep," he grumbled.

"First a kiss." She leaned over the side of the bed, her little braids dangling near her cheeks as she slapped a kiss on his forehead. "Night, Maxi," she sang as she scooted back into bed.

"Good night, Zuzu," he responded, punching the pillow twice and settling in.

He was almost asleep when bedcovers rustled. Blankets dragged across him. A pillow landed near his head, and Zuzu tripped over his chest as she tried to get to it.

He was too tired to demand that she go back to

bed, so he helped her settle down and covered her with a blanket.

"Good night again, Maxi," she whispered. "I love you."

What else could he say but "I love you, too"?

Chapter Fifteen

Christmas lights.

The bane of Charlotte's existence.

She hated hanging them with a passion that rivaled her passion for cooking.

She couldn't put the job off forever. No matter how much she wanted to. Friday morning, she did what she had to and dragged the box of tangled lights from the bedroom closet. She was perched on a stepladder attempting to hang Christmas lights from the eaves of the porch when Cade walked across the street. She saw him coming, but she had to make a choice between finishing the row of lights or letting them dangle while she greeted him. Since she wasn't sure how well they were attached, she decided to finish what she was doing.

"Morning, Charlotte!" he called, jogging up the stairs, his uniform crisp, his coat hanging open to reveal his uniform shirt and badge. Unlike Max, he never wore a tie. "Do you have a minute?"

"I will once I finish this," she grunted as she

stretched to hook the last part of the string into place.
"There." She hopped off the stepladder. "What's up?"

"Just wanted to ask you a few questions before I
headed into the office."

"Official questions or unofficial?"

"Official."

"Does that mean you can't have a cup of coffee
and a pumpkin scone?" That's what she'd bribed
herself with when she'd been trying to get motivated
to put up the lights. Every year it got harder to want
to decorate for Christmas. Every year she did it
anyway.

This year she was rewarding herself with scones
and coffee.

"I always have time for your baked goods, Charlotte. You know that." He grinned, taking his hat off
as he walked into her house. He was a true gentleman, but she wouldn't have expected anything else.
His family had been in Apple Valley for five generations. Their roots in the community went deep, and
their reputation had remained untarnished by
sordid stories or dark pasts.

She took a scone from the cooling rack, poured
coffee into a mug, and handed both to Cade. "There
you go."

"Thanks." He bit into the scone and groaned. "I
could eat a dozen of these."

"I'll pack you more, but you have to share with
your family."

"If I didn't love them so much, I'd keep the
scones to myself." He sipped coffee, eyeing her over

the rim of the cup. There was something calculating in his eyes, a sharpness that usually wasn't there.

"What's going on, Cade?" She handed him another scone and bit into one herself.

"Have you had any conversations with Daisy lately?" he asked casually, pulling out a chair and gesturing for her to sit.

"No," she responded quickly. Then realized it wasn't the truth. "Actually I did. She stopped by the day after your wedding. She wanted to buy some of my double chocolate delight cupcakes."

"Did you sell them to her?"

"Of course not. You know the rule." She'd explained it to him the same way she'd explained it to everyone else who'd wanted to buy the cupcakes. He'd been a lot less disappointed than most people had been.

"I do. I'm not sure you remember it though." He took a last sip of coffee and dumped the remainder in the sink.

"What's that supposed to mean?"

"Max had one of those cupcakes yesterday."

"Accidentally," she protested. "I didn't even realize I'd made one until it was too late."

He eyed her for a moment, his dark blue eyes filled with amusement.

"What?!" she demanded.

"How does a person accidentally make a cupcake?"

"You know what I mean." She bit into the scone. She didn't want to say more than that. He might think she was protesting too much.

Not that it really mattered what Cade thought. He'd keep it to himself. Unlike most people in town, he was very good at protecting information. "I guess I do. It was sort of a Freudian slip, right?"

"Ri . . . *Wrong!*"

"You just keep telling yourself that, Charlotte." He grinned.

"Think what you want," she huffed.

"I will."

She grabbed the dish towel and tossed it at him. "You're a rat, Cade."

He laughed, taking her by the arm and walking to the front door. "I'm a friend. To both of you. I just want to make sure neither of you is hurt."

"We're both adults. I think we can avoid hurting each other without too much effort."

"That's what Tessa said. She also said I should keep my nose out of it and let the two of you figure things out. I decided not to listen."

"There's nothing to figure out, so you wasted your time coming over here."

"I came over to ask you about Daisy. I did. The other questions were bonus."

"Why *did* you ask about Daisy?"

"She was parked in front of Zim's house the other night. Max saw her as he was leaving."

"That was . . ." She was going to say "after midnight," but she didn't want to admit that Max had been at her house that late. "Strange."

"Max thought so. He questioned her about it. She said she was on her way home from the library and saw his car. She wanted to ask him about the break-in at your place and make sure that you were okay."

"Interesting."

"Especially since you don't know her very well. Or have you guys become chummy since my wedding?"

"No, but that doesn't mean she wasn't telling the truth. It's possible she really was concerned."

"You're right. That's why we ran the prints we found at your house before I spoke with you. I wanted to make sure we didn't have another suspect."

"You don't think she has something to do with the break-in?"

"She asked a lot of questions about your case, Charlotte. She wanted to know what evidence Max collected. She seemed to be fishing, but we're not sure what she thought she'd catch."

"Maybe she's guilty and wanted to know if you were getting close to arresting her? Is that what you're thinking?" Charlotte asked.

"I'm thinking a lot of things, but I don't have any proof yet. I want to talk to a few of Daisy's coworkers and friends. Maybe they have information about her that will help the case."

"It seems strange to even call it a case. Nothing was taken. Nothing was destroyed. If it was Daisy—"

"She broke the law and will have to pay the penalty for that. I'll give you a call if we learn anything, okay?"

"Just be careful, Cade. This town is small, and if people think I've been accusing the town librarian of a nefarious act, I'll probably be blacklisted. My baked goods will go stale because no one will be willing to buy and eat them. Maybe—"

"Don't worry, Charlotte, I'm pretty diplomatic

when I want to be." He patted her shoulder. From the look on his face, he was trying desperately not to laugh.

Of course, it was funny to him.

He'd spent his childhood in Apple Valley. He was the golden son, the hometown hero, the guy most likely to succeed. He seemed to do everything right all the time. No missteps. No reason for the gossips to talk. Even his marriage was the perfect match. When he and Tessa announced their engagement, there'd been a town-wide celebration. The prodigal daughter and the good old boy together forever? It was the perfect ending and the perfect beginning and the perfect everything in between.

Charlotte didn't have the luxury of town loyalty. Sure, people liked her. In another twenty years, they might even start thinking about her as homegrown. For right now, though, she was still the transplant from Montana, and she had to be a lot more careful about what she did and said.

That was one of the reasons why she had to get the stupid Christmas lights up even if she didn't have a drop of holiday spirit in her. Every other house on Main Street had lights in the windows, around the doors, draped from the porch, and around every tree in the yard. Charlotte didn't have the time or patience for full-on decorating, but she'd put up lights for the very first time after moving to Apple Valley. Zim had knocked on her front door two weeks before Christmas and asked why she was such a Scrooge. He'd made no bones about the fact that she was bringing down the entire neighborhood by not decorating her house.

Once she'd assured him that hadn't been her intention, he'd offered to help her hang a few strands of Christmas lights. She'd agreed. The holiday decorating tradition had been born, and in a place like Apple Valley, traditions never died.

And there she was, three Christmases later, hanging lights by herself. No Christmas carols or hot chocolate. No laughing conversation. Just her and the darn tangled lights in the box she'd left near the front door.

She dragged the whole mess outside. One more free strand. That was all she needed, and the porch would be finished.

Or she could just throw all the lights away and forget it. She'd be the only house on Main Street with nothing to honor the holiday season aside for the lone string of lights that hung listlessly from half the porch.

Not that Zim would let that happen.

If she didn't get the lights up soon, he'd be over to help. If that happened, they'd be hanging lights from every available surface. Porch, windows, eaves, trees, fence. Maybe even the dried-out grass, if he could find a way to do it.

She yanked at the tangle of lights, only half noticing a father and daughter on the sidewalk a couple of hundred yards away. She probably wouldn't have noticed them at all except for the fact that the man was jogging behind his daughter's pink Big Wheel, his long stride shortened to stay just a little behind. They made a cute picture. The little girl sporting a pink bike helmet and fluffy pink coat and the man . . .

The man!

Wow!

Black running pants and a black long-sleeved T-shirt, his gray down vest closed over a broad chest. Her gaze drifted to his face, and she found herself looking into the most incredible blue eyes.

"Max!" she called without meaning to, her heart tripping all over itself with excitement. She was supposed to be avoiding the man. That was the plan for the day. She'd made her deliveries early, so she could put up the lights and get out of Dodge. When Max came to pick her up for dinner, she'd be out . . . Christmas shopping.

Sure. That sounded good.

Not that she had anyone to shop *for*. She usually gave neighbors and friends baskets of baked goods for Christmas, lots of nice little goodies to share with friends and family who were coming for the holidays. By the time Christmas arrived, her cupboards were bare, and the scents of baked goods had faded from the kitchen. Last year she'd come home from Christmas Eve dinner at the McKenzies, and the house had the musty smell that old abandoned homes got when they hadn't been lived in for a while. It had been depressing and sad, and she'd felt so lonely that she'd gone for a drive. She'd made it all the way to the Idaho border before she'd felt like turning around.

"Char-lotte!" Zuzu squealed, pedaling the Big Wheel for all she was worth. Dark curls peeked out from under the helmet, her cheeks bright pink from the cold. She looked adorable!

Charlotte dropped the tangled lights and walked across the yard. "Look at you, Miss Thing! You're a regular speed demon."

"I'm not a Speed Demon. I'm Zuzu!" Zuzu stopped half an inch shy of Charlotte's foot and pulled off her helmet. "See!"

"You sure are! Are you out for a ride?" She made a studious effort to avoid looking at Max.

He didn't seem to have any qualms about looking at her.

He moved right into her space, his arm brushing hers as he leaned over to take the helmet from Zuzu's hand.

"Tell her why we're here, Zu," he said.

"I didn't cry one time at the doctor, so I get cookies. Maxi is going to buy me a hundred-zillion," Zuzu announced.

She climbed off the Big Wheel, the cuffs of her pink pants half-tucked into blue snow boots.

"That's a lot of cookies," Charlotte responded, taking the hand that Zuzu held out.

"I like cookies. Maxi likes cookies, too. Right?" She looked up at Max, and that was the exact moment that Charlotte looked at him, too. It was a mistake, because he was watching Zuzu, and he had the softest expression on his face. A sweet kind of besotted-and-I-don't-know-how-it-happened kind of look that made Charlotte's heart melt into a puddle.

"I love cookies. Among other things," he murmured, his gaze cutting to Charlotte, his eyes going from soft to burning hot.

Her heart wasn't the only thing that melted. Her insides turned to mush, every thought she'd had about canceling dinner flying out the proverbial window.

"That's . . ." she started to say, her voice huskier than she wanted it to be. She cleared her throat and tried again. "Nice to know. Come on, Zuzu. Let's go get those cookies."

She headed across the yard, nearly running in her haste to get away. The sad thing was, she could have run a million miles and still not escape, because the problem wasn't Max. It was her.

Max carried Zuzu's Big Wheel across the yard and set it on Charlotte's porch right next to a tangled mass of Christmas lights. It would take time and patience to separate the strands. Maybe he'd take a shot at it after he had one of the cookies Zuzu had been begging for *all day long*.

He stretched his calves and shoulders and walked into the house. He'd needed a fast-paced run after his doctor visit with Zuzu. He'd thought it would chase away the sick cold feeling in his chest.

It hadn't.

But then he'd had to keep pace with Zuzu. No running until his lungs heaved and sweat poured down his face, he'd maintained a slow steady pace that matched Zuzu's excited pedaling. He hadn't worked out any of his tension or worry, but he'd worn Zuzu out for sure. She didn't know it yet, but she'd be going to bed early. He'd called in a favor a few days ago, and asked Emma to babysit while he was out with Charlotte.

She'd seemed happy enough to do him the favor.

But then he'd sat with her scumbag of a father more than once in the past year.

The man was mean as a pit viper, and Emma hadn't been able to keep caregivers for more than a few months at a time. She'd have probably had to give up her job if she hadn't finally found a registered nurse who was willing to put up with the crap her dad dished out. The guy was former Navy. He knew how to deal with problems. When he took a day or two off, Emma hired someone else or asked a friend to fill in. Max had done it a time or two.

He didn't know much about nursing, but he knew a lot more than most about dealing with scum. The old man must have sensed it. He'd taken a verbal swipe or two, but mostly he'd stayed quiet and compliant. Compared to Rick, taking care of Zuzu was a piece of cake.

The problem was, Emma had been looking more and more exhausted lately, the circles under her eyes getting darker, her cheeks hollowing out. She needed a few nights away from her father. What she didn't need was to spend a long evening chasing a nearly four-year-old around. He hadn't had it in him to ask Ida, though. Emma was all he'd had.

He followed the sound of voices into Charlotte's kitchen. Several unfrosted cakes were cooling on the counter, and one of those fancy wedding toppers sat on the kitchen table.

"Getting ready for the Henderson wedding?" he asked, lifting the topper and studying it. Lynette Henderson came from money, and her father hadn't spared any expense when it came to her wedding. At least that's what the gossips were saying.

Max wouldn't be attending the nuptials. He hadn't been invited.

Not surprising as he and Lynette had dated a few times before she'd hooked up with Calloway Johnson.

"Yes. I already have all the sugar flowers made. I just have to buttercream the layers and lay the fondant."

"The way I hear it, the wedding is going to be one for the records."

"Lynette is trying to outdo Tessa and Cade."

"Even if Lynette spends more money and has fancier things, she won't be able to outdo what Cade and Tessa achieved," he responded. He didn't really care what Lynette did. The sooner she was married off and the gossips stopped talking about her shindig, the happier he'd be. He'd been hearing too much information from too many people who seemed overly concerned with things like dresses, silverware, and place settings.

"Lynette has to try, though. She insisted her cake have at least one layer more than Tessa's and a dozen more flowers."

She opened the pig-shaped cookie jar and took out a large cookie. "Here you are, Zuzu. Sit at the table, okay?"

"Cookies!" Zuzu scrambled up into a chair. Charlotte had already helped her out of her coat, and she looked cute as a button sitting there with her big blue eyes and pink overalls.

The cold hard knot in his chest grew about seven sizes.

Charlotte took another cookie from the jar and

handed it to Max. "You look like you need some sugar."

"What I need," he said, taking the cookie and glancing at Zuzu. She'd shoved half the cookie in her mouth and had crumbs all over her face. "Is the truth."

"You're worried, aren't you?" She took milk from the fridge and poured some for Zuzu. "Want some?"

"No. Thanks." He bit into the cookie. Sugar and cinnamon, the outside crisp, the inside chewy, it was the best cookie he'd ever had. "But I'll take another one of these."

She handed him a second cookie, her eyes gentle as a summer rain. "You didn't answer my other question."

"About my being worried? I am."

"Why?"

"It's complicated."

"It doesn't have to be."

"What's that supposed to mean?" He finished the second cookie.

Charlotte grabbed his hand and tugged him into the pantry. "You had the paternity test today, didn't you?" she whispered.

"Yes."

"Then there's nothing complicated about it. If she's yours—"

"That's what's complicated, Charlotte." He raked a hand through his hair, wishing he could have had the run he'd been craving, pounded out some of his tension on the pavement. "I don't want kids. I've never wanted kids."

"Funny," she responded, glancing through the

doorway. Zuzu was clearly visible, what was left of the cookie lying on the table, the cup of milk in her hands. "I would have given anything to be a mother."

"I'm sorry, Charlotte. I don't mean to sound like an assho—"

"You don't." She smoothed her loose cotton sweats, brushed crumbs from her sweatshirt, shifting uncomfortably in the sudden silence. "I mean, there's no crime in *not* wanting children."

"There's no crime in wanting a houseful of them, either." He moved a step closer, inhaling vanilla and cinnamon and the sweet scent that always seemed to cling to Charlotte. "That's what you'd like, right?"

"No," she started to protest, and then laughed. "Okay, I'll admit it. I always thought I'd have six or seven kids. I had this silly dream about living out in the country on a couple of acres. I thought Brett and I could have chickens, cows, horses, and a mess of children to love."

"What happened?"

"Dreams die, Max. I'm sure you've lived long enough to know it." She didn't sound bitter or angry, just resigned.

"How long were you married?"

She stiffened, her soft lips pulling into a tight hard line. "Six years. He died just shy of our seventh anniversary."

"That must have been tough."

"He was diagnosed with cancer and died a month later. It was a lot quicker than we thought, and I guess if there is a blessing in any of it, that's it." She twirled a strand of hair around her finger, pulling it taut and then releasing it. It sprung free in a tight curl that he desperately wanted to touch.

"I'm sorry, Charlotte."

She shrugged, and he got the distinct impression that she wasn't sorry. "I think it's the way he would have wanted it."

"So, you had nearly seven years together. That's plenty of time to have a few kids. Why didn't you?" He knew it was the wrong question to ask, but he asked it anyway. He wanted to know how Charlotte had ended up where she was, alone in a house that should have been filled with all the things she'd once dreamed of.

She swallowed hard, glancing out into the kitchen again.

He thought there might be tears in her eyes, and he touched her arm, felt the coiled muscles beneath the cotton fabric of her sweatshirt.

"That's a really personal question, Max."

"We've kind of been getting personal, if you haven't noticed." He let his hand drift down her arm, wove his fingers through hers and tugged her so close he could feel the heat of her body and the tension that radiated out from her. "The thing is, dreams die. It happens all the time, every day to all kinds of people. You're just not the kind of person who lets them go easily. So what happened? Could you not have children? Did your husband not want them?"

"Brett *had* kids. Four of them. He neglected to tell me about that before we were married. He also neglected to tell me that he was still married to his first wife. When he went on his long trucking runs, he'd spend days and weeks with them while I waited at home praying for his safety."

"When did you find out?"

"The twenty-seventh of November. Our seventh wedding anniversary. He'd been gone three days, and his lawyer stopped by to talk to me about a will that I didn't even know existed. Brett left the house and everything in it to his other family. He left all his money to them. I had nothing but my clothes, my most recent paycheck, and a note from Brett that said he knew that I'd be fine." She shrugged as if it didn't matter, but he knew it did. Just like he knew she still wanted the country house and the gaggle of kids.

"You didn't contest the will?"

"What would be the point? He was right; I was going to be fine one way or another. Besides, I didn't want to hurt his other family any more than they already had been hurt."

"Your husband should have been the one who thought about that long before he married you," Max growled. If the guy hadn't been dead, he'd have tracked him down and taught him a thing or two about how to treat a lady.

She shrugged again, her gaze skittering away. "Looks like Zuzu wants another cookie. I'll get her one, and then I have to get back to hanging Christmas lights."

He followed her back into the kitchen, unconsciously watching the subtle sway of her hips.

"Zuzu, don't climb on the chair," she said gently.

He tore his gaze away from the soft swell of her

hips, saw that Zuzu had dragged her chair to the counter and was trying to reach the cookie jar.

"Zuzu, you know better than that!" he said a little more harshly than he'd intended.

Zuzu took it the wrong way.

Her little face crumpled, and she started the god-awful wailing she'd demonstrated the first night she'd spent at his house.

He picked her up and awkwardly patted her back. He wasn't hardwired to be a father, but he'd seen enough good dads to know that they did this sort of thing. Pat the back. Wipe the face with a paper towel. Tell the kid she could have another cookie.

The last worked.

Zuzu sniffed back more tears, pressed her hands to his cheeks, and looked deep into his eyes. "You're a special boy, Maxi," she said.

He chuckled and took the cookie Charlotte held out.

"I bet you say that to all the boys who give you cookies," he responded, passing the cookie to Zuzu.

"Thank you!" She wiggled. "Put me down now."

"*Please* is a nice word," he said, echoing words his grandmother had said often in the first few months after he'd moved in with her. He'd forgotten that until just that moment.

"Please put me down," Zuzu responded.

He set her down, and she hurried back into her chair.

She looked happy as a clam.

"You're really good with her, Max," Charlotte said quietly.

"She's an easy kid to be good with." That was the

honest truth. Morgan must have done something right, because Zuzu was a wild child, but she was also sweet as pie.

Or sweet as one of Charlotte's cinnamon sugar cookies.

He took one out of the cookie jar.

"Do you mind?" he asked. "We had to be at the doctor at nine. After I exploded the oatmeal I was cooking for Zu—"

"An oatmeal explosion?" Charlotte laughed.

"Yes, and don't ask me to explain how it happened. I don't think I can. The end result was a huge mess and me leaving the house without breakfast. I'm starving."

"I can make you some lunch. Zuzu is probably hungry, too."

"We'll eat when we get home." He grabbed her hand before she could open the refrigerator. "Besides, you've done enough for us, and I'm going to make it up to you."

"If you're talking about dinner tonight—"

"I'm talking about those Christmas lights. My grandmother loved Christmas. It was her favorite time of the year. I used to spend hours untangling Christmas lights for her." He'd hated every minute of it for the first two years. After that, he'd begun to like the tradition.

"I always thought it would be fun to have family to visit during the holidays."

"I wasn't visiting. I lived with my grandparents through high school and most of college."

"Were your parents—"

"An incarcerated drug trafficker and a self-centered user who spent more time trying to find someone to take care of her than she spent taking care of me."

"I'm sorry." She touched his arm.

Heat shot through his blood, pounded hard in his chest.

He could have yanked her right into his arms, kissed her until they were both breathless, but Zuzu was munching her cookie, he was still holding his, and the moment wasn't right.

Which was a crying shame, because Charlotte had very, very kissable lips, and he would have been more than happy to taste them again.

"Don't be," he said, his voice gruff and just a little hard. "My past brought me here, and I wouldn't change it. Even if I could."

She nodded solemnly. "I get that."

"But you'd still like to change your past?"

"I don't know. Sometimes maybe."

"What would you change?"

"I'd be a little less trusting, I guess. A little less desperate."

"I can't imagine you desperate."

"Then you don't have a very good imagination." She laughed, her eyes sparkling.

"You really are beautiful, Charlotte. You know that?" he said, the words just kind of slipping out, because she was and he thought she needed to know it.

She blushed, her cheeks going a deep shade of pink.

"Max—"

"Save it for later, okay? I've got to get those lights

untangled for you. Otherwise you'll be stuck with Zim's help."

"And have a yard covered with Christmas lights?"

"It might be an interesting look."

"Yay!" Zuzu squealed. "I's gonna help with Christmas lights!"

"Not until you finish your cookie, drink your milk, and wash your face," Charlotte said, turning her attention to the little girl.

That was Max's cue to leave.

He'd had an entire morning of little-girl antics. He should want the break, but he actually didn't want to leave behind the warm kitchen, the sweet smell of baked goods, Zuzu, Charlotte. They all seemed wrapped up together, tied with a bow that he thought might just be called home.

Chapter Sixteen

Max walked out of the kitchen, and Charlotte could finally breathe again.

Thank goodness!

She needed to get oxygen to her brain and clear her thinking, because right at that moment, the only thought running through her head was that it would be really nice to kiss Max again.

"But that wouldn't be good, Zuzu. Not at all," she murmured as she wet a dishcloth with warm water and wiped the little girl's face.

"Cookies *are* good," Zuzu protested.

"You're right. They are."

"You have some." She shoved what remained of her cookie at Charlotte, smashing it against her stomach.

"Careful, Zuzu." She took the cookie and wiped off her sweatshirt. She'd once thought twins would be fun. A few minutes with Zuzu, and she thought maybe they would just be exhausting.

"Let's go to make Christmas tree lights!" Zuzu

hopped down and raced across the room, her overalls brushing the floor, her little legs churning and arms pumping.

"Slow down, Zuzu," Charlotte called, but Zuzu was on a mission, and she didn't seem eager to stop. Charlotte chased her into the living room, following her across the floor and scooping her up as she reached the door. "You don't even have a coat on, silly girl."

"I's not silly!" Zuzu scowled. Which only succeeded in making her look adorable.

No wonder the child had Max wrapped around her little finger. "Maybe not, but you're going to be cold if you don't put on your coat before you go outside. You don't want to freeze, do you?"

"Yes."

Charlotte laughed, and carried Zuzu back into the kitchen. "Well, *I* don't want you to freeze. You can't eat cookies if you turn into a snowman."

"I can't?" Zuzu shoved her arms into her coat and went to work trying to zip it, the tip of her tongue peeking out.

"Of course not. Snowmen don't eat."

"They don't?"

"No. They just stand out in the cold all day long. They don't even get to ride Big Wheels." She brushed Zuzu's hands away and helped her with the zipper. Zuzu took mittens out of her pockets and thrust her hands into them.

"I don't want to be a snowman," she said solemnly.

"Then it's good that you're all bundled up." Charlotte held out her hand, and Zuzu took it.

"Where's Momma?" Zuzu asked as they walked to the front door.

How should Charlotte answer that?

Obviously, Zuzu already knew the facts. Maybe she needed more. Maybe she needed some reassurance that Morgan was coming back, that she wasn't going to be without her forever. "She's in Las Vegas, Zuzu. Remember?"

"Is she a snowman? 'Cause I think she maybe is a snowman."

The question startled a laugh out of Charlotte. "Why would you think that?"

"If she's frozen, she can't drives to me."

"She's not a snowman, Zuzu. She's just busy finding a job. She'll come for you as soon as she can."

"You know what? She's got to find a job cause of Papa Tom. He died."

"That's sad."

Zuzu nodded. "You know what else?"

"What?"

"Papa Tom told me about a little girl who almost got eaten by a mean old wolf."

"Red Riding Hood?"

"Pink Riding Hood. 'Cause I like pink." Zuzu tried to open the front door with her gloved hands, but the metal knob kept slipping. "The mean old wolf tried to eat her, and she karate chopped him. Chop! Chop!"

"Wow!"

"I'm going to karate chop the bad man if he comes. Chop! Chop!"

Bad man?

Was she serious or playing a childish game?

Charlotte crouched down so they were eye to eye. "What bad man?"

Zuzu glanced around the room. She wrapped her hands around Charlotte's head and pulled her closer, whispering in her ear, her breath tickling Charlotte's cheek. "He's under the bed."

"What bed?"

"My bed. Momma says he'll come out and gobble me up. She says he likes little girl hearts and brains. He eats them for dinner."

"Zuzu! That's not true!"

"It is! Momma told me!" Zuzu jerked back, crossing her arms over her chest, her chin wobbling.

"Your momma was joking." And it had been a really mean joke. Who told her kid that a monster lived under the bed? No one Charlotte knew, that was for sure. Certainly no one she respected.

She wanted to track Morgan down and tell her what an idiot she was.

Not that it was any of her business how the woman raised Zuzu, but a story like that? Told to an impressionable three-year-old? That was just cruel.

"No, she wasn't. The man is under my bed. I heard him last night." Zuzu's eyes were big as saucers.

No doubt she'd heard something.

Probably Max's big ugly tom scurrying after a dust bunny.

"You probably heard the cat. They like to go under beds."

"Pete likes the couch."

"Does he?"

"He likes the counter, too. Ida makes him get down."

Zuzu seemed to have forgotten all about the bad man under the bed. Charlotte opened the door and followed her out onto the porch.

Max stood near the box of lights. Somehow he'd managed to free one strand from the tangled mess. Apparently he hadn't been joking about spending his Christmases practicing the skill.

"You did it!" she cried, taking the strand. "I could just . . ."

Kiss you was on the tip of her tongue.

"I'd like that a lot," he responded with a wicked smile.

"You don't even know what I was going to say."

"I know *exactly* what you were going to say." His gaze dropped to her lips, and she blushed.

Darn her fair skin!

"I think I'd better put these up before they tangle again," she mumbled, turning away and hanging the end of the string from one of the hooks, because she was definitely *not* going to kiss the man.

"And I think we'd better head out. Much as I'd like to spend the rest of my day here, I have a hot date tonight, and I need to get ready for it."

Surprised, she met his eyes. "You have a date?"

"A very hot date," Max responded, eyeing her intently. "You did tell me that you didn't want to have dinner as friends, right?"

"Right. I'm glad you found someone else to go out with," she muttered, draping the lights from nails she and Zim had installed her first year in the house.

"I'm pretty excited about it," he responded, a hint of amusement in his voice. "It's a full moon tonight, so we're going to picnic in Riley Park. Not quite as romantic as a camping trip, but I'm going to make it work."

"It's going to be ten degrees out tonight," she pointed out, because she might have been just at teensy bit jealous.

A picnic in the moonlight sounded romantic and just a little heavenly, and there was a small part of her that wanted to be the woman he was taking.

A small part?

A huge part!

"That's part of my evil plan, Charlotte. My date and I will have to stay close to keep warm." He tugged her in so that there wasn't a bit of space between them. Like magic, she could feel their combined body heat chasing away the cold.

God, it felt good.

He felt good.

She wanted to stand right where she was for the rest of the day.

Heck with that.

She wanted to pull him into the house and kiss him senseless.

"I have my grandmother's old fur throws," he murmured, his lips brushing her ear, his hands smoothing up her spine and back down again. "The ones her mother used when she rode in a horse-drawn carriage. I'm going to spread them out on the ground in this quiet little place I found. It's right at the base of the hill that leads to Apple Valley Community Church."

"Near the cemetery? I'm sure that will be extremely romantic."

He chuckled, the sound vibrating through her. "Not even close to the cemetery. It's in a little clearing in the middle of a copse of trees. We'll lie in the moonlight and sip wine and eat cheese. We may even hold hands."

"That sounds . . . nice."

"There's just one thing I need. Maybe you can help me with it."

"What's that?"

"I'd like to bring something special. A treat of some kind. Something a woman might really enjoy."

Great. Now he was asking her to help him with the hot date he planned to have in the moonlight. "Cheesecake?"

"I'm thinking she's more of a chocolate kind of girl." A smile hovered at the corner of his lips.

"I have a nice recipe for chocolate cake. It's simple and tastes good with or without frosting," she offered, mostly to convince herself and him that she was glad he was going out with someone besides her.

"That sounds fantastic."

"I can make the cake this af—"

"If you give me the recipe, I'll make it."

"You're kidding, right?"

"You think I can't cook?"

"I've seen your kitchen, Max. You don't have any ingredients. Unless you want to make a cake out of cardboard and eggs."

He smiled. "I think I can manage to find what I need at the grocery store."

"The thing is, I usually don't give out my recipes."
Too many people complained when she did. Nothing ever tasted the same, and everyone insisted she'd left out an ingredient or two.

"Can you make an exception if I promise I won't share the recipe with anyone?"

"I don't think—"

"*Please* is a nice word, Maxi," Zuzu piped in.

"You're right, Zuzu," he responded. "Can you please make an exception, Charlotte?" He smiled into her eyes, and she couldn't think of one reason why she shouldn't.

"I guess. Since you said please."

She ran into the house, because that seemed so much easier than staring into his eyes wondering what it would be like to be the woman he made chocolate cake for.

Man! She had it bad, and she wasn't even sure how it had happened. She hadn't intended it to. She'd planned to keep her distance, keep her focus, and refuse to veer from the course she'd set for herself after Brett's death.

She grabbed an index card from a drawer in the kitchen and jotted down the recipe.

All set! She'd hand it to him and send him on his way.

Good riddance to bad company. Only the company hadn't been bad. It had been pretty darn good, and she'd enjoyed every moment of it.

"Idiot," she muttered as she walked back outside.

Sam and Zuzu weren't alone on the porch. Daisy was there, her brown hair pulled into a messy bun, her eyes big behind her thick-lensed glasses. She didn't look like a criminal who'd been breaking into Charlotte's house, but Charlotte couldn't forget what Cade had told her.

"Hi, Daisy!" she said, her voice squeaking just a little at the end.

Nerves.

They did that to her.

Daisy didn't seem to notice. Her gaze was on the index card, her eyes bright and glittery. Maybe even a little crazed. "Hi, Charlotte. I'm sorry for interrupting. It's my lunch break, and I wanted to talk to you before I have to be back at the office."

"About?" She handed the index card to Max.

Daisy watched the transaction, her brow furrowed. "What's that?"

"Nothing," Charlotte responded quickly. If she admitted that she'd given Max a recipe, Daisy would beg for the double chocolate delight recipe again. "You were about to tell me why you're here, remember?"

"Of course, I remember," Daisy snapped. "I'm here about a wedding cake."

"You're engaged?!" Charlotte glanced at Daisy's left hand. She couldn't see a ring bulging out from under the leather glove, but that didn't mean there wasn't one.

"I'm going to get married," Daisy responded, offering a brittle smile. "I'd like to choose the cake and topper today."

Let the woman who might have broken into her house order a cake with her?

That wasn't going to happen.

"I'm sorry, Daisy. I have a lot of work to do for

the Henderson party. Next week would be better for me."

"What if it's not better for *me?*"

"Then I guess you'll have to find another baker to make the cake." She hoped Daisy would take her up on the offer.

"You know what I think? I think you don't want to let me order my cake because I'm not engaged yet," Daisy huffed.

"I had no idea—" *that you weren't engaged* was what she planned to say, but Daisy cut her off.

"I thought you were a really nice person, but I'm beginning to see that I was wrong."

"But—"

"Go ahead. Make the Henderson cake. I'll come back next week. *If* you have the time for me then."

"I told you—"

"I'll see you then." Daisy stalked away, her entire body vibrating with the force of her indignation.

"Talk about not getting a word in edgewise," Max murmured as Daisy got into her car and peeled away from the curb. "She didn't even give you a half a chance to speak."

"She's pissed."

"That's the understatement of the century." Max tracked Daisy's retreating car. "She was angry as he"—he glanced at Zuzu—"heck."

"I don't know why. I've always been really nice to her."

"You're always really nice to everyone, Charlotte. It's past time that someone was nice to you." He tucked the recipe in his pocket and led Zuzu to her Big Wheel. "We have to get out of here. Thanks for the cookies and milk. We really enjoyed them, right, Zuzu?"

"Yes!" Zuzu agreed.

Charlotte smiled. "I'm glad you liked the cookies. Thanks for stopping by. I'll see you—"

"At six. Dress warm," Max cut in as he lifted Zuzu onto her Big Wheel.

"Dress warm for what?"

"Our picnic in the moonlight," he responded. "You haven't forgotten already, have you?"

"I thought you were taking your hot date there."

"I am, but only because she refused to go out to dinner as friends." He dropped a quick hard kiss on her lips, gave Zuzu a gentle nudge toward the town center, and started jogging along behind her.

"We are not going on a hot date!" Charlotte shouted after him.

He probably heard, but he pretended not to, his gaze fixed on Zuzu.

Darn the man!

He'd set her up.

She should be upset about it, but she was smiling as she finished hanging the lights and humming Christmas carols as she walked inside the house and made a pot of tea.

Making a cake was not supposed to be difficult.

Was it?

Max looked at the lumpy, gooey mess that he'd dumped onto a plate and scowled.

"Yucky!" Zuzu said, peering over the edge of the counter and staring at the brown goop.

"You think?" The sarcasm was lost on Zuzu.

She wrinkled her nose and frowned. "Yes."

"Then it's good you don't have to eat it." He used a spoon to try to pile the mess into something that resembled a cake. All he succeeded in doing was splattering batter on the wall. "Sh—oot!"

He'd been trying to clean up his language.

Little pitchers had big ears.

At least that's what Ida had said when she'd heard him cuss in front of Zuzu. She had a point. If he wasn't careful, Zuzu would be wandering around town spouting words no three-year-old should know.

"You made a mess!" Zuzu accused, her gaze sharply focused on the flecks of chocolate that dotted the walls.

Someone knocked on the door.

Emma. It had to be. She was early, but he wasn't going to complain. The last hour of Zuzu's chatter had driven him almost to the brink of insanity. She'd talked so much, he'd been tempted to invest in a pair of earplugs.

He yanked open the door and let Emma in.

Her eyes were shadowed, her hair pulled into a high ponytail. She wore dark blue jeans and an over-sized sweatshirt. No makeup. No snide look in her eyes. She could have been ten or fifteen rather than twenty-five.

"You look like hell," he said. "Are you sure you're up to babysitting?"

"Thanks," she growled. "Yes. And watch your language around the kid."

"I've been working on it."

"Hmph!" She carried a huge duffle to his coffee table and dropped it there.

"You planning to spend the night?"

"I'm planning to entertain a precocious three-year-old."

"And you thought you needed an entire bag of tricks to do it?"

She tucked a loose lock of hair behind her ear and looked at him like he was an idiot. "From what I've heard, I may need more than that."

"What's that supposed to mean?"

"Jordyn Lancaster told Tate Gordon that Zuzu is the smartest kid she's ever met."

"She told me the same thing." As a matter of fact, the young nurse had said it at least a dozen times during Zuzu's appointment. "Why was she saying it to Eli and why did Tate say it to you?"

"We ran into each other at the district courthouse today."

"You got another speeding ticket?"

"I've only gotten two, Max, and you're the one who issued them," she responded with a scowl.

"I've got to do my job. No matter—"

"Yeah, yeah. Save it for someone who cares." She tightened her ponytail and crossed her arms over her chest. "As I was saying, I was at the courthouse, and I ran into Tate. He mentioned how impressed Jordyn was with Zuzu."

"So Jordyn and Tate are an item now?"

If so, Max was surprised.

A divorce lawyer turned college professor, Tate

lived on the east edge of town with his three kids. His wife April had died a few weeks after the youngest was born. That had been Max's first year in town. He'd heard lots of talk about the couple and their perfect marriage, perfect children, perfect house on the edge of town. There wasn't a woman in Apple Valley who hadn't thought Tate would marry again before the year was out.

He'd need someone to care for his poor daughters. Or so the blue-haired ladies at the diner had said.

Over and over again.

Tate hadn't remarried. The girls were doing just fine, and the gossips had finally shut up about the situation. Hopefully Tate didn't ruin that by entering the local dating arena. Since he and Max were friends and hunting buddies, it was only right that Max let him know that.

"He helped Jordyn with her divorce last year. She *says* that she and Tate are dating, but you know how she likes to exaggerate things."

"More than rabbits like carrots. More than the Red Hat club ladies like their purple shampoo."

She laughed. "Thanks, Max."

"For what?"

"Making me laugh. I needed it."

"Bad day with your dad?"

"Bad day all around." She unzipped the duffle and pulled out Play-Doh. Twenty-four different colors. "But I'm going to put it behind me. Zuzu and I are going to have a blast tonight. Aren't we, hun?"

"No," Zuzu responded, shoving her thumb into her mouth and clambering onto the couch. She'd already taken her bath. He'd done his best to brush her hair, but it was sticking out in about five different directions. Despite his best efforts to get her into one of the pretty new pairs of pajamas the historical society had brought, she'd insisted on wearing the god-awful footy pajamas she'd arrived in. He could see a little hole in one foot and another under the arm.

She looked like a ragamuffin.

A very angry ragamuffin.

"Sure you are, Zu," he cajoled, because there was no way in hell he was missing his date with Charlotte. "Emma is a fun person."

"Not tonight she's not," Emma muttered under her breath, but she walked back to the bag and pulled out a coloring book with a princess on the front cover. "That's okay, Max. She doesn't have to have fun with me. I can have fun all by myself." She dragged a brand-new box of crayons from the duffle. "I'm going to color princesses—"

"I'm a princess," Zuzu said, the words muffled by her thumb.

Emma didn't seem to have any trouble understanding her.

"I know—"

"Don't feed her delusion, Em. She'll be wanting to walk around in a crown all day."

Emma rolled her eyes. "Obviously, you don't understand, Max. Every girl is a princess. Right, Zuzu?"

Zuzu nodded, her eyes wide.

"That's why we're going to make crowns, too!"

Emma pulled out some weird Styrofoam-looking crowns and a bunch of glitter glue.

"Wow!" Zuzu said with obvious wonder. "I want pink."

"That's good, because I like yellow." Emma extended her hand and Zuzu took it.

They walked into the kitchen together.

Max grabbed the wicker picnic basket that Tessa had lent him when he'd called and asked her advice about dinner with Charlotte. The thing had cups, plates, an old-fashioned Thermos, and containers for food. It was a relic of the past, probably something Tessa had saved from the shop her sister and brother-in-law had once run.

It fit the occasion.

But that was Tessa. She loved reusing old things, making them work for new situations.

He carried the basket into the kitchen and set it on the counter. He'd already filled the Thermos with wine, put grapes in one container and cheese that Ida had provided in another. Gourmet. According to Ida, that was the way to go. He'd consulted both women. That probably surprised him as much as it surprised them.

This date mattered, though. More than others he'd been on.

That might mean nothing or it might mean everything.

He wanted to find out.

Oddly, because he'd never felt the need to do it with any other woman he'd dated, he wanted to impress Charlotte. Not just the normal kind of good impression that everyone attempted when they went on a date. He wanted to make the kind of impression that stuck in Charlotte's mind, made her remember the night long after it was over. Tessa and Ida knew more about Charlotte than anyone in town, but even they'd been at a loss as to what her perfect first date would be.

He'd come up with the idea of a picnic.

They'd come up with everything else.

Cheese. Grapes. Wine.

Chocolate.

He looked at the mess he'd left on the counter.

"What in the world is that?" Emma asked, poking at the congealed mess.

"Cake."

She looked at the chocolate that coated her finger, sniffed it, her nose wrinkling. "Are you sure?"

"Yeah. I'm sure. I even used one of Charlotte's recipes."

"I love Charlotte!" Zuzu crowed as she climbed into a chair and lifted one of the Styrofoam crowns.

"You and everyone else. If *I* didn't like her so much, that would totally annoy me," Emma responded. She nabbed the index card Max had left on the counter and studied it. "This looks easy enough."

"That's what I thought, but if it were, I'd have cake instead of goo."

She nodded, setting the card back down. "Don't feel too bad. Charlotte gave me a recipe for pumpkin scones about a year ago. I followed it exactly, but my scones were more like hockey pucks than food.

I tried to feed them to Dad's chickens. Even they were too smart to eat them."

"Yeah. Well, I'm not going to serve this to Charlotte. That's for sure." He dumped the mess into the trash.

"Good thing I stopped by her place to get some treats for Zuzu." She ran back into the living room and returned with a brown paper bag.

She thrust it into his hand. "Here you are."

"What is it?"

"Brownies and cookies. Maybe a cupcake or two. When I told Charlotte I was coming over here, she donated what she had left from her day to the cause."

"I can't feed her stuff she baked." But he sure wouldn't mind eating it.

"Would you rather scrape the goo out of your trash can and hand that to her on a plate?"

"I'd rather that da . . . rn cake had turned out." He opened the bag, took out two plastic-wrapped brownies. "I can smell them through the wrappers."

"I know. My stomach has been growling all the way here." She sighed longingly.

"Want me to leave you one?" Sharing a brownie with Charlotte might prove to be a lot more interesting than having his own.

"Nope. I'm just as happy with whatever else is in there." She snatched the paper bag back. "And I can tell you right now, that I'm going to eat every single thing that's left after Zuzu has her snack."

"Don't give Zuzu too many sweets. She'll have trouble sleeping."

"Good to know," she muttered, dropping the bag

onto the counter. "Fill me in on the kid. What time does she go to bed?"

"Eight-thirty. Earlier if you want. I did everything I could to wear her out today."

"She ate dinner?"

If canned spaghetti counted as dinner, she had.

"Sure."

"Max—"

"She ate. She had a bath. We checked under the bed three times to make sure the bad man wasn't there."

She nodded like that made perfect sense. "What about her M-O-M?"

"What about her?"

"If she calls, should I put Zuzu on the phone with her?"

"Yes, but she won't call until after Zuzu is asleep. Don't wake her to talk to Mor . . ." He glanced at Zuzu. She seemed engrossed in trying to make the crown fit her head, but that didn't mean she wasn't listening. "Don't wake her if she's asleep."

"Got it. Anything else I need to know?"

"Pete is prowling the neighborhood. He'll scratch at the door when he's ready to come in."

"I love Pete!" Zuzu said.

"I think you love everyone, kid," he responded, kissing her on the head. "You be good while I'm gone, okay?"

"Don't go, Maxi." She grabbed his hand and held on tight. She'd been left by her mother, and he thought she must be terrified that he was leaving her, too.

"It's okay, Zuzu. I won't be gone long." He picked

her up, patted her back the way he had a dozen times before. Every single time, it felt more natural. Every single time, she cuddled just a little closer, relaxed just a little more. He'd become her lifeline, her provider, her . . . *father figure?*

That scared the hell out of him, but he couldn't do anything less for the kid than what he was doing, because Zuzu deserved so much more.

"Where are you going, Maxi?" She laid her hand on his face and looked into his eyes, just like she always did.

"Out with Charlotte. Remember? We talked about this."

"I want to come, too."

"You're going to stay with Emma and make crowns."

"No!"

"Zu—"

"It's okay. I've got this," Emma cut in, taking Zuzu from his arms.

Or trying to.

She clung like a monkey.

He had to pull her arms away, and he felt like a cad and a loser when she started crying.

"Better get your stuff and get going," Emma said over the sound of Zuzu's sobs.

"Maybe—"

"She's going to be fine. If she doesn't calm down in a few minutes, I'll give you a call."

She thrust the basket into his hand, gave him a little shove between the shoulder blades.

He went, because he'd told Charlotte that he'd be at her place at six, but there was a big part of him that thought he should stay.

Chapter Seventeen

Good golly!

The woman was holding out a dead rat.

At least that's what it looked like to Charlotte.

Apparently, Gertrude thought it looked like a trendy fashion statement.

"I'm telling you right now, she needs to wear the fur hat. It adds just a touch of whimsy to the outfit," Gertrude griped, her hands fisted on her hips, her orange hair standing on end. Just beyond her shoulder, the living room window sparkled with red, green, and blue Christmas lights. Zim had stopped by as soon as Max left and insisted on hanging them.

They looked pretty against the evening dark.

The hat, on the other hand, looked like roadkill.

Charlotte was tempted to tell Gertrude that the 1920s fur cap that she was offering looked like something Max's old tomcat might have dragged in, but she didn't want to offend the woman.

Besides, the clock was ticking, and Max would be there any minute. She needed to get the McKenzies out of her house before then, because she did *not* want him to know that Tessa and Gertrude had stopped by to offer Charlotte fashion advice.

Gertrude's idea, apparently, and it was a little embarrassing that a seventy-something-year-old woman thought Charlotte needed help figuring out what to wear on a date.

"Whimsy? Give me a break, Gertrude. Charlotte doesn't want to look whimsical," Tessa responded, rolling her eyes and sighing. "She wants to look elegant and sophisticated, right?"

"Umm . . ." Charlotte glanced down at her dark blue skinny jeans and mint green sweater. If they were elegant and sophisticated, she had it made.

"Elegant? Sophisticated?" Gertrude spat. "Please! Go ahead, Charlotte, put the hat on."

"Don't. The thing looks like a dead rat, and that's *not* a good look on anyone," Tessa pronounced emphatically. "Is it, Alex?" She glanced at her nephew.

He sat on the couch, the cookie Charlotte had handed him when he'd arrived with his aunts loose in his left hand. His right fingers tapped a rhythm on his thigh. He nodded his head in time with it.

"Alex?" Tessa prodded. "What do you think about Gertrude's fur hat?"

He raised his head, looked into Charlotte's eyes, his gaze steady for just a heartbeat before it drifted away. "It looks like a dead rat."

Tessa laughed. "That's one of the many things I love about you, Alex. You're always honest."

He nodded, his fingers still tapping away. "Charlotte doesn't need a hat. She's pretty without one."

"Thank you, Alex," Charlotte said, oddly touched by his pronouncement.

"Well," Gertrude huffed. "If you are going to all gang up against me and my hat, I'll just head on home and put it away."

"What we should all be doing is going home." Tessa glanced at her watch and frowned. "Max will be here any second now."

"If you and Alex are leaving, I'll stay." Gertrude thrust the hat into Tessa's hands. "I need to make sure Max knows the rules."

"Gertrude," Tess warned. "Don't start."

"Start what?"

"Anything. That's what. Charlotte is a grown woman. Max is a grown man. They don't need you to stick your nose into their business."

"That's not what you were saying when we decided to come over and see what Charlotte was wearing on her ho—"

"Gertrude!" Tessa warned, shooting Charlotte an apologetic smile. "Sorry about my aunt. She's—"

"Standing right here, and if there needs to be any apology for me, I'll be the one doing it!"

"Right. Fine. Obviously you're in one of your ornery moods. Come on, Alex. Let's get out of here." Tessa took her nephew's hand and led him out the front door.

"Have fun, Charlotte," she said with a kind smile. "And don't overthink things. Just relax and go with the flow and see where it takes you."

That wasn't going to be easy, considering that she was already overthinking things.

"Okay," she replied, because she didn't have time to explain all the reasons why her heart was thundering and her thoughts were racing. She didn't really want to explain. She liked to keep her private life private. She'd never told anyone about her marriage or Brett's betrayal.

Until Max.

She'd told him everything, and she didn't quite know how to feel about that. Relieved? Worried?

"Call me tomorrow morning and fill me in on the details," Tessa called over her shoulder as she and Alex made their way across the yard.

Two down. One to go.

She met Gertrude's eyes. "You really don't have to stay, Gertrude."

"Does that mean you want me to go? If it does, why don't you just say it without beating around the bush?" Gertrude demanded.

Charlotte was about to utter an emphatic *yes, I want you to leave,* when Max pulled into the driveway. She couldn't see him through the darkness, but her insides went all hot and liquidy at the *thought* of seeing him.

This picnic thing?

It was a bad idea. A really, really bad idea.

Max got out of the car, waving as he walked across the yard. "Good evening, Ms. Gertrude."

"Don't Ms. Gertrude me, you cad!"

"What'd I do?"

"It's not what you've *done.* It's what you might be *planning* that I'm worried about!"

"What I'm planning," Max said calmly, "is a nice

quiet picnic under the stars, so I really hope that you're not planning to come along."

"I'm sure I'm not invited, but I feel the need to warn you—"

"Gertrude," Charlotte finally managed to cut in. "There's no need to warn anyone."

"That's what all the girls think about ten seconds before they're barefoot and pregnant, standing over a hot pot of gruel because it's all they can afford."

Max laughed. "You sure do know how to spin a tale."

"What tale? It's the way it always works. The guy just wants to get in the girl's—"

"You know what?" Charlotte said hastily. "I'd better get my purse and lock up so we can get out of here."

She ran into the house, grabbed her purse, and took a few deep breaths. At the rate things were going, this night was going to be a disaster.

"Ready?" Max stuck his head in the open doorway. "Is she gone?"

"Tessa came and dragged her back home." He grabbed her coat from the back of the sofa and helped her into it, his fingers sliding against her nape as he adjusted the collar.

"I'm sure she was fighting and screaming the whole way."

"Something like that." He smiled, but there was a hint of anxiety in his eyes.

Not because they were going out. Charlotte was certain of that. The guy had been on more dates in the past few months than she'd been on in the past three years. If anyone should be nervous, it was her.

"What's wrong, Max?" She touched his arm.

"Zuzu wasn't happy when I left."

"She didn't like Emma?"

"I think she did. She just didn't want me to go."

"Then you shouldn't have."

"I had to."

A simple statement, but she heard a boatload of meaning in it. Zuzu would go back to Morgan eventually. Maybe not tomorrow or the next day, but at some point it was going to happen.

"I'm sorry, Max. This is going to be tough. No matter which way things work out."

"I know." He opened the Corvette door and helped her in.

"We could go back to your place and bring Zuzu out for ice cream or something."

"This is our night, and it's going to be a good one. So how about we stop talking about Zuzu?" He shut the door and ended the conversation.

They drove to the town center in strained silence.

So much for a nice romantic evening.

If Charlotte had wanted one, she would have been disappointed.

Fortunately she hadn't wanted one.

Much.

Max parked close to the sheriff's department, the Christmas lights that hung around its windows mocking the tense mood in the car.

This was a mistake. She should never have agreed to go with Max. Relationships were trouble. At least in her life they'd always been.

He turned off the car engine, took a deep breath. "I'm sorry, Charlotte. The situation with Zuzu is making me tense, but I don't have any right to take it out on you."

"It's okay." It was. Especially because it had reminded her of what a big mistake she was making.

"No. It's not okay." He sounded so sincere. He looked sincere. "But I'm going to make it up to you. I already carried the stuff for the picnic into the park. Let's go relax and enjoy the evening."

He got out of the car and rounded it while she sat like a lump, her heart beating a heavy sickening beat.

She wanted to go into the park with him, lie under his grandmother's furs, and look at the moon that was just rising over the mountains. She wanted to listen to him talk about Zuzu and Morgan and all the reasons why he was stressed and worried. Heck, she'd be happy to listen to him talk about anything. She loved his voice. She loved his hands. His smile.

He opened her door and smiled quizzically. "You ready?"

"Max, I really don't think this is a good idea."

"I know." He took her hand and tugged her from the car.

"Then why are we doing it?" Somehow her right hand settled on his chest, and her left hand settled on his shoulder.

"Because you haven't told me no, yet."

That was her chance, her opening. He was handing it right to her. He was even waiting for her to take it.

She knew what she should say. It was on the tip of her tongue, but the words wouldn't come. "I can't, because I don't know what I want."

"That's a cop-out, Charlotte."

"It's the truth."

"Here's the truth." He covered her right hand with his, pressed it closer to his leather coat. She could almost swear she felt his heart beating beneath the thick fabric. "We always have choices in life. To be safe or to take chances. I'm choosing to take a chance on you. On us, because I think we're going to be good together."

"What if we're not?"

"Then what have we lost?"

Everything.

Heart. Soul. Dreams. All of them dying.

It wasn't worth it. Not even for whatever she and Max might have together. And she thought he was right. Whatever it was, it would be good.

The silence went on a moment too long. She could feel it. Feel the way his body tensed. See his eyes cool. His hand slipped from hers, and her opportunity to choose slipped with it.

"It's fine, Charlotte. I'm not the kind of guy to push myself on someone."

He wasn't. She knew it. And she knew that he wouldn't show up at her house with Zuzu asking for cookies again or put locks on her doors or talk about picnics under the moonlight.

"Come on. I'll take you home." He pivoted and walked to the other side of the car.

She felt cold. Not just because of the frigid temperatures, either. It was the same kind of cold she'd felt the day after she'd married Brett. She'd woken up beside him, her blood running ice cold through her body as she looked at the man she planned to spend the rest of her life with. He'd drunk himself into a stupor after their wedding, and she'd had to tuck him into bed like a child.

You made a mistake, her mind had whispered.

It whispered the same thing as Max got behind the wheel of the car.

She could see how it was all going to play out. He'd drive her home, drop her off, watch as she walked into her house. She'd peek out the living room window as he drove away and wish that she'd had the guts to give things a go.

Once he was gone, she'd pull out the boxes she'd dragged from the attic and finish going through them. She'd already seen dozens of things that Mary had left behind. Old photos and dresses and even a diary.

One day Charlotte would be gone and another woman would find her things boxed up with no one to claim them.

How pitiful was that?

"Charlotte, since we're not going on our picnic, I'd really like to get home," Max said wearily.

She got in the car, closed the door, her movements wooden and stiff.

Just tell him you want to go on that picnic! her brain shouted, but her mouth stayed firmly shut all the way back to her empty little house.

He opened her car door. He even walked her to the porch.

But he didn't tell her she was beautiful, he didn't

kiss her good night. When he said good-bye, it sounded like forever, and that should have been fine.

She peeked out the window as he drove away. Just like she'd known she would. When his car disappeared from sight, she dragged the largest of the boxes into the living room and knelt on the floor, lifting out one item after another and telling herself that the tears that were rolling down her cheeks were for the woman who'd left the box. Poor sweet Mary who'd died alone in a nursing home because she hadn't had any family.

Yeah.

That was *exactly* why she was crying.

She swiped at her face.

She was a coward, and because of it, she was going to die a lonely old woman. If she were lucky, she'd find a nice young lady who'd be willing to visit her in her old age. She'd leave the house to her, and the whole darn cycle would repeat itself.

Or . . .

She could pull up her big-girl panties, go over to Max's place, apologize for being an idiot, and ask him for another chance.

It should be that simple.

It *could* be that simple.

She just had to let it be.

What Max wanted to do was hit the local bar and drink a couple of beers. But even if he hadn't had Zuzu and Emma waiting for him at home, he wouldn't have done it. He never drank when he was pissed, sad, or lonely. Bad habits were easy to form and not so easy to break.

He wasn't ready to return to the apartment though. Emma would wonder why he was home so soon, and he'd either have to explain or annoy her by refusing to.

He'd avoid both by staying out for a little while.

Not too long. If he wasn't with Charlotte, he wanted to be home with Zuzu. She needed him a lot more than he'd thought, and he couldn't quite shake the feeling that he'd failed her in some vital way by leaving her with Emma.

He parked behind the sheriff's department, grabbed his duffle from the back of the Corvette, and yanked his running clothes out. The building was quiet this time of evening. He walked in the back entrance, changed clothes in the locker room, and walked out without bumping into anyone.

Good thing.

He wasn't in the mood for talking.

He ran two laps around Riley Pond, the soft lap of water against land oddly soothing. The full moon stood a hairsbreadth above distant mountains, dark clouds just beginning to edge out its golden glow. He could feel a hint of moisture, smell snow on the still evening air. A winter storm was moving in. The first one of the season. There'd be at least a dusting by morning. Zuzu would love that.

High on the hill overlooking the park, the nativity glowed in its lone spotlight. He had to grab the picnic stuff anyway, so he headed in that direction, running full speed across dry grass and into the copse of trees. He grabbed the basket and blankets, his breath heaving, his heart pounding. He'd worked off a lot of steam, cleared his head a little.

He trudged up the hill anyway, bypassing the old cemetery with its gleaming white headstones and wrought-iron fence and heading into the church's front yard. Baby Jesus lay where he always was, Mary and Joseph smiling down on him, the angel perched in its place. He should go home and get Zuzu, bring her back to see the nativity again. She'd been begging to visit the baby and angel. He hadn't found the time. He'd better. Soon enough, Morgan would return, and Zuzu would be back where she belonged. Max would be free. No kid to worry about. No woman taking up too much of his thoughts.

He should be thrilled, but he just felt hollow and empty.

The church door opened, and Jethro walked outside, a stack of books in his hands.

"Good evening, Max! Finished your picnic already?" he asked as he walked down the porch stairs.

"Who told you?" Max responded.

"Natalie. I believe that Gertrude told her, and it was probably Ida who let her know."

"And by now the entire town is talking about it," Max muttered.

"Something like that." Jethro smiled. "Usually you don't let the gossips bother you. What's going on?"

"The picnic didn't happen."

"Hmmmm."

"Hmmmm what?"

"You were worried about leaving Zuzu, weren't you?"

"A little." A lot actually. And he probably shouldn't be lying to a man of God.

"And Charlotte was probably worried about trusting you with her heart."

"I wasn't asking for her heart. I was asking for a relaxing evening."

"It's probably the same thing to Charlotte."

"Charlotte is an intelligent woman. I think she knows the difference between one date and forever."

Jethro nodded but didn't say anything. He just stared at the nativity as if it held all the secrets of the universe.

"She *does,* Jethro."

"Do *you?*" the pastor finally said, looking straight into Max's eyes.

Max laughed, the sound rusty and tight. "I think you've known me long enough to know that I've got no problem understanding the difference."

"Then why are you telling yourself you only want one date with Charlotte?"

"I'm not." He smoothed his hair, wiped sweat from his face.

"But you're not telling her you want more, because you're just as afraid as she is."

True and true.

Not that he planned to admit it to Jethro. "Since when did you get a counseling degree, Jethro?" he asked lightly. He liked the guy. He wasn't going to argue with him, but he wasn't going to have deep philosophical discussions about relationships with him, either.

"I got it the same time I got my doctorate in theology. I mostly use it for solicited marriage counseling. But I'm always happy to throw it around when I decide to give unsolicited advice to friends."

"Are you giving me advice?"

"Why not? In for a penny, in for a pound, right?" Jethro shifted his pile of books into one hand and pointed down the hill. Christmas lights sparkled from almost every visible house and business. "Did you know that after the first mayor of Apple Valley lost his wife, he decided to never celebrate Christmas again? That first year after Miriam died, there wasn't one decoration in town."

"And?." He shifted impatiently, looking down the hill to the town he'd grown to love so much. It looked like a holiday greeting card, the scene old-fashioned and beautiful.

"Most people say Daniel was so heartbroken, that he was sure that he'd never feel joy again. Refusing to celebrate was his way of making that feeling a reality."

"I'm sure you have another theory."

"You're right. I don't think Daniel's actions had anything to do with not wanting to feel joyful again. They were all about hope. Or lack thereof. Daniel didn't have any left, and he didn't *want* to have it. Not without his wife."

"Got it," Max said, still not sure where this was heading and a little too tired to try to figure it out. "If the history lesson is over—"

"It's not about history, Max," Jethro said seriously.

"It's about not repeating past mistakes. One of the things that I've found in my years of ministry is that there are often second chances in life. Third chances are harder to come by."

"Meaning?"

"You've been plugging along, living your life, thinking that you don't need anyone or anything to complete you. I think you're finally learning that you're wrong." He glanced at the nativity, a smile hovering at the corner of his mouth. "It's probably a strange realization to come to. Even a disconcerting one. It's going to take you a little while to come to terms with it. Charlotte, though, she's always known she needs more. For her, Apple Valley is a second chance to have the things that are really important. Don't screw it up for her."

The last surprised a real laugh out of Max, and all his tension seeped away. "Are pastors allowed to say *screw*?"

"I'll check the manual later," Jethro responded with a chuckle. "You heading home? I can give you a ride."

"Thanks, but my car is parked at the station. Besides, a little more fresh air will do me good."

"More likely, it will turn you into an ice pop. It's cold out tonight. Looks like we've got snow heading our way. Natalie will hate that."

"She doesn't like the cold, huh?"

"She doesn't like being stuck in the house while I plow out the long driveway." Jethro smiled, but his eyes were tired.

"I can give you a hand if you want. It'll make things go faster."

"Nice of you to offer, Max, but you have other responsibilities. Speaking of which, we'd both better get going. See you Sunday?"

"I'll try to drag myself out of bed." Actually, he wouldn't have any trouble doing that now that Zuzu was around. She woke at the crack of dawn.

"Try hard. We have a great Sunday school program. Zuzu will love it."

"Zuzu loves—" His cell phone rang. "Excuse me for a second, Jethro?"

"Sure."

He grabbed it from his vest pocket, glanced at the number. Emma. Probably desperate for him to return so she could go home. "Hello?"

"Max?!" Emma screamed into the phone, Zuzu wailing like a banshee in the background. "You need to come home. Now!"

In the years he'd known Emma, he'd never heard her even close to hysterical. Right then, in that one word, he heard enough panic to make his blood run cold.

"What's wrong?"

"Zuzu fell down the stairs. I think her arm is broken, and she's got this huge lump on her head. The ambulance is on the way."

"What stairs?! How?!" He pivoted, ready to run back down the hill and across the park.

Jethro grabbed his arm. "I'll drive you."

He nodded, his heart in his throat.

"Zuzu was tired. She fell asleep early, and I did, too. We were in the living room with the light off, and I heard someone wiggling the doorknob. I opened the door and saw someone running down the stairs. I followed, and Zuzu . . ." Her voice broke. "Just get here, Max. Okay?"

She disconnected.

"Emma!" he yelled into the phone, as if that would do any good.

"It's going to be okay, Max," Jethro said as they ran around the side of the church and raced to the parsonage.

"I hope you're right."

"I know I am," Jethro responded with so much confidence Max could almost believe that the pastor was somehow tied into something greater than himself, clued into the plans of a divine creator, that he had some in with God, and that he could arrange for Zuzu to be just fine.

Please, let her be okay. I'll go to church every Sunday for the next forty years if she is, he silently bargained. He wasn't sure it would do any good, but he was willing to try anything.

It took too long to get to Jethro's old Jeep and it seemed to take even longer to get the beast of a vehicle started.

By the time the engine sputtered to life, Max was about ready to jump out and run back home.

"Hold on," Jethro commanded.

"Wh—?"

The Jeep jumped forward, did a tight U-turn in the driveway, and sped down the hill toward town.

Chapter Eighteen

Something was wrong. Really, really wrong.

Charlotte turned onto Ida Cunningham's long driveway, the sound of sirens drifting through the station wagon's closed windows. In all the time she'd been in Apple Valley, she'd heard sirens just a few times. Once because there'd been a three-car pileup on the freeway. Once because a bunch of teens had accidentally set fire to an old barn at the edge of town. A few other times that she couldn't recall the reason for.

Whatever was going on, it was close.

She glanced in her rearview mirror, surprised to see an ambulance racing up behind her. She couldn't pull over without slamming into a bunch of trees, so she stepped on the gas, the station wagon shaking as she zipped forward.

Lights shone from every window in Ida's house, and Charlotte's first thought was for the older woman. Had she had a stroke? A heart attack?

No. There she was, wearing a long nightgown and bathrobe, waving the ambulance toward the garage.

Zuzu!

Oh, dear God! Charlotte hoped not.

She yanked the steering wheel to the left as the driveway widened, allowing the ambulance to pass. No sign of Max's Corvette. He must have gone out after he'd dropped her off.

She jumped out of the car, leaving the keys in the ignition and the motor running.

"Charlotte! Thank goodness you're here!" Ida rushed toward her. "Where's Max?"

"I don't know. He dropped me off and—"

"Well, hopefully he's right behind you. We really need him here."

"What's going on?"

"Zuzu is hurt. She was following Emma down the stairs and tripped."

Charlotte's heart nearly stopped at the words. "Is it bad?"

"That's what we're trying to find out." Even in the midst of the crisis, Ida seemed calm. "Emma left her where she fell, afraid of injuring her further if she tried to carry her into the apartment. She's standing up, screaming for her mother, Max, and you between shrieks. Hopefully she'll calm down for you, and we can figure out where she's hurt."

Headlights illuminated the garage door and the bottom of the stairs that led to Max's apartment. Emma stood on the bottom step, holding Daisy's arm. Zuzu stood on the ground just below them, two EMTs crouched in front of her, trying to convince her that a cervical collar was a good idea. Zuzu was having nothing to do with it. Eyes shut tight, mouth open wide, she looked like she was about to start those horrible screams that one of Charlotte's friends had once told her about. The ones that came from the deepest depths of a child's terror or hurt.

Charlotte dropped down in front of her, ignoring an EMT's warning to back off and let them do their jobs.

"Zuzu," she said gently. "What's wrong?"

Zuzu just kept screaming, a horrible swollen lump on her head seeming to pulse with every screech.

"Zuzu?" she tried again, touching Zuzu's cheek. "Did you fall?"

Finally Zuzu opened her eyes and reached for Charlotte with her right arm, her left arm hanging loosely at her side.

"Charl-lott!" she wailed. "I falled right down the steps and hurted my arm."

"It's okay. These nice people are going to take you to the doctor."

"I don't want no doctor. I want Maxi!"

"Shhhhh." Charlotte lifted her carefully, wincing as she got a closer look at the huge lump on Zuzu's head. "Max will be here soon."

"Ma'am," the older of the two EMTs said, "we'd like to get this collar around her neck. Just to be on the safe side."

"What do you think, Zuzu? You want to have a cool necklace on?"

"No," Zuzu sobbed, dropping her head to Charlotte's shoulder and shoving her thumb in her mouth.

The EMT moved in and eased the collar on anyway.

"There you are, little one. It's fine, see?" he said gently.

Zuzu didn't respond. She'd closed her eyes, her body nearly limp against Charlotte's.

Had she passed out?

Was she breathing?

"I'm going to take her into the ambulance and get her vitals. Don't worry, Mom," the EMT said as he took Zuzu from Charlotte's arms. "She's in good hands."

"I'm not Mom," she responded, but she felt like she could have been, fear knotted so tightly in her stomach she thought she might be sick.

They carried Zuzu into the ambulance, and Charlotte followed, hovering near the gurney as they checked Zuzu's blood pressure, looked in her eyes, touched her head and her shoulder.

"Dislocated," the younger of the two said.

"What's dislocated?" Max climbed into the ambulance, his face ashen, his eyes dark with worry.

Charlotte was so glad he was there, so relieved, her knees nearly buckled.

"You the dad?" the older of the two EMTs asked.

Max hesitated, then nodded.

"Her shoulder is out of the socket. Looks like she might have caught her arm on something as she was falling. It probably kept her from breaking her neck. We'll transport her to Sacred Heart. Which one of you wants to ride along?"

There was no question that it would be Max.

Charlotte stepped back, dismissing herself before she was dismissed. "I'll—"

"Meet us at the hospital? I could really use your help there, Charlotte," Max said quietly. He looked worn-out, and Charlotte couldn't have denied him any more than she could deny Zuzu.

She nodded. "I'll follow the ambulance."

She hurried to the station wagon and got behind the wheel.

"Hold on, Charlotte!" Ida called. "We're coming, too."

"In your pajamas?" Charlotte asked as Ida climbed into the passenger seat.

"I'd say I'm more covered than most young people these days," Ida responded, cinching her bathrobe belt a little tighter. "Besides, this is an emergency. If the *Apple Valley Times* wants to snap a couple of pictures of me in my nightclothes and run a story about the town's wild mayor, let them do it."

"I think they're going to have an even better story to run," Emma said as she opened the back door and nudged Daisy in. "*Local librarian turns to a life of crime.* Has a cool ring to it. Don't you think, Daisy?"

Daisy wailed in response, her cries almost as loud and uncontrolled as Zuzu's had been.

"I am not a criminal!" she managed to gasp between sobs.

"Right. Because most law-abiding citizens use credit cards and bobby pins to open locked doors."

"I wasn't—"

"You were, too!" Emma barked. "You thought the apartment was empty because Max's car was gone and all the lights were off. You thought it was the perfect opportunity to break in and take what you wanted. What were you going to do? Steal his computer and television?"

"No!"

"Well, you were there to steal something!"

"Now, let's not throw around accusations without knowing all the facts." Ida interrupted the argument. "I'm sure Daisy had a logical reason for being here tonight. Why don't you explain it to us, Daisy? So we'll all understand."

The car fell silent as Charlotte did a three-point turn and followed the ambulance back down the driveway. They were on the freeway before Daisy spoke. When she did, her voice was so low, Charlotte could barely hear it.

"I needed the recipe for double chocolate delights," she whispered. "I saw Charlotte give it to Max, and I just had to have it. I've been waiting years for Jerry to propose. I know he wants to. He just needs a little extra incentive."

"First of all, Max doesn't have the recipe, Daisy. I gave him one for an easy chocolate cake, but the other recipe is in my head. I never write it down. Second of all—"

"Please," Emma interrupted. "Let me. Second of all, Daisy, even if you'd gotten the da—"

"Language," Ida warned.

"Even if you'd gotten the darn recipe, it would have all been for nothing," Emma snapped. "Because cupcakes can't make a man propose any more than sitting in this car with you can make me stupid."

"Emma!" Ida chided. "Be kind."

"Why? If she hadn't been fiddling around with Max's door, I wouldn't have run after her and Zuzu wouldn't be hurt." Her voice shook with anger and, Charlotte thought, the aftermath of adrenaline and fear.

"I didn't mean for anything bad to happen!" Daisy cried.

"You can tell that to Cade. He's meeting us at the hospital. You can also tell him that you were responsible for the break-ins at Charlotte's place, because you were. Right?"

"I just wanted the recipe! If Charlotte had agreed to give it to me—"

"Enough," Ida commanded. Not loudly. Just a quiet command that swept through the car and seemed to steal all fight from both women. "Obviously, mistakes were made, and restitution will have to be offered. For now, though, we have a little girl to worry about. The rest of this can wait."

She was right.

At that moment, Charlotte couldn't have cared less about Emma's accusation or Daisy's confession. All she wanted to do was get to the hospital. The ambulance had left her in its dust, the station wagon no match for the faster vehicle. She puttered along the nearly empty freeway, snow swirling in the headlights. The way things were looking, she'd be driving home in a snowstorm on her bald tires, but even that seemed inconsequential in view of what had happened.

Within minutes snow covered the asphalt.

She slowed the station wagon to a fast crawl, leaning forward to peer through the deepening storm. At the rate they were going, they might reach the hospital sometime before Zuzu's eighteenth birthday.

Then again, they might not.

"Can't this thing go any faster?" Emma leaned over the seat, fingers beating a fast tattoo on the seat.

"Not if we want to stay on the road. My tires are shot. I need to get new ones. I just haven't had time," Charlotte admitted.

"Wonderful," Emma huffed, dropping back into her spot. "Not only did I nearly let a kid I was babysitting die, but I'm going to spend the next three hours stuck in a car with . . ." She didn't finish.

Charlotte had a feeling she'd been about to make some snide comment about being stuck in the car with America's Most Wanted librarian.

"You didn't almost let Zuzu die, Emma. She fell down the stairs. Children do that all the time," Ida reassured her, but Emma didn't seem convinced.

"She landed on concrete, Ida. Most kids don't do that. Most don't dislocate their shoulders or nearly knock themselves out." She paused and took a deep breath. "I just really, really hope she's okay."

"She'll be fine, dear," Ida responded. "Trust me. A dying child cannot scream like that little girl did. Not for any length of time anyway. She'll be a little bruised and a little sore, but she'll be up to most of her old antics, driving poor Max crazy by tomorrow morning. Won't she, Charlotte?"

Charlotte wasn't as confident as Ida, but she

didn't plan to tell the others that. "Of course! She'll probably be begging for cookies for breakfast and insisting on riding her Big Wheel down Main Street in the snow."

"Showing off her bruised head to everyone who'll take a look," Ida said with a little laugh.

"Using it to get every shop owner on Main Street to feel sorry for her. She'll get all kinds of treats," Charlotte added.

"I hope you guys are right. I'll never forgive myself if she has some kind of long-term problem because of the fall she took."

"The biggest problem that Zuzu has isn't the knot on her head or the dislocated shoulder," Charlotte responded. "It's that her mother isn't here."

"I couldn't agree more," Ida said. "Morgan has lost all sense of priority. Fortunately, Zuzu has Max. She has you. She has me and all the people in town who have grown to love her. Even if Morgan never came back for her, she'll be okay."

"*Okay?*" Emma snorted. "She'd be better off. Morgan is no prize as a mother. Zuzu deserves a lot better. If she sticks around here, she'll have it."

"We can't know for sure that being here will be better for Zuzu," Ida responded.

Emma laughed harshly. "Of course, we can. Morgan is a loser. She dropped her kid off with someone who was a virtual stranger to the child and went off to wait tables at a casino. There's no pretty way to say that, Ida. No way to paint it into a nice little Apple Valley picture."

"You sound bitter, dear."

"I'm a realist."

"In the midst of your realistic assessment of the situation, don't forget to extend a little grace. Morgan made a mistake. That's the truth of the matter, but she may rectify it once she finds out about the accident."

"By what? Coming back? Too little too late. She should have all her parental rights taken away. That's my opinion anyway," Emma said with a quiet huff.

"It's your opinion because you're just plain mean. Just like your dad." Daisy chose that moment rejoin the conversation.

Not the best time, and probably the worst subject she could have chosen.

But Charlotte was certain she knew it.

"I may be mean, but at least I'm not a sneak and a trespasser!" Emma retorted.

"Girls!" Ida cut in with an exaggerated sigh. "I thought we just agreed this wasn't the time for arguments."

They weren't girls, and they hadn't agreed, but neither said that to Ida. They shut up and stayed that way until Charlotte finally turned into the hospital parking lot.

She chose a spot close to the emergency exit, and they all filed out. Except for Daisy, who huddled in her seat, arms wrapped around her waist, a forlorn look on her face. "I'll just stay here. I'm sure that Max won't want me there after what I've done."

"Stop feeling sorry for yourself and come on!" Emma yanked her out of the car.

"I'm not feeling sorry for myself."

"Okay, then, you're putting on an act, so we'll leave you out here and you can make your escape."

"I am not going to make an escape," Daisy sputtered, her face mottled red as they walked into the emergency room lobby.

Cade was already there, sitting in a vinyl chair nursing a cup of coffee. He stood as they approached. "Tough time getting here, huh?"

"My tires—"

"Are bald. Max mentioned that three times. He doesn't want you driving home in this. One of the guys from the station is putting chains on Max's Vette and bringing it over here, so you guys will have a safe ride home."

"How's Zuzu?"

"The doctor already popped her shoulder back into place and had an MRI of her head done. She's in triage for now. Max asked me to take you back there when you arrived. You"—he pointed at Daisy, and her face lost every bit of color—"stay right here. We have a few things to discuss."

He took Charlotte's arm and walked her through a doorway and into a wide hall. Rooms opened up to either side, the sounds of televisions and conversation drifting out from a few of them. Soft music played through a centralized PA system. A Christmas carol, but Charlotte was too nervous, her stomach too tied up in knots to really listen.

When they reached the end of the corridor, Cade stopped at a closed door. "This is it. I'm going to let you go in alone."

"So you can deal with Daisy?"

"And so you can deal with Max."

"You heard what happened?"

"Not all of it. Max just told me that you'd decided against the picnic, and that he'd taken you home before Zuzu fell. He probably wouldn't have mentioned it, but Jethro showed up a couple minutes after the ambulance arrived. We were talking, and he mentioned that Max had been up at the church by himself when he heard the news about Zuzu."

"I'm an idiot."

"No." He shook his head, gave her a quick hug. "You're cautious. There's nothing wrong with that."

"There is if I miss out on something great because of it."

"I'm tempted to say that Max won't be a great thing."

"You don't think he will be?"

Cade studied her for a moment, his gaze intent but open. He knew her as well as anyone, and she'd always been able to count on him for honest advice. "Truth?"

"Of course," she managed to say past the tightness in her throat and the sudden dryness in her mouth.

"Max is a good guy. I can't say he'll never hurt you, but I say that if he loves you, he'll do whatever it takes to make things work. He'll move heaven and earth to make you happy, and he won't ever purposely let you down." He scowled. "And just so you know, it hurt like hell to say all those nice things. If you tell him I did, I'll deny it. Now I really do have to go. Daisy needs to be dealt with."

"You were right about her, Cade. She admitted

she's been breaking into my house looking for my cupcake recipe."

"You and those cupcakes, Charlotte," he said with a smile. "I might have to ask the town council to ban any mention of them."

"And trample the right to free speech?"

"If it prevents people like Daisy from going nuts, it might just be worth it." He grinned. "I'll check back in later. Tell Max to give me a call if he needs anything before then."

"I will."

He walked away, and *she* took a deep breath, bracing herself for the moment when she walked into the room, saw Max and Zuzu, felt her heart jump in acknowledgment. She'd made a lot of mistakes in her life. She'd *paid* for a lot of mistakes.

This wouldn't be one of them.

She knocked softly.

The door opened immediately, and she looked into Max's eyes. They were hollow and old, his gaze raw with anxiety.

"Hey," he said softly. "I thought I heard you out here."

"I was talking to Cade." She tiptoed over to the bed. Zuzu lay sound asleep, the lump on her head slightly smaller and much more colorful than it had seemed before, an IV line attached to her hand. "How's she doing?"

"She'll be in a sling for a few days, but the shoulder should heal fine. The doctor said the head injury looks superficial."

"*That's* superficial? It's the size of a small ostrich egg," she protested.

"That's what *I* told *him*."

"What did he say?"

"He told me that when I got a Ph.D, I'd probably be better able to know the difference between serious and not."

"Nice bedside manners."

"We're old hunting buddies. Last year I came home with an eight point buck, and he got nothing. I think he's still a little upset about that." He slid an arm around Charlotte's waist, tugged her into his side.

God, he felt good. All hard muscles and warmth. At some point he'd changed into running gear, the fabric of his shirt soft against her cheek. "You've been running."

"I needed to clear my head."

"Of me?"

"That," he responded, shifting so that they were face-to-face, "would not be possible. Even if I wanted it to be."

"I'm sorry."

"For what? Digging yourself so deeply into my brain that I can't get you out of it no matter how hard I try?"

"For being a coward." She touched his cheek, her hand slipping to the curve of his jaw and resting there. "I wanted that picnic so badly, Max. It scared me."

"Are you still scared?" He pressed her palm to his stubbled skin, his calloused hand familiar and wonderful, and she had this feeling way deep in the depth of her soul that he could be everything she'd ever wanted if she had the courage to let him.

"I have never been more terrified in my life," she

whispered, her heart beating so fast she thought it would fly right out of her chest.

"Don't be," he responded. "I would never hurt you. Not intentionally."

"Funny, that's exactly what Cade just said to me."

"Did he?" he murmured. "Because, about twenty minutes ago, he told me that he'd knock my head off if I so much as thought about breaking your heart."

"Nice." She laughed, and Zuzu shifted, the bed-sheets rustling.

"Charl-lott!" she called weakly, lifting her right hand beseechingly. "I needs you to hold me."

"I don't know—"

"It'll be okay," Max said. "Just sit in the bed with her."

She climbed in, leaning against the headboard as Zuzu crawled into her lap. She smelled like anti-septic and little girl.

"Better?" Charlotte asked, patting her back.

"Yes." She dropped her head onto Charlotte's shoulder. "Where's Mommy?"

"On her way," Max responded.

Charlotte met his eyes. "You finally reached her?"

"She called me back while we were in the ambulance."

"Was she upset?"

"She's worried about the head injury, but she said Zuzu has loose joints and that this isn't the first time her shoulder has popped out. I told her that would have been nice information to have."

"And?"

"She said something I can't repeat in front of the kid. Then she told me that she's going to get a flight out as soon as she can. Hopefully she'll be here by morning, but with the snow—"

"Snow!?" Zuzu squealed. "I wants to see!" She bounded up, nearly slamming her head into Charlotte's chin.

"So much for being weak and injured," Max muttered, snagging her by the waist before she could jump off the bed and rip out her IV line. "Slow down, kid. You're going to hurt yourself."

"I already did that. Now I needs to see the snow," Zuzu responded with such a serious look on her face, Charlotte laughed.

"Knock-knock!" a tall red-haired doctor called from the open doorway. Dr. Eli Winters had grown up in Apple Valley. After attending medical school in Maryland, he'd returned. Charlotte didn't know much more about him. Except that he had a weakness for gingerbread and pumpkin muffins. "Looks like our patient is feeling a little better. That matches what we're seeing on the MRI." He glanced at a clipboard as he walked into the room. "Shoulder looks good, too. Since Zuzu isn't vomiting or showing any signs of a concussion, I think it's safe to send her home. A nurse is on the way in to take out that IV. She'll bring the aftercare instructions with her."

"Thanks, Eli." Max grabbed the footy pajamas Zuzu had been wearing from a chair. "I really appreciate you moving so quickly on this."

"Thank me by not getting in my way when we go hunting next year," the doctor replied. "I'm having a hard time living down the fact that a city slicker brought in a bigger buck than I did."

"You didn't bring in any."

"Thanks for the reminder, Max. I'd forgotten that little detail." Eli smiled and ruffled Zuzu's hair. "Are you ready to go home, Zuzu?"

"I'm not going home. I'm going to see a snow," Zuzu informed him.

"Have you ever seen snow before?"

Zuzu shook her head, her eyes big in her pale face.

"Then you're in for a treat."

"A cookie treat?" she asked, her whole face lighting up. "I love cookies."

"I don't see why you can't have a few cookies." Eli laughed.

"That's because you're not going to have to deal with her at three in the morning when she's wired up from sugar," Max growled, but Charlotte could see the amusement in his eyes.

"Payback sucks, man! You have my cell phone number if Zuzu has any trouble when she gets home. Call me if you need to." He walked out of the room, and Max tugged Zuzu's pajama pants up her legs.

"We going?" she asked.

"As soon as the nurse takes that needle out of your hand."

Zuzu's eyes widened, and her face went from happy to terrified.

"You shouldn't have—" *Mentioned that*, Charlotte was going to say, but Zuzu's high-pitched scream drowned out the words.

Chapter Nineteen

Three hours.

That's how long it had taken to get released from the hospital and make the drive—what should have been a twenty-minute drive—home. Max glanced in the rearview mirror. Charlotte had squeezed into the backseat, smashing herself in beside Zuzu and holding the little girl's hand.

They'd fallen asleep like that about a half hour into the ride, the slow soft silence of the winter snow and the easy snail pace of the drive lulling them both into dreams.

"We're home," he said softly. Zuzu didn't budge. Neither did Charlotte. She looked dead to the world, her head bent toward Zuzu, her hair a wild mass of dark waves around her face.

He touched her shoulder, his hand moving along her nape and tangling in her hair.

"Charlotte?" he called quietly.

"Is this the part where a kiss wakes the sleeping

maiden?" she murmured sleepily, a smile hovering at the corner of her lips.

"Yes," he whispered, kissing her deeply, with every bit of the longing he felt.

"Wow!" She sighed. "That was . . . wow!"

"It seems to have woken you up, so I guess we're good." He offered a hand, tugging her out of the car.

Snow fell on her dark hair and dusted her fair skin, wet flakes sticking to her lashes and her cheeks.

He brushed them away, his palm resting against cool silky flesh. "God, you're beautiful."

"What I am"—she laughed lightly—"is freezing."

"We'd better get inside, then. You want to open the door, and I'll get Zuzu?" He handed her the keys, watching for a moment as she walked away.

"I thought you were getting Zuzu," she called over her shoulder.

"I'm good at multitasking," he replied as he un-buckled Zuzu and lifted her from the car seat. She snuggled into his arms, her head under his chin, her right hand on his cheek. He could feel the little sling that the nurse had fitted her with.

He'd been scared out his mind when he'd gotten the call from Emma, but Zuzu didn't seem any worse for wear. According to Daisy, the kid had only tumbled down the last four or five steps. Max wasn't sure how accurate that information was, since Emma had been sitting on Daisy's back holding her for the police when Zuzu went down.

Still, if it were true, that explained why Zuzu hadn't been hurt worse. It also explained why Zuzu was bouncing off the walls about three minutes after she'd been unhooked from the IV, acting and playing just like she always did. She'd even spent the first twenty minutes of their ride home begging for cookies and asking if they could build a snowman in the morning. Max had said they could. He'd promised hot chocolate and snow angels and all sorts of things that he wanted to give her.

Everything was fine. Except that Morgan was on her way back to town to get her daughter, and Max wasn't quite sure how he was going to say good-bye.

He got Zuzu a drink of water and gave her some children's Tylenol, then tucked her into bed. He stood watching her while she drifted off to sleep, thinking about how empty the room was going to be soon, how quiet the apartment.

Being a father was hard work, but he finally understood why men did it and why the good ones never resented the time spent and the sacrifices made.

"Is she asleep?" Charlotte whispered from the doorway.

"Yes."

"Come on, then. I made coffee, and you have all the ingredients for French toast. You look like you could use both."

"That bad, huh?" He slung his arm over her shoulder as they walked down the hall, and she settled in at his side like she'd always been there and always would be.

That cupcake had done the trick.

Or her perfume . . . that luscious mix of sugar and vanilla that clung to Charlotte's skin and hair and lips.

Or . . . just Charlotte.

Even without the cupcake and perfume, she was addictive.

"You couldn't look bad if you tried," she responded, tugging him into the kitchen and pulling out a chair. "Sit."

She set a cup of coffee in front of him, and he grabbed her hand. "I'm the one who owes you dinner, remember?"

"I think we can forget about that now. Morgan will be back tomorrow, and Zuzu will go home, and our lives will go back to what they were before she came."

And saying those words was just so sad Charlotte had to turn away, busy herself at the fridge pulling out eggs and cream and a half loaf of bread.

Max's phone rang, and he answered.

He didn't say much. Just *yes* and *no* and *whatever helps you sleep better at night,* but there was a curtness to his voice, an edge to it that she'd never heard before.

She turned, met his eyes.

"Morgan," he mouthed.

His ex must have said something he didn't like, because he frowned. "Look, Morgan. Even if she's mine, she's yours, too. She might not be in the hospital, but she's asking for you. Right. I'm sure she will. See you then."

He slammed the phone into the receiver, raked a hand over his hair.

"What's going on?"

"No flights here because of the snow. Morgan is using that as an excuse to stay in Vegas. I guess once she got my message that Zuzu was being released from the hospital, she decided it wasn't an emergency and she wasn't needed. She says she'll lose her job if she misses the next two days of work. She has three days off at Christmas. She'll be here then to pick Zuzu up."

"Are you going to let Zuzu go with her?"

"Assuming she comes, you mean?"

"You don't think she will?"

"I think that Morgan thinks she will. I think she even loves Zuzu, but I don't think Zuzu has ever been her priority. Her husband probably did all the childcare work, and that's probably the way she liked it." He shrugged. "If Zuzu is mine, I'm going to petition for custody. I don't think Morgan will fight me. If Zuzu isn't mine . . ."

"What?"

"I'm going to treat her like she is. I'll still petition for custody. I'll still do everything I can to make sure she has the life she deserves. If I lose, at least Zuzu will know I gave it my best shot."

"You're a good guy, Max."

"Not really, but I'm going to do everything I can to be a good father." He touched her cheek, smiled into her eyes. "There's something else I've been thinking about being ever since I ate that cupcake of yours, Charlotte."

"What's that?" she asked, her mouth dry, her heart pounding wildly.

"Yours," he murmured, his lips brushing hers once. Twice. The third time, she slid her hands through his hair, pulled him in for a deeper kiss, one that shook the world and made firecrackers explode behind her eyes. One that could have gone on forever and still not have lasted long enough.

Her body melted against his, her hands sliding to his shoulders, his back, his spine.

He groaned, pulling away and resting his forehead against hers.

"Keep kissing me like that, and I'll never get you home," he muttered.

"I'm not sure I want you to," she responded.

"Ida's standing by her phone, waiting for me to call and ask her to watch Zuzu while I deliver you to your place safe and sound, and that's exactly what I'm going to do."

"Okay."

She wasn't disappointed. Much.

"Of course, if we took a detour on our way there, who'd know but us and Ida? As long as we stick close to the apartment just in case Zuzu wakes up looking for us, there's no reason why we can't take a little side trip."

"What kind of trip are you talking about?" Not that it mattered. She was pretty sure she'd be willing to go anywhere with him.

"The kind that involves a picnic basket and fur blankets and a little wine."

"It's snowing," she protested.

"And Ida's yard is lined with evergreens. We'll spread a fur under one, and sip a glass of wine, and watch the snow fall. Just for a little while, Charlotte. Just long enough to start figuring out what it means."

"The snow?"

"No." He smiled gently, his hands skimming down her arm, his fingers lacing with hers. "Belonging to each other. What do you say?" he whispered. "Are you up for it?"

There was nothing she could say but yes.

Nothing she could do but blush when Ida arrived and warned them about frostbite and staying warm during their mini-picnic.

Nothing that would ever compare to the fragrant scent of pine, the cold crisp air, the snow that fell all around, and the hope that filled her heart as she and Max walked across the yard, found an old, thick-boughed pine, and spread the fur beneath it.